Praise for *A Right*

T0014002

"*A Right Worthy Woman* is a remarkable and stirring novel, a story destined to be told. Ruth P. Watson brings to vivid life a woman who changed history, a woman both determined and fascinating, a woman named Maggie Lena Walker. From the heartbreaking opening line to the closing scene, the reader is on a transformational journey as Maggie Lena Walker revolutionizes both Richmond, Virginia, and women's history. Inspiring and rich with detail, this is your next book club read."

—Patti Callahan Henry, *New York Times* bestselling author of *The Secret Book of Flora Lea*

"A stirring fictional account of a remarkable figure . . . Watson's love of Maggie shines through."

—*Kirkus Reviews*

"Illuminating . . . This appealing portrait would be perfect for a high school classroom."

—*Publishers Weekly*

"This fascinating historic novel reimagines the life of Maggie Lena Walker, a real person who went on to become the first Black woman to establish and preside over a bank in the United States. Not one to rest on her laurels, she also founded a newspaper and a department store."

—*New York Post*

"This rich, captivating saga takes readers to 19th-century Virginia."

—*Women's World*

"A luminous work of historical fiction chronicling the trailblazer's life."
—*The Atlanta Journal-Constitution*

"History that's never been told is being shared by master storyteller Ruth P. Watson in such an epic way."
—Brenda Jackson, *New York Times* bestselling author

"It is my distinct honor and pleasure to support this inspiring novel based on the life and times of Maggie Lena Walker, who was one of Zeta Phi Beta Sorority's esteemed honorary members, inducted into our beloved organization in 1926."
—Dr. Valerie Hollingsworth Baker,
25th International Centennial President of
Zeta Phi Beta Sorority Inc

"A character this richly complex and relentlessly determined deserves a place in the pantheon of great American entrepreneurs. . . . Although our complicated racial history runs through this story, the author's skill as a novelist makes Walker's journey as enjoyable as it is inspiriting."
—Pearl Cleage,
award-winning playwright and bestselling author
of *What Looks Like Crazy on an Ordinary Day*

"In *A Right Worthy Woman*, Watson lovingly crafts a jewel of a story to bring life back to Maggie Lena Walker—a genius Black financial wizard of Jim Crow–era Virginia. Readers will prize her amazing legacy as a welcome and crucial addition to the growing collection of historical fiction about unsung Black women's lives."
—Piper Huguley, author of *By Her Own Design*

"Watson has given us an extraordinary journey of a determined woman who, against the odds, reminds her community what can be accomplished when united around a common vision."

—Kaia Alderson, author of *Sisters in Arms*

"Maggie's story is one that needs to be told, not only to understand the past, but to inspire the present. Author Ruth P. Watson rivets the reader with rich period detail and emotional impact. *A Right Worthy Woman* is a literary journey to the deep and dark recesses of our history, one that we all would be better for taking."

—Tracey Enerson Wood, author of *The Engineer's Wife*

"Watson masterfully connects the reader to Maggie Lena Walker's world in an impactful manner and gives voice to Walker's innermost feelings and frustrations as she traversed the hazardous journey of being a Black woman, wife, mother, advocate, and entrepreneur in the Jim Crow South. This nineteenth-century voice needs to be heard today in the twenty-first century!"

—Dr. Cassandra Stroud Conover,
former district attorney of Petersburg, Virginia

"The story of Maggie Lena Walker as masterfully told by Ruth Watson is about daring to dream the unimaginable and achieving it. It is set in a different time, yet its fundamental theme—that understanding the socio-economic and financial drivers of our time is essential for building resilient families and economically viable communities—remains as relevant today as it was in her time. Maggie Lena Walker's story is of global significance as a mirror of the experiences of the African diaspora."

—Dr. Renosi Mokate,
executive chairman at Concentric Alliance

A RIGHT
WORTHY
WOMAN

A Novel

RUTH P. WATSON

ATRIA PAPERBACK

New York   London   Toronto   Sydney   New Delhi

An Imprint of Simon & Schuster, LLC
1230 Avenue of the Americas
New York, NY 10020

This book is a work of fiction. Any references to historical events, real people, or real places are used fictitiously. Other names, characters, places, and events are products of the author's imagination, and any resemblance to actual events or places or persons, living or dead, is entirely coincidental.

Copyright © 2023 by Ruth P. Watson

All rights reserved, including the right to reproduce this book or portions thereof in any form whatsoever. For information, address Atria Books Subsidiary Rights Department, 1230 Avenue of the Americas, New York, NY 10020.

First Atria Paperback edition February 2024

ATRIA PAPERBACK and colophon are trademarks of Simon & Schuster, LLC

Simon & Schuster: Celebrating 100 Years of Publishing in 2024

For information about special discounts for bulk purchases, please contact Simon & Schuster Special Sales at 1-866-506-1949 or business@simonandschuster.com.

The Simon & Schuster Speakers Bureau can bring authors to your live event. For more information or to book an event, contact the Simon & Schuster Speakers Bureau at 1-866-248-3049 or visit our website at www.simonspeakers.com.

Interior design by Dana Sloan

Manufactured in the United States of America

1 3 5 7 9 10 8 6 4 2

Library of Congress Cataloging-in-Publication Data
Names: Watson, Ruth P., author.
Title: A right worthy woman : a novel / Ruth P. Watson.
Description: First Atria Books hardcover edition. | New York : Atria Books, 2023.
Identifiers: LCCN 2022054545 | ISBN 9781668003022 (hardcover) |
ISBN 9781668003039 (paperback) | ISBN 9781668003046 (ebook)
Subjects: LCSH: Walker, Maggie Lena, 1864-1934—Fiction. |
LCGFT: Biographical fiction. | Novels.
Classification: LCC PS3623.A8736 R54 2023 | DDC 813/.6—dc23/eng/20221110
LC record available at https://lccn.loc.gov/2022054545

ISBN 978-1-6680-0302-2
ISBN 978-1-6680-0303-9 (pbk)
ISBN 978-1-6680-0304-6 (ebook)

To all the hardworking, courageous women who envisioned what could be, and who sacrificed their intelligence, time, and energy for the love of friends and family and for the betterment of their communities.

When it comes to success the choice is simple. You can either stand up and be counted or lie down and be counted out.

—MAGGIE LENA WALKER

A RIGHT WORTHY WOMAN

CHAPTER 1

RICHMOND, VIRGINIA

1876

AT TWELVE YEARS OLD, my childhood immediately ended. On a chilly February day, Daddy's body was found floating facedown in the raging, icy James River. I was forced to forget about playing outside after school and instead focus on helping my mother, who afterward would stare hopelessly at the sky, searching for God, and crying herself to sleep at night. Nothing was ever easy again.

The night Daddy died, Momma kept glancing at the old wooden clock on our kitchen wall.

I remembered the worry in Momma's eyes when the clock read 6:45 p.m. Daddy always arrived home by half past five each evening. She had tried to stay calm, but none of it was normal. She'd paced the rough floorboards that she always kept shined to a high gloss, tracing and retracing her steps across the kitchen.

Daddy had left home early that morning before daylight to work for the St. Charles Hotel. He loved his work and would stand ramrod-straight

1

whenever he'd speak of his job. And each morning, Momma would watch him from the front door in the murky darkness before dawn as he moved swiftly along, with his lunch tucked tightly under his arm, until he was out of sight. His shift at the hotel started at 6:00 a.m. and ended at 5:00 p.m., and Daddy never complained.

That night, the hard knock on the door had made us all shudder. I rushed to open it.

"Oh no, child, you let me get it," Momma had said, right behind me.

She looked around and laid her eyes on the rifle beside the front door. She hadn't picked it up, but I'd gone and stood close to it in case there was a problem. Bracing herself, Momma opened the door cautiously. A white Richmond police officer stood there, and immediately she knew something was terribly wrong.

"Mrs. Mitchell?" the officer had asked. She nodded in affirmation. "Can I come in?"

"Yes, sir, come on in," she'd said, her voice trembling, hesitantly glancing over her shoulder to find me beside the rifle, my eyes on her, curious about this interruption in our routine. The policeman had entered, looking like a Confederate soldier in his navy-blue swallow-tailed coat with a raised leather collar and faded blue trousers. A truncheon at his side, he had his hand on it, ready to use it, even though only Momma, Johnnie, and me were at home.

Momma turned to me and said brusquely, "Get back, child." Fear exuding from her wide eyes.

I, stubborn as usual, hadn't budged, moving closer to Daddy's rifle. Though still young, I was old enough to know how mean the Richmond police officers could be to colored folks, and I had known, even at that age, that I should not and would not move.

"I've got some bad news," the officer had said, stepping into the hallway, kicking dirt off his boots onto Momma's spotless floor. He'd continued into the kitchen, Momma following.

"What is it, sir?" Momma had asked, wiping her hands on her apron.

He told Momma that Daddy had been found floating in the James River. "Drowned," she mumbled. Momma stood stock-still.

Then she asked, "How did it happen, sir?"

The officer narrowed his eyes and said, "We think it was suicide."

Momma started to tremble. Her hands shivered like a leaf as she tried to maintain her posture.

"Thank you," she said quietly and went to the front door to open it for him, all the while keeping her composure. When the officer walked out the door, she closed it cautiously behind him.

The instant he was gone, she turned around, glanced at us, and slumped down to the floor. We rushed over to her and held her in our arms, tears sliding down Johnnie's and my cheeks. Momma didn't believe a word the officer said. And she knew no one would even care.

"He didn't drown, and he didn't commit suicide," she murmured.

Now, every night she is lonesome and tired, mourning for Daddy while worrying herself to the bone for us.

❖❈❖

Since then, all I do is think about Momma. Will she be all right without Daddy? Will we ever be able to afford a full meal? Only one slab of bacon remained hanging in the small smokehouse in the back. When my brother Johnnie, only six, whined about being hungry, there was not much I could do. The flour was running low in the kitchen and the lard was just about gone, too—everything had to be rationed. A half a biscuit with a little apple butter would do.

Momma's eyes were red from crying silently. All I wanted to do was comfort her. But there's no rest or comfort when you're suddenly the only parent and support for two children.

Before Daddy died, Momma had already been laundering rich white folks' clothes for some time, to add to what Daddy brought home from his job. When it became our only way to survive, Momma needed Johnnie's and my help to not only grow her business but keep our family afloat. And I worried I would have to leave school and work full-time as other poor colored children had to do.

So, we worked. My puny, pruned fingers dried up, and my skin cracked from being in boiling-hot water. The rose water and fatback grease Momma told me to rub on them had little effect, and my brother cried because his hands ached. The potash soap was rough on the skin. My knuckles blistered from rubbing stains out of Momma's customers' fine clothes on a washboard.

Momma kneaded each garment like a loaf of bread on the tin washboard. Her wrinkled hands immersed in steaming-hot water, she'd press and roll the clothes until all the stains were gone. And she taught me how to do the same thing.

It was like a supply-chain line—all of us had a responsibility. Johnnie's job was to keep the fire going under the pots, so that when the clothing was transferred from the soapy pot into the rinsing pot there'd be no wasted time.

Momma was proud of her children—with few complaints, we had become a part of her laundry production line. She was proud of all that we accomplished, and constantly told us so. "I know it is hard, and every day I thank the Lord for my children."

One of the secrets of Momma's well-earned reputation for outstandingly fresh laundry was the addition of a dash of water scented with rose petals and lavender to the final rinse. It gave the clean clothing an inviting smell and a crispness that lasted.

Our day always started before daybreak. With our eyes half-shut, we got the clothes done in the early morning chill and left them hanging on the clothesline, swinging in the wind. So, after a breakfast of grits, which kept us full all day, together Johnnie and I would walk swiftly through the dense trees and onto the cobblestone road, hoping to reach school before our teacher rang the late bell.

Each day after school, Johnnie and I would rush home to help Momma deliver the day's laundry. She would have the clothes ready by midafternoon, having ironed and starched them while we were in school.

Momma had four main customers, each of them snobbish in different ways, and all of them so wealthy they practically owned the town. Mrs. Thalhimer, the wife of the man who owned the biggest and most popular department store in Richmond, was the richest. She had a house full of servants, yet she hired my mother, Lizzie Mitchell, to do her laundry.

Each time we went to Mrs. Thalhimer's house, I strained my eyes to see beyond the confines of the kitchen and the butler's pantry where we left the basket of clean clothing. If no one was watching, I'd peek around the kitchen doorway to admire the paisley wallpaper and tall ceilings in the grand parlor. I knew the rest of the house had to be magnificent, with large rooms filled with the finest furnishings, including paintings brought over from Europe. On one of the parlor walls in later years was a masterpiece that I learned was by Monet. I would get glimpses of these things and had determined that one day I would have a fine house just like this.

One rainy evening, we unexpectedly saw Mrs. Thalhimer herself, who normally would have been out playing whist with her friends. Even when she was home, she spent little time in the kitchen, which was where we entered, through the back door, being oh so careful not to scuff up her meticulously shined wood floors. The thunderous downpour had probably brought her home tonight.

"Hello, Lizzie," Mrs. Thalhimer said, nodding in Momma's direction. Momma's name was Elizabeth, but most folks called her Lizzie. "How are you today? And you too, Maggie?" She smiled down at me.

"We're fine, thank you. Still mourning Willie's passing, of course, but we're getting by," Momma answered with her head hanging down.

Mrs. Thalhimer was wearing a long, buckled, sky-blue dress. She had a waist so tiny I could probably have wrapped my hands around it. Did she eat? I wondered. She was elegant and effortlessly exuded confidence. A queen— and she carried herself in that manner. After thumbing through the basket of laundry we had delivered, she kindly reached in her dress pocket, pulled out a small pouch, and gave Momma a few coins for the day's work, which clanged as they fell into her hand.

My eyes studied everything around me, especially the furniture in the nearest room, cushiony and fine, with intricately carved wood. I had never seen anything like it. I was in awe of all of it, and couldn't hold my tongue any longer to ask, "Mrs. Thalhimer, how can I live like you?"

"Hush, child!" Momma scolded, giving me a disapproving look with those deep, dark eyes of hers. "Don't bother Mrs. Thalhimer with your silly questions."

But Mrs. Thalhimer appeared to be amused by my brashness and smiled. She glanced over at Momma. "It's important for her to ask questions. How else will she learn?" Then she turned her attention to me, saying, "You appear to be a bright girl. How could that happen, you ask? Keep asking questions and keep a sharp eye on your mother. Work hard like her, doing the best you can. Then save your money."

I smiled and nodded, listening intently to her advice. I knew, of course, that the chances of me or any other colored person ever living in a house like hers were close to nil. But I was pleased by Mrs. Thalhimer's remarks and decided right then and there that I would strive to give truth to her words. I knew the few coins she gave Momma was hardly enough for much.

On the way home, I could see the tension building in Momma's face. First the creases and then frowns. She felt I had said the wrong thing; colored girls were not to speak without being spoken to, and I had done the unspeakable. Although she didn't say much, the side eye she gave me and her tight jaw were enough to worry me about a whipping when I got home.

When the scolding came, her voice rose: "You said that like you were a white child, and you know better."

I lowered my head sadly and didn't say anything.

Momma said, "The next time you go anywhere with me, keep your mouth shut."

I thought to myself, *Why couldn't a colored girl ask a question, too?*

CHAPTER 2

1876–1885

AS WE LEFT THE OFFICE of the Independent Order of St. Luke in Jackson Ward, a thought occurred to me: *Dead men can speak, even from the grave.* Everything Daddy had done for us was on my mind, and he was more than worthy of a proper burial. The Order, as we sometimes called it, was a fraternal order that was noted for addressing the needs of the community. Burial costs were one of the things residents often depended on them to provide assistance for, since funerals were expensive and most people couldn't add that cost into an already depleted budget.

Our home was not in the heart of Jackson Ward, a predominantly colored neighborhood, but it was close enough. It was a few blocks over, hidden behind a street lined with a canopy of red maple trees, fern twigs carpeting the walkway. My daddy loved it because it was close to downtown and near his job. Our beloved community in Jackson Ward was flourishing with newness and small businesses. And we were proud of having made a good home for ourselves despite the almost constant upheaval of everyday life that still lingered fifteen years after the end of the Civil War. The Independent Order of St. Luke, which helped to support and uplift our community, was right in the heart of it all.

Momma's eyes drooped at the thought of asking the members of the Order for help, but where else could we go? And she was grateful for their services, but meticulous when we sat down with the undertaker an hour later. Taking special care in all the details for Daddy's burial, she told the undertaker, who was dressed in a weary black and dry as a prune, how she wanted Daddy's hands placed. "I want them down beside him and not across the chest. He didn't sleep that way," she said, and the undertaker nodded in agreement.

I was so impressed with the services that the Order provided, I thought about their kindness all the way home. It wasn't long before I started attending their meetings at the First African Baptist Church, where Johnnie and I went to Sunday school every week. My curiosity had gotten the best of me.

My very first visit to one of the Order's meetings at the church stirred something in me. My determination to be free from a life of subservience developed over time. I had seen firsthand the assistance that the Independent Order of St. Luke had given us for the funeral and burial costs for Daddy. They offered other humanitarian services to colored people, trying to help them find better jobs and writing letters to the government demanding to change laws that restricted their ability to better themselves. I wanted to be involved.

There, I gazed studiously at the crowd who attended the meetings. All of them businesslike and concerned about the community. Men and women alike worried about the citizens living in Jackson Ward and other smaller colored communities nearby. I was concerned, too. And even though Momma allowed me to attend the meetings, work at home did not stop. The laundry business came first.

When I was not needed for chores at home, I spent what time I could at the Independent Order of St. Luke. I'd ask questions. Lots of them. Each time I went there, I'd come home with a mountain of ideas for how colored people could do better for themselves and for their community. Though Momma worried about me and my ideas, she was also very proud of how ambitious my dreams were.

She was also proud of the skills I was developing through my volunteer work for the Order. I learned office skills—filing, taking notes, bookkeeping—and I even inquired about starting a youth branch of the Order, something the members joyfully agreed to. Clearly, I was on a mission, not just of self-improvement but of improving the world in which colored people lived. And folks at the Order were starting to notice me.

✦C✦

Momma continued to work herself ragged for us. I marveled at seeing how, despite how tired she appeared, Momma never seemed to stop. I knew that when I grew up, I wanted to be like her, strong-willed and independent. She was intent on making a good life for us, no matter how difficult it was. More than once I had heard her say, "A little hard work is good for you. It will make you stronger as the days go on." And she was proud. She'd kept her head high when she'd approached the men at the Order about Daddy's funeral, and she did the same with the undertaker, never waning away as some women do when speaking to men. She was going to do whatever was necessary for the betterment of my brother and me. "We're going to make it, Lord," she would mumble to herself at times while staring at the ceiling.

Momma said she was always very tired and wished that we could reclaim the easier life we'd had before Daddy died, but her own mother had schooled her well in the need to keep her head out of the clouds, to focus on what was real, and to take on every task with determination. Getting the job done was important, but more critical was doing the job the best we could. That, Johnnie and I had come to realize, was the only way to get ahead in life.

In many ways, I was a perfectionist like Momma—especially when it came to learning. I was a good student. I wanted to know about everything and how to apply all that knowledge. I was especially attentive when it came to conversations about economics, particularly as it applied to our lives. "Why do things cost so much?" I would ask. "We work until our fingers ache and still there is not enough money to buy so many of the things we need— forget the things we want. They're all so expensive. Why do white people seem to have all the money?" I would either be called impertinent or was ig- nored, but no one ever had a satisfying answer to any of my questions. I think that was the reason I found attending the Independent Order of St. Luke meetings so compelling.

Often, I found myself wondering how it was that stores and vendors put such a high price tag on things that cost very little to make. The potash soap that Momma used to wash her customers' clothes came from combining animal fat and ashes, by-products of regular household practices. Yet some people sold one bar of that soap for more than it took to make an entire tray.

I took all my questions to the Order meetings. Some folks would turn up their noses when I offered my ideas, but knowing I was the youngest in the room did not stop me. One night, one person blurted out, "You think you white or something?" Another said, "What do someone your age know?"

I wasn't sure who made the comments, but I stared hard in the direction the voices had come from and didn't look away for a minute. I mimicked the glare Momma gave me when I was out of line. All coloreds, no matter how light-skinned, were second-class citizens in Richmond—and in the world. And just as they had questions, so did I.

I told Momma about that exchange. "Child, do not worry your little head about things like that," she said. "Just leave them up to the good Lord."

I frowned. My mother had been raised in a home among independent white women who took risks and worked secretly to defeat the Confederacy. It was something she was proud of and spoke about often, yet it was clear that in her heart she had settled for things as they were. White women could make a difference; coloreds could not.

I was determined not to settle. I enrolled in the Richmond Colored Normal School, which trained colored high school students to be teachers.

As soon as I earned my teacher's diploma in 1883, I had devised a plan to use it and my education to make a difference in the world. I would not be silenced.

◆◆◆

I often thought about the coins Momma received from the laundry work we did. Some weeks it was enough and at other times it didn't amount to much. But how to turn them into more wasn't something I was taught in school or anywhere else. As a teacher at the Valley School, I couldn't help but try to change that with my own students. For three years, I stood before my class with a few coins in my hands.

"Do you know what this is?" I'd ask the class.

"A penny!" one of the little boys hollered out loud, forgetting to raise his hand.

"That's right. And what can a penny buy?"

"An egg?" they hurled back at me.

"And what else?" I would ask, encouraging them to think about the world around them. "What does five pennies equal?"

"A nickel!"

"How many nickels equal one dollar?"

The children paused to think, some of them writing on a sheet of paper and others counting on their hands, all of them trying hard to visualize the coins.

Finally, one of them said, "Twenty, Mrs. Mitchell."

"Right. What can we buy with a dollar?"

"A lot," a little girl answered, eyes wide with wonder. Then she added, "My momma can get a lot of things with a dollar."

"So, the more money one has, the more they can buy." I'd look around to see if they were paying attention before continuing: "You can get a dozen eggs, a pound of beans, a bushel of potatoes, sugar, and flour with just one dollar. We started with a penny, and we could only afford one egg. Now we can get a lot more. Small things can build into greater things, more sustainable things, that can help us live a little better, a little easier."

It was not long before those little exercises were making the children think critically about their well-being, and what it cost on a daily basis to live in their parents' house and why knowing how to count and make money was essential to their quality of life.

One Wednesday, as I was finishing up for the day to leave for a meeting of the Independent Order of St. Luke, I stood smiling to myself, feeling like I was making a difference. As I packed up, I invited another teacher to join me at that evening's Order meeting. She accepted.

CHAPTER 3

1885

THE INDEPENDENT ORDER of St. Luke meeting started at 6:00 p.m. I rushed to pack up from the day and straighten up my classroom to head over to the church for the meeting. My students had been quite inquisitive. They wanted to know how to make money and increase it over time. Their little eyes were ablaze with curiosity. "Are we going to be able to spend the money we've saved on land?" "Can we have a business like the white people?" So, I made sure to change my plans for the next day to include all the questions they had about money and buying. It would be another exciting way to learn math.

Being active in the Independent Order of St. Luke inspired me. From my very first meeting, the discussions about our youth and the needs of our community had me ready to roll up my sleeves and work. The Juvenile Branch had grown and so had the membership. They had allowed me to add a voice in the room, and most importantly, the voice of a woman. When they helped bury my daddy, I knew they were doing good in the community. My participation in the Order had led to me being the speaker for the night. I had quickly gained the trust of the other members by offering suggestions whenever possible for how we could improve our services. And I didn't mind the challenge of taking the lead. It had been my idea to get our youth more involved, knowing their parents would follow and, in that way, help to increase our funding. It sounded a little unrealistic at first, but as I began to invite strangers to the meeting, and some of them stayed, the other members began to see me as a vital part of the Order.

"The increase in membership, along with the additional funds, has been a blessing to our community! They've allowed us to help more families bury their kin *and* pay the undertakers for their services!" I said loudly, trying to bring the meeting to order. Slowly, the overlapping conversations dwindled as I repeated myself over again until I finally held everyone's attention.

The enraged attendees' anger began to subside, and the outbursts concerning the cost of undertaker services in Jackson Ward ceased. Two undertakers in attendance, dressed all in black, stood up and clapped, and others stood and joined in with them. Burying our deceased at no charge was about to come to an end in Jackson Ward. Fannie Tweedy, the wife and owner of the most prominent funeral parlor director, threw her hands up in the air in elation, as her husband continued to applaud, and thunderous gratitude was heard across the room. Finally, the in-kind services were no longer necessary.

As my eyes panned over the elated crowd, I noticed that Armstead Walker was sitting motionless. *What would rouse him?* I thought. Yet I was still captivated by his lack of expression and stately manner. There was something alluring about him, and I simply could not tear my eyes away.

I didn't believe in love at first sight then, and I didn't still when my heart raced the first time I truly set eyes on Armstead Walker. A regular at the Independent Order of St. Luke meetings, Armstead was well dressed in a dark suit and bow tie, sitting quietly at the back of the room, when he caught my eye. His upright, muscular frame was very distinguishable from where I stood on the podium. He was a handsome man with a thick mustache and a face so smooth it appeared waxed. However, it was rare that I ever noticed him smiling, because he always seemed to maintain a stoic countenance. I wasn't sure if it was his demeanor or his beauty, but the crowd surrounding him seemed very ordinary in comparison. This was certainly not the first time I'd had that feeling when he was in attendance.

Armstead sat judiciously and patiently, waiting for me to give my report. The rest of the group was a bit raucous as a cacophony of voices bounced around the room.

Armstead listened respectfully to the concerns of the people and their questions. When he did offer an opinion, he had an astute comment for every subject. This impressed me even more. If he was ever frustrated, it was impossible to tell. Armstead had a poker face, as they called it. You could not tell when he was moved. And after the loud outbursts and chitter-chatter of the members, the observations he shared were easy on my ears.

Most of the meetings were well planned and followed close to the agenda, but talk of burials seemed to bring out the worst in the attendees. Many of them complained about not being able to pay the high cost associated with the undertakers' prices, even with help from the Order's burial fund. The undertakers held their ground on their prices, refusing to lower them any further.

"Maggie, we've solved half of the issue, but what about the undertakers overcharging us?" one of the members stood up and said.

"Maybe we can have a discussion with the undertakers at another meeting."

Mr. Walter Jones, an undertaker, said, "Ain't nothing to discuss. We have given you all too many services for free already."

Voices were raised again, and the meeting grew out of control.

"There's money enough to pay for their services. We have funds in our account," I stated again.

The crowd calmed down, and after a series of additional concerns, tabled until the next meeting, we adjourned. Most left with a smile on their face.

I couldn't help but look for Armstead as folks began to leave the church. I found him sitting, stoic yet poised, still looking at me. I secretly wondered if he was married. Without knowing the answer, I felt physically drawn to him, my heart begging me to move closer.

At the close of the meeting, the usual folk who hung around to discuss matters and debate were in the room. I boldly strolled over to Armstead Walker, who was just standing to leave, and introduced myself.

"Good evening. I am Maggie Mitchell. How are you this evening?"

He beamed and held out his hand for a handshake. "Armstead Walker. Nice to finally meet you, Miss Mitchell. I've heard your name many times, and heard you speak, of course," he said, gesturing to the podium. "Yet somehow, we've never been officially introduced."

As he spoke, I glanced over him, looking for a wedding band or any signs of marriage, things married men did like shifting their eyes from side to side, cautious of their surroundings and who might be watching them. But his eyes remained on me, oblivious of the surrounding voices. I slyly glimpsed down at his hands. His hands were rough as someone used to hard labor, but there was no ring on his finger.

"You can call me Maggie. No need to be so formal. I'm glad we finally had the chance to meet properly," I said. "What do you do when you're not attending these meetings, Mr. Walker?"

"In that case, 'Armstead,' please," he said, pressing a hand to his chest. "I guess you could say I'm a builder. I work mainly in this community. I have built a few of the structures that house some of the businesses here in Jackson Ward," he said modestly.

I knew of his company and the precision used in their Jackson Ward renovations. However, I had never met the man who owned the business. He was one of several Walkers attached to the premier Jackson Ward construction company.

"And what do you do, Maggie?"

"I'm a teacher," I answered proudly, sticking out my chest. "Some evenings I come to the Order to volunteer and offer my services, but my passion is getting young people ready for the world."

He listened like he was truly analyzing my every word. Then he said, "Education is very important. Many children struggle with reading and arithmetic; simple things, like counting money correctly. You are a blessing to those children, I'm sure." His compliment made me blush, but I caught myself and tried to remain serious. However, I couldn't help but admit to myself that I was mesmerized by his hazel-brown eyes.

"Well, Mr. Walker, I appreciate your compliment. Yet I feel there is so much more to do in the community. The Order needs as much help as it can get. It does such important work yet has trouble sustaining itself."

He nodded. "We all do," he said and peered around the room. "Well, Miss Maggie, it seems we are going to be the last people in here if we don't get to going soon."

"It seems you are right," I said, scanning the room as well. It was practically empty. "It was nice meeting you," I said, ready to turn away and head home.

"May I walk you home?" Armstead asked, and then I really couldn't help the smile that spread across my face.

Armstead was more than just handsome; he was a gentleman.

"Thank you. I would like that," I said and pulled my shawl up around my shoulders, ready to brace myself against the brisk evening air.

Behind us, two men were still chatting. We could hear the bass tone of an undertaker's voice as we left the building saying, "Funerals ain't cheap. We have expenses, too. You have no idea how much time it takes to prepare the body."

"Have you forgotten? I have a funeral parlor, too."

Their voices faded and the sounds around us shifted as we left the building and moved farther away. By the tenor of the conversation, we could sense the discussion would certainly last awhile. Their concern was always about business, as if our people were not dying every day.

"They might have to lock up the church on those two," Armstead said, smiling.

"I sure hope not," I kindly replied.

Armstead positioned himself on the outside of the cobblestone sidewalk as we strolled down the street. The street lanterns lit the pathway as we headed home. Armstead cautiously looped my arm in his as an escort would. I was a bit uncomfortable at first and could feel the tension rising, yet I didn't pull away.

"Are you married?" I asked finally, knowing he might not have taken my arm if he was married or in a relationship, but needing to be sure. The magpies, my name for people who always had a negative opinion about things, were always paying close attention, lurking behind closed doors, curtained windows, and around building corners, and I didn't want to give them anything to gossip about. Most everyone in Jackson Ward was associated and word traveled fast.

"No, Maggie, I am a single man. I guess I've been working too much to find the time to court anyone seriously." My doubts seemed to unravel and dissolve.

As we strolled down the uneven sidewalk, we passed by other couples who'd left the meeting and they nodded or smiled at us. I was rarely seen out with anyone and seeing me with a suitor was clearly a pleasant surprise to them.

"Maggie, I assume you must have a suitor. I hope he understands I mean no harm. I just don't want to see a lady walking home alone," Armstead commented, being less bold with his information-seeking than I was.

"No, I don't. I am always working myself. I haven't made the time."

I noticed a smile subtly spread across his face. I had been approached by men before, yet none of them appeared to be my type. I desired someone with my entrepreneurial goals, someone who cared about the community. Armstead spoke with excitement as we discussed the restoration of Jackson Ward. His voice came alive as he described the amount of time it took to make sure the buildings were constructed soundly and with a flair for their community. His biggest concern had been the way the price of lumber seemed to be increasing by the minute.

"The community is growing, Maggie, and I love being in the midst of it all." What he shared made me feel optimistic about the growth of Jackson Ward.

As we got closer to my house, I slowed my stride and looked up, as if I was trying to see all the stars lighting up the universe before going inside. I didn't want the night to end. I was enjoying Armstead's company so much.

Armstead looked up at the sky, too. "It is a clear night. You can see every star in the sky," he said.

"I love to look up at the gibbous moon and the bright stars. It's like God is smiling down on us," I said, pointing out the Big Dipper and Little Dipper to him.

"Maggie, you are something else," he said, and we both giggled. "I hope God is watching."

"I am sure my momma is," I said, knowing she was probably peeking from behind the window sash, waiting patiently for me to arrive home while watching the old wooden clock.

As we approached my house, I said, "This is where I live."

He faced me. "Thank you for allowing me to walk you home."

I smiled. "It was my pleasure, Armstead. I've enjoyed the company."

As I placed my foot on the stairs to go up to the front door, Armstead asked, "Do you think I could come by sometime and maybe take you to the Virginian to hear some music?"

I was fidgety, but also glad to hear his proposal. I searched my purse for a key, and realized the door was almost never locked. "I'd love to do that," I answered in my normally confident yet now shaky voice.

As I placed my foot on the next-to-last step up to the porch, Armstead came up the stairs behind me. I turned around and gazed at him, sort of wondering where he was going.

"May I pick you up on Saturday night?" he asked. I deliberately paused before answering.

"Yes, Saturday is good," I said with apprehension, as if I had a list of other callers.

Armstead grinned. "Is seven o'clock a good time?"

"Well, yes, seven is fine," I said.

"Unless you'd like to have dinner before the show?" I nodded yes. "In that case, I think six o'clock would be better. We can grab a bite to eat and then go over to listen to some music."

"That's perfect," I said.

"I will see you on Saturday evening then," he said, smiling.

Armstead waited for me to open the front door, and once I put one foot inside, he turned to go back down the steps, a smile of accomplishment barely concealed on his face. Once he was back on the sidewalk, he attentively waited for me to go inside the house. As I stepped through the door, I glanced back at him, and he was still there. When he caught a glimpse of me, I turned away quickly, and closed the front door.

He only lived two streets over from me, which would make it easier to visit. When I finally got myself together, I peeked out the front door, but he was long gone.

I could smell the pungent but satisfying aroma of coffee wafting through the house. I dared not go into the kitchen because I knew Momma was in there, but she called out to me before I could make my escape. "Is that you, Maggie?"

"Yes, ma'am," I replied and went into the kitchen, where she sat sipping a cup of coffee. I took a seat at the table. "Momma, I think I like that guy."

"What's so special about him, darling?"

"He seems to be a good man."

"Now, what makes you feel that way?"

Momma sipped her coffee and waited for me to gather my reasonings. "Well, he has purpose. He cares about the community and is helping to restore things in Jackson Ward."

"Remember, you had a good daddy."

"I know, Momma, and he has some of the same qualities," I said, smiling shyly, blushing.

"You have to get to know him, chile. Don't be too quick to love. Things are not always as they seem."

I smiled. "Momma, Armstead is different, I know it. And I want to see him again."

Momma shook her head and smiled back. Then she looked up toward the ceiling, something she always did when she was talking to God.

CHAPTER 4

1885

THE WEEKEND CAME FAST. I tried on everything in my armoire before choosing a deep crimson bustled dress with pleats and a tight corset to accentuate my waist and lift my bustline. I added a little pressed powder to my cheeks and cinnamon blush for color. Standing in front of the mirror, my bright skin reflected the lights. For this special evening, I wanted to be radiant. Momma sensed he was special, since I had never spent so much time getting dressed before. My hair and makeup were perfect. I always cared about appearances, but this evening I wanted to be sure that I was the center of Armstead Walker's attention.

Momma watched me as I added a little more cinnamon powder to my cheeks.

"That's enough, you're already pretty," she commented.

"Just a little dot, Momma."

She stood observing my every move, determined.

"Momma, how did you know Daddy was the one?" I asked, still pressing my hair in place.

"You will know, chile, you will know," she said, and she sat down on the side of my bed.

"What's wrong?" I asked her, after she hesitated to answer me.

"Willie Mitchell was really too good for me."

"Momma, I know that couldn't be true," I said and put the final bobby pin in my hair.

"Well, chile . . ." she doubtingly said while I twirled in front of the armoire admiring myself.

She tapped the bed. "Come sit down beside me for a spell."

I sat down next to her, and she cleared her throat.

"In 1863, when the Confederate Army, on the verge of surrender, marched into Richmond, their men exhausted and despondent, the Van Lews opened their home to the soldiers. A flush of fear swept over the entire mansion. And every servant, including me, dreaded what might happen," she said.

"That Saturday afternoon," she continued, "when the first group of soldiers appeared inside the house, waiting to be fed, the pungent stench of sulfur wrought by exploding gunpowder filled the air, almost but not quite powerful enough to overwhelm the smell of sweat and fear and wet wool. The men were fatigued, most of them filthy, some wrapped in bloody cloth bandages.

"It was known by every member of the household that Ms. Elizabeth Van Lew had secretly worked to advance the Union cause throughout the war, hiding soldiers in the cellar of her home and showing them great kindness. Yet still she needed to treat the Confederates as honored guests. Ms. Van Lew instructed her servants to serve the soldiers a soup of pork and vegetables. She didn't believe in what they stood for, and she was no stranger to their evildoing, but she had to keep up appearances.

"Most of the soldiers were rude to the women serving them. But I made sure that they were properly cared for. Many were from poor homes themselves and had only seen their mothers and sisters set the table. Servants were far outside their range of experience. Now they groped the women who

tended to them. I hated their behavior," Momma told me. And she was surprised when one of the soldiers chastised another for grabbing her buttocks.

"'You got a thing for this nigga girl?' the offending soldier asked," Momma
said. "'We are all hungry,' my defender answered. 'Leave her alone and allow
her to serve our food.'

"I stole glances at him, careful not to be caught looking at him openly.
He seemed different from the others. He said thank you when served and
was generally polite to everyone. After the men were full and relaxed, most
of them fell asleep on the floor. The solicitous one, though, graciously offered
to help me move the dishes from the dining area into the kitchen.

"Later that evening, with the household settled and quiet, the soldier
who had come to my aid sat at the kitchen table, writing in a notepad. He
encouraged me to take a seat at the table. Though apprehensive, I did. He
introduced himself to me, telling me that he was a writer and hoped to be
a reporter one day. He reached for my hand and told me how much he admired my beauty. For years, I had gently rebuffed Willie's advances. Now, an
educated white soldier was giving me the same kind of attention, his eyes
paying the same compliments. The more we chatted in the kitchen that night,
the more relaxed I became, my anxiety slowly slipping away. At least not all
Confederates were evil, I thought."

"Weren't you going to tell me about Daddy?" I interrupted.

"I want you to know the whole story."

Momma continued: "The soldier's name was Eccles Cuthbert. He came
back to visit me many times after our first encounter. One day, Willie watched
from a distance as me and Eccles stood on the veranda. Willie later told me
that he had to resist calling out when Eccles pulled me close to him.

"The next day, Willie asked to speak to me in private. He looked directly
into my eyes and without hesitation said firmly, 'Look the other way, girl.
A white man is nothing but trouble for a colored girl.' But his warning did
absolutely no good. I could not deny my attraction to the handsome soldier,

who began showing up often for the evening meal. We would disappear after dinner into one of the many places we knew we could be alone, uninterrupted.

"Soon enough, I was growing, with you inside, a child the entire house staff knew belonged to Eccles Cuthbert. And now he had gone up north to pursue a career in journalism, having found employment working for the *New York Herald*. Occasionally, a letter would arrive 'For Elizabeth,' in care of Ms. Van Lew—who would dutifully pass it on to me without comment. Sometimes the envelope held a bit of money, but eventually there was a message that made me cry. Seeing my pain, your Daddy's heart ached for me. He was the first one there to assist on July 15, 1864, when the old midwife showed up to deliver my baby." She paused, grinning.

"When you came out, so much paler than me, everyone knew for sure that you belonged to Cuthbert. Shortly afterward, Eccles finally came for a visit. It would be his last. I was left alone with a little white baby. I named you Maggie Lena, after an enslaved woman I had loved as a child.

"Willie, your daddy, quickly came to love you and would often hold you tight in his arms. He always treated you as his own. Because he was so attentive to my child and because my loneliness was so sudden and profound, I began to appreciate Willie more, and as time wore on, he became more attractive to me. He was an unusually kind man, one I'd put off for years, but now I was falling in love with him. Willie was a great man, one I don't think many will find. I just hope Armstead will be worth everything you are putting into this date. Courting can be tricky."

I smiled. I knew about my biological father, Eccles, but she had never spoken about how Daddy had pursued her. He was surely a man on a mission.

❖❍❖

Armstead arrived around 5:30 p.m. that Saturday, earlier than expected. Momma met him at the door. To me, Armstead seemed more handsome than he had appeared at the Order meeting. His perfectly pressed suit fit him like that of a distinguished gentleman, and his shoes shone so bright they sparkled. All I could do was stare.

"Come in," Momma said.

I stood at the top of the stairs watching, my nerves twitching uncontrollably. With sweat on the palms of my hands, I took my time coming down. And for that moment, I had Armstead's full attention. He gazed up at me as if he was in the presence of royalty, and I smiled cordially. He didn't stop staring until Momma called out his name.

"Mr. Walker, I am Maggie's mother. I hear you live around here." Armstead couldn't take his eyes off me, yet Momma had gotten his attention. While he spoke to Momma, he would casually peer at me as I slowly made my way down the stairs. Momma noticed and glanced at me as well.

"Yes, ma'am, I live two streets over. I could walk here in ten minutes," he answered, giving her the attention she demanded.

"Did you walk tonight?" Momma asked, examining him with her suspicious dark brown eyes. She didn't know him and was careful about who her children associated with, even though I was already a grown woman who'd been teaching nearly three years and helping to pay the bills.

"No, ma'am, I have my carriage outside. I wanted to make sure Maggie was comfortable and we could move swiftly from the restaurant to the Virginian." She peeked around him at the carriage parked in front of our home. I knew Momma was impressed, but she kept a stoic face. Only a few people drove coaches in Jackson Ward or had stables attached to their home to store them along with the horses, and we were surprised he was one of them.

Momma didn't ask many questions, but she did want to know where we were going. Armstead assured her we would stay in the Jackson Ward area. "Now have her home at a decent hour," she said.

"I will, Mrs. Mitchell," Armstead assured her, smiling at me as he took my arm to lead me out to his carriage.

We started our evening close to home. Armstead steered us to a restaurant only a few blocks from my house. As we walked toward the entryway I inhaled. When we entered, the staff greeted him warmly. Clearly, he was a regular there. The elegantly set tables were consistent with the class he'd exuded even at the Order meetings. Like most places in Jackson Ward, it was a colored establishment, and it was filled with the clinking of utensils on plates and waiters and waitresses moving swiftly through the large room, cautiously carrying food with an aroma that had us salivating.

Armstead led me to a table he'd reserved for us. I had never attended with a date, but I had been there once before. It was the finest restaurant in the Ward. My expectation was a quiet table for two in the corner somewhere so we could talk privately, but we took our seats in the center of the room. It seemed to me that Armstead wanted the other diners to recognize us as a couple.

As we waited to be served, it appeared quite a few people were peering at us, and I had to ask, "Armstead, this is a nice place, and the atmosphere is perfect. Is there a reason you chose a table in the center of the room?" We were seated right beneath the large crystal chandelier that folks often admired. For a moment, I felt the light was directly upon me.

"I thought the center would be a perfect place to sit."

"What might you be saying?" I asked him.

"Well, most of us in this part of Richmond know each other. We do business together and we fraternize at the barbershops and hair salons. Sometimes when you are in the corner of a room, the impression is you've got something to hide. We don't have those worries. Anything we do tonight is not a secret. You see, I admire you and enjoy being with you. Besides, I love the center table."

I struggled to contain my smile, yet I knew my cheeks were pink from blushing. Armstead was transparent about what he wanted and was not concerned with the naysayers, the magpies who might gossip about how poor my family was compared to his and make assumptions. Armstead didn't seem to care about any of that. I had always been that way myself. I felt if we handled ourselves in a professional and honest manner, regardless of our status, coloreds would continue to advance. And why not? Jackson Ward was already being talked about in the *Virginia Star*; they called it the Black Wall Street of the South. The Greenwood community in Tulsa, Oklahoma, was similar, as Blacks there strived to build their own wealth and to keep the money in our communities. And just like in Greenwood and the Auburn Avenue community in Atlanta, it was working. We had everything we needed right in Jackson Ward.

The menu had everything you could want, from roasted chicken to lamb. I had skipped meals all day to appear svelte in my dress, but now just the scent of the food being served around us caused my stomach to growl. Armstead took the lead and ordered a glass of red wine for each of us, professing the taste would prepare our tongues for the meal to come. He was a sophisticated man, one many a woman in Jackson Ward would love to have dinner with.

Our eyes met across the table and he reached for my hand. The wine made my head spin. I struggled to find something to say.

"Are you familiar with Peter Woolfolk?" I asked. "He and Otway Steward helped me understand racial progression and led me to believe that I could dream."

"What do you mean by that?" Armstead asked, sipping sweet red wine from the long stemware.

"Well, Mr. Woolfolk was formerly enslaved, and I admire the way he turned his life around. Once freed, he became a teacher and started the *Virginia Star* with Mr. Steward, who was also a teacher. Transformation was at the center of their belief, and I believe it, too. We grow as a community when we have a thirst for knowledge and an undying ambition to be more than we are. Those of us who are educated must lift ourselves and our people up from the degradation and ignorance that whites have forced us into, and then help others to realize their value and their potential as well."

Armstead leaned in to listen to me. It was as if I had opened a door of awareness he had never heard from a colored woman. "Maggie Mitchell, you amaze me. You are speaking about the things I think about much of the time. I haven't heard most women speak on these topics. It brings me much joy that I can talk to you about them." I could imagine other women only amusing him with talk of family and love. I had other things on my mind, too, and didn't mind sharing them.

"There are a lot of women like me, we just need men like you to listen."

He smiled. "Oh, is that so?" I never had a problem speaking out about things I was interested in. And many women would do the same if allowed.

"Armstead, I'm sure you know well that colored women pay attention and want the best for their families and their communities. But we are often too quiet about the things that matter to us, like the right to vote, afraid of retaliation or repercussions. So, we remain silent to keep the peace. Even white women are afraid to talk openly around their men."

"To keep the peace means to be silent?"

"Yes, Armstead." He nodded his head in agreement.

"We've got to do better," he declared, saying it in such a way that I knew it meant he was giving thought to change.

We paused our conversation while the waiter took our food order. Even after he left the table, Armstead was still gazing at me as if I had awakened a concern in him. I sensed from his pensive gaze that he wanted to continue the conversation. So, I broke the silence.

"Most of us colored women are cautious about sharing our feelings with anybody, including our male friends."

"Maggie, these are matters that have kept me up at night from time to time as well. Jackson Ward is a good place for us. I am impressed by the progress we have made, by what I see around me. And I love building more and better for my people. But to go further, I believe we need more women like you."

"We're here, in Jackson Ward. We just need the courage—and support— to raise our voices with yours."

I watched him closely, searching his face for any indications of jealousy or anger. Men are often threatened by intelligent women, especially those unafraid to speak their minds. They'll squint their eyes or frown deeply, furrows forming across their forehead, and then I know to be cautious. These are all signals that a woman has said too much. And in most cases, the "offending" woman will cover her mouth in contrition and apologize for what she said. But not me. My boldness was part of the reason I hadn't had many male callers. They felt I was too forthright for a woman. Most of them would prefer I walk behind them, and just let things be as they've always been. And at times, I might agree. But I saw none of those signs in Armstead's expression.

However, even when I was fourteen years old and working at the Independent Order of St. Luke, I eagerly shared my ideas. At first the men would cut an eye toward me, as a gesture to be quiet, and others would rudely talk over me as if I had not spoken a word. However, with time, things changed, and they began to take me seriously.

"Maggie, what made you want to be a teacher?"

"I believe education is vital for the betterment of our people, but more importantly, education can open doors with others as well. We all should have a yearning to learn something, whether it is a skill or history. I love to teach children because they have a natural thirst for knowledge. We can learn something from everything around us. To teach is an honor."

"I feel we'd make a good team, Maggie," Armstead said, looking at me as if we were the only two people in the room.

"Oh, really?" I said, but inwardly, I agreed with him.

"You know, Maggie, I love your assertiveness, your ideas, and even your bold comments. Most of the women I've known remain silent on most subjects and expect me to take the lead, making decisions and standing for all of us even in matters that involve the state of our community's prosperity. You are a lot like my momma, who was very active in our household and in the community. My daddy made sure her voice was heard, and that we all listened and acted upon her words. And I believe in the same thing. You are something else, Maggie Walker," he said, shaking his head and grinning, "and I'm happy you allowed me to take you out tonight."

I gave myself a moment to take in his words, and a smile spread across my face as I felt joy fill my heart.

The waiter served us plates of lamb chops, sweet potatoes, and turnip greens then. Armstead grabbed my hand and said grace. I wasn't sure I could smile any wider. Putting God first was important to me.

I had observed his interactions with other people, and it was quite clear he was a man with an unmistakable vision. He knew what he wanted, and he was not going to settle for less. I began to think that I had finally stumbled upon a stable and honest man. One who would allow me to do the things I wanted to do in life. One who would be my real partner.

After such a satisfying meal, we decided to skip the chocolate cake and ice milk that was typically served for dessert, and Armstead had a cup of coffee while I finished the red wine I had been sipping on. As he escorted me back to the carriage, he asked, "Do you want to go listen to some music? It is still relatively early."

We had arrived at the restaurant around 5:55 p.m., just five minutes earlier than we anticipated. Yet three hours had passed, and between the conversation, delicious food, and the bustle of the excellent wait service, I was a bit exhausted.

"It is almost nine p.m., and we have been talking for hours. I would love to listen to some soft music, but perhaps another time. I don't think I could handle any more tonight."

"I must admit, I'm a bit disappointed. I wanted to swing you around a couple of times on the dance floor."

I smiled at his comment and said, "Okay, let's go for a little while."

✦c❧✦

The clicking of the horses' hooves on the cobblestone sidewalk pulled us down the street one block to the Virginian. It was a hangout spot for the community, and on occasion, professional acts would perform there.

Millie and Christine McCoy, the conjoined twins, had performed there before they retired. They danced and sang to an unsuspecting crowd of attendees. Most of the people left upset after seeing their act. Instead of jovial conversations about the entertainment, the audience had felt sorry for them. Some of them had loudly vowed to never come back to the establishment. The jazz trio that followed their act relaxed the crowd, but the performance of the conjoined twins was a hard memory to get beyond. The hour we spent inside the club was uninteresting. We enjoyed being together, but neither of us could get into the entertainment hired for the night. So we decided it was time to head home. Despite the disappointments, I couldn't help wishing the evening was not ending.

"Look up at the sky, Maggie. It's a clear night and the moon is bright again." Pointing up, Armstead said, "There's the Big Dipper." I glanced up at the sky, knowing it was the start of something new for me. The stars twinkling made it a perfect evening. The moon seemed to shine right on us like a spotlight. As Armstead pulled me close into his arms, he kissed me lightly on the lips, right in front of Momma's front door. I nearly melted.

"Can I call on you again this week?" he asked, staring into my eyes.

"I'd love that," I answered.

"How about I come over on Friday evening? We can do whatever you'd like."

Before I opened the door, he grabbed my hand and pulled me into his arms again and kissed me deeply on my lips. When Momma swung open the front door with a bang, he quickly let me go. We stood still, gazing at one another.

"Good night, Armstead," Momma said pointedly, as if I were a teenager.

"Good night, Mrs. Mitchell. Maggie, I'll see you on Friday," he said, and waited for me to go into the house. As soon as I closed the door behind me, Momma started peppering me with questions about my evening. She wanted to know all the details, but I gave her just the highlights and she seemed a bit puzzled that I didn't share more. Not that it mattered what she thought about Armstead. Although having Momma in my corner would make everything so much easier.

"So, I take it you had a good time," Momma said inquisitively.

I smiled. "Yes, ma'am. I had a great time."

Respectfully, I was a grown woman.

CHAPTER 5

∼◦⦙◦∼

1885–1886

AS I AMBLED DOWN SECOND STREET into the businesses and shops, folks greeted me with a smile. Each of them soon turned into a frown, shadowed with apprehension, when I brought up the subject of their money and savings.

Mr. Thomas, a prominent man in the community who owned a welding business, attended all the Order meetings. At the mere sight of me, his forehead creased, and a sudden but deep frown appeared on his face. I approached him humbly and as honestly as possible concerning the difficulties we were experiencing at the Order. We discussed things like the diminishing presence of the Order and the lack of funds available to cover the services we often provided to members of our community. We couldn't afford to assist with services such as doctor's visits or prescriptions. Most people created their own concoction instead of visiting the pharmacist. And the assurance of a burial fund had everyone talking.

He stared at me with disgust etched plainly across his contorted and weathered face, and said, "Maggie, every damn time I'm approached by y'all sitting over yonder"—he pointed over my shoulder toward the St. Luke building—"begging is involved."

Mr. Thomas's business made a sizable amount of money from Jackson Ward's residents. A master welder, he was the builder of the locally hand-manufactured cast-iron porches, distinct with their rich ornamental ironwork. He always had work and lacked for nothing. It wasn't too much to ask him to spare what he could for our efforts, for his own people.

"Mr. Thomas, we need assistance from everyone in the community. And we should all be proud to support our own. St. Luke's needs you, and all the other business owners here in Jackson Ward, to dig deep down in your pockets and make a contribution."

The veins in his neck protruded. Just the idea of giving money to an organization—or anyone—had struck a nerve in him. I had been expecting this reaction. I stood unyielding, glaring back at him, knowing he would have bitten me had he been an animal.

"Can I count on you for your support?" I asked again without even wincing. He was tough, but I knew how to work with him. "Mr. Thomas, all the beautiful ironwork fences adorning the front porches across Jackson Ward are your creation, as well as the cast-iron frying pans and pots in each kitchen. We appreciate you and your work so much. All we are asking for is your courteous donation."

"Hell, Maggie. You don't know how to give up, do you? All right, I'll contribute something." Again, he pointed in the direction of the Independent Order of St. Luke and added, "But y'all need to learn how to manage the money we are putting into that organization."

"We do a lot of good with the funds we receive, Mr. Thomas."

"Hell, you know how to get to a man, Maggie. You just push us into a corner." All the while he reached down into his pocket.

He sighed and handed me some greenbacks, which I accepted gracefully, recording the amount in my journal. Most of the other business owners were just as reluctant, but he appeared to be more frugal than the rest, even angry at times. My experience was, the more money a person had, the harder it seemed for them to part with it.

"Thank you, sir," I said before leaving, and he hurled back, "But you're not welcomed." It was always his response. I smiled as I continued canvassing the businesses on Second Street.

❖c❖

Armstead and I were becoming more involved, but at the same time I was busier than ever working as a teacher while also dealing with disgruntled business owners like Mr. Thomas. None of them seemed to understand how important contributing to the Order's fund was for the community.

Sure, most of the money was being used to help with burials, but we were also putting together a fund that residents could borrow from to purchase a home or establish a business.

After long hours teaching and fund-raising for St. Luke's, I couldn't wait for nights on the porch with Armstead when I would lie my head on his muscular chest and watch the stars and lightning bugs, and listen to the crickets chirping as if the night were theirs. Every night, he hated leaving me, and I hated that he had to go home. Often, I'd been told that opposites attract, but we were not so different. I had come to trust Armstead completely. We talked about everything and most times we had the exact same concerns for Jackson Ward, commenting on the same things printed in the *Virginia Star*, our neighborhood newspaper. Armstead believed in working hard to change the colored economic condition. And we both wanted a family.

"Today, I felt like a wheelbarrow."

"What are you talking about, Maggie?"

"I spent some time at Mr. Thomas's business, and he was as stubborn as usual. He will hold on to his money until the very end. I felt I was pulling a load when I was trying to get him to make a contribution. He knows there are certain goods and services every thriving community should have. All he ever worries about is his money. He's got to be one of the most well-to-do men in Jackson Ward."

"I like seeing my money grow, too," Armstead replied adamantly as we sat on the front porch that evening.

"For me, there is very little left to save. I contribute to the Order's fund and then I manage to put a little aside," I said.

"Together we could have more," he proclaimed.

I didn't comment, but silently thought on what he'd said and wondered how that might be possible. *What if we had a bank of our own in our community? Together, our pennies could become dollars.*

Armstead was everything I wanted in a man and a partner, but I was not alone in this. There were other single ladies in town with their eyes on him, and some of them would share their bitter thoughts with me on it. Ella, a friend of Armstead's, simply told me one day as I was knocking on the neighbors' doors soliciting membership for the Order, "Armstead could have any woman in Jackson Ward. You know what folks are saying? That he chose you because you are so damn light, as close to white as any white woman around."

At first, I could only look at her. I wondered, if I was a darker woman, would that truly make a difference? How interesting people were when it involved their true feelings. But as Ella stood firmly with her hands on her hips, nothing she could say would keep me from doing what I'd come to do for the community.

So, I gazed right into her beady dark eyes and said, "No, I wouldn't say that much, Ella. My light skin has nothing to do with it. I think what we have is love and true understanding." She turned her nose up and removed her hands from her hips, walking away as if I'd hurt her feelings and not the other way around. *She* insulted *me*, I thought.

Was it so hard to believe that Armstead was attracted to me because I was beautiful and we shared the same goals and concerns? He had been quite vocal, letting me know how much he admired the way I persisted in sauntering up and down the cobblestoned streets in uncomfortable buckle-heeled shoes in my attempt to help the members of the community. Afterward, my feet would ache from all the walking.

It was strange hearing about her disappointment in our relationship. She obviously didn't know Armstead at all. He treated my dark momma with the utmost respect and the one lady he almost married had been as brown as the cocoa Momma put on her cake. We had something special, and all the jealous women could sense it. I was as colored as they were and unapologetic about the lighter shade of my skin. I'd never considered passing as white, like many other paler coloreds had done. I was colored, through and through.

Roger, a man who had chased after me for over a year, said derogatory things about me, too, once he realized I was happy with Armstead. He was like Ella, jealous.

"You don't like men because you are fancying around as if you are a man. Maggie Mitchell, you are unladylike. No man is good enough for you. And you are always standing toe to toe with us acting as if you are in control. You need to stay in your place and start acting like a woman. Why don't you learn to give your love to a man like me instead of the got-damn community, like you're always talking about?"

Roger was a boisterous man, and careless, always saying whatever he was thinking. He was tall, dark-complexioned, and extremely attractive, but he lacked self-control. His comments were a bit extreme, and they upset me. He couldn't get used to the way I pursued things. I often made him furious because I was so assertive. He would roll his eyes at me. But I hadn't lived in the home of Ms. Elizabeth Van Lew without learning a thing or two. Although I was around six when we moved out of her home, Momma always shared stories of her exploits with me. And fear was not something I ran from. My mother was strong as a bull, and just as stubborn. Besides, I believed that, as a woman, I could get more accomplished than most men.

❖<>❖

Armstead had an authoritative presence at the Order meetings. He would sit in the same place and only comment when needed, but he was never out of place. Once he introduced me to his family, I knew where he had gotten his class and sophistication. His parents were warm and welcoming, and Armstead was the spitting image of his dad, who was a hardworking builder, just like his son.

Between teaching and my social work at the Independent Order of St. Luke, we struggled to find time together.

At the next meeting, all eyes were glued to me as I spoke on increasing juvenile involvement and expanding our outreach in the community. Folks squirmed, wondering how we could make progress in a short period of time. "Things take time," one of the ladies sitting with a grimace on her face said. Though she seemed to be speaking about the community's progress, I knew to expect more than just a bad attitude from her.

After the meeting, I heard her speaking to Armstead. "Why are you still running around with Maggie Lena Mitchell? Just because she acts like she is something special doesn't mean she is, or that she deserves to be with you." She said it without any hesitation or concern that I might be listening a short distance away.

Armstead cleared his throat and replied, "Maggie is my special friend, and in fact I am her suitor."

"Haven't you noticed *me* all these years, Armstead?" the lady said.

"I haven't paid much attention, no. Work has been my priority. There are plenty of men waiting for a chance to take you out. Give one of *them* a chance."

The obstinate woman boldly mumbled, "I know you adore me. I've seen the way you look at me." But she shuffled away in a huff all the same.

He scratched his head and turned away. Finding me there, he said, "I must admit it: people are never interested in you until they see you with someone else. I'm sorry about that, Maggie. Are you okay?"

I nodded my head yes.

"Are you ready to leave, my dear?"

We left the meeting together, as we had done for months.

When I glanced back over my shoulder on the way out, the same lady was showing all her teeth to two businessmen, who'd just been deep in conversation. The two undertakers, who were surely loaded with money, since there was a death nearly every day. *May she find peace and happiness with one of them,* I thought. *And finally leave Armstead alone.*

❖◦❖

On warm nights, Armstead and I often took the long route home, walking through the winding back alleys. Stopping along the way, Armstead kissed me deeply and I, longing for more from him, became embarrassed by the heat building between my legs. "Let's go by my house first," he begged.

"I can't. Momma will kill me," I said. It wasn't just Momma. I wanted him to treat me with respect. Armstead had always been a starched gentleman, and I was not going to ruin it. He agreed, and once we'd calmed down again, we resumed our walk down the cobblestone street and around the ancient limestone buildings past the homes in Jackson Ward.

As was now our custom, we sat for hours on my front porch talking and watching the galaxy. When Momma was not around, I would lay my head on his chest, and it was my peaceful place. The fireflies sparkled every now and again against the dark. When the rain poured, we'd sit in the quietness of the parlor, knowing that anything we said would be heard, because Momma was listening.

When Armstead dropped me off at home that night, Momma asked me, "Why is that man around so often?"

"He enjoys visiting me."

She bit her lip and squinted. "I hope you are not allowing him to do anything you might be ashamed of."

"Of course not, Momma."

"Just remember, child, anything you do in the dark will soon come to light."

I knew she was right. She had given me the same speech often. She wanted me to have more than she ever did, and I wanted more, too. It was the reason I gave more of my time as a volunteer at the Independent Order of St. Luke. I had been honored with the title of secretary, but that wasn't enough. I was determined to make a difference in the lives of coloreds. I had work to do. Since I'd started teaching, Momma had stopped doing laundry for rich white women. I was determined to bridge the economic gaps, and that required a commitment from the entire community. Armstead, unlike Roger, admired me for this effort. I never doubted that he only wanted the best for me.

I had already started talking to the parents of my students in Jackson Ward about the importance of understanding money and how to begin to save it. My students were inquisitive and wanted to understand the differences between the white and colored communities. Most, if not all of it, was based around greenbacks. Explaining hard work and progress to them was difficult.

"Why should we work any harder?" a little boy asked. "My daddy said things haven't changed. They will always hate us."

Tears welled up in my eyes because there was truth in his conviction. I pulled myself together.

"Child, things are changing. Some changes are quick, and others are slow. Do you know what I mean by that?"

The little boy seemed puzzled, so he put his hands in his pockets and stood straight, listening, yet I could see the confusion in his eyes.

"Remember how you kept trying to pull down the latchstring to turn on the lights? Some days you would jump up and touch the hanging string, but grabbing it was too far out of your reach. And I can remember you falling on your knees a couple of those times. In spite of that, you tried it again the next day and the next."

He started to smile. "I remember that!" he exclaimed. And his voice was jovial.

"Then one day after many tries, you could touch it. You grew, child."

"I did, and I grabbed it, too." He spoke happily.

"If you change your thinking and start believing things will be different, you will grow. You've got to keep reaching."

"I can do it, Miss Mitchell."

"If we try, child, anything is possible. There will not be a white man or any man that can hold you back. Your determination along with your growth worked in your favor."

"But how does getting taller help with a white man?"

"Good question, child," I said, realizing it was all coming together for him.

"You didn't allow your height to stop you from trying. Every day, you would jump as high as you could to touch that string, and each time you got a little bit closer. Then one day it was easy for you. It's like playing stickball: you keep trying until you strike the ball."

I was amazed I still had his attention. At times he'd grin, and then glance into space as if he was thinking, and I knew something was happening inside his brain.

"And when you play stickball, you keep trying to hit the tiny ball until you finally do it, and each time it becomes easier. Life is challenging, child, but you will never know what you can do without trying."

A few days later, I met that little boy's daddy at the corner market and couldn't let the opportunity slip by to gently challenge him about what he was teaching his son.

"Mr. James, do you have a minute?" I asked him.

"What ya need, Miss Mitchell? Need help carrying your groceries?" he asked.

"I just want to speak to you about your son, Moses."

He grimaced. "That boy better not be acting up in school. I done told him—"

"No, sir, he is a fine child."

Immediately the lines across his forehead and his frown softened. "What is it, then?"

As we walked around inside the market, I told him, "Along with reading, writing, and arithmetic, we are hoping the children will dream of a better future for themselves and learn how to accomplish it. We want the students to be ambitious, to feel they can be business owners and earn decent wages. Jackson Ward is growing and improving our quality of life every day, and they can grow and improve with it."

"Well, that ain't true. It is hard for us coloreds. Why are you telling them to dream when you know that the white man will hang them dead in the street for nothing at all?" he asked adamantly.

"We have successful colored businesses in Jackson Ward, and I believe your son is smart enough to open his own one day. That is, if you would provide a little encouragement."

He stopped walking and gave me a warning glare. "Are you trying to tell me how to raise my son?"

"No, not at all. I just wish you would try to encourage him to find a trade or something he can do to make his own money."

It took him a while before he spoke again. "Well, Miss Mitchell, I expect I could do that," he said humbly.

"You know, it is so much easier to work toward your own goals than someone else's."

"Miss Mitchell, I promise, I will tell my boy to think on what he might want to do and try to help him achieve it, if I can."

"Mr. James, the Juvenile Branch of the Independent Order of St. Luke meets once a month, sometimes twice. If you need any help or support with Moses, we are a group of sound-minded people, who care about our youth."

I shouted, "Halleluiah!" after he'd left. This was my first victory in convincing a parent to foster their child's economic growth. Jackson Ward was growing, and colored businesses were sprouting up everywhere. For that to continue, the next generation needed to be a part of it, too.

Mr. James and his son weren't the only ones I was hoping to reach, but it was a start. And it bolstered me for the work still ahead. In school, I challenged my students intellectually, making them think about what they could do once they were no longer in school. I wouldn't allow them to focus on the way whites continued to suppress us. Instead, we discussed ways around the oppression.

I remembered stories Momma shared with me about Ms. Elizabeth Van Lew, and the fearless way she had spied on the Confederates for the Union soldiers.

Momma said, "She was too far ahead of the rest of the world."

Those stories at the kitchen table eating fried potatoes and scrambled eggs will forever linger in my mind.

Momma said, "One day, Ms. Van Lew took off in the early morning. It was still dark as coal outside, only a few stars in the sky, and the dew was wet on the ground. She carried a pistol with her whenever she took to the woods, tucked into the waistband of her skirt."

"Going into the woods in the dark?" I asked.

"Oh, yeah. She had gotten word from a strange man that the Confederates were holding a Union colonel or someone hostage in a makeshift fort yonder between Richmond and Petersburg. She took off on one of her horses, didn't even think about the carriage, and headed east. She was back before daylight, and a man was with her, in torn Union soldier clothes. That man stayed down in the cellar until he was healthy. Then one night, when everyone was quiet, he took off and we never heard a word from her about him."

"Didn't folk know about her?"

"Chile, Ms. Van Lew knew how to lie. When the people came looking for the man, she put on a show I had never seen before. She told them she'd alert them if she saw or heard anything. And then she offered them a cup of hot coffee to warm them up. All that time, the man was down in the cellar, quiet as a mouse. Lord have mercy, she was a fearless woman."

"She must have prayed all the time."

"I never seen much of that, but she was always gazing at the sky. I s'pose it was God she was talking to. We did everything we could to help her. And she helped us coloreds. Chile, life ain't easy for some of us, including white people."

"What do you mean?"

"Folks knew she was up to something, and she ignored their hatred, and kept doing what she did. I'm sure she is still taking care of those in need." Momma laughed and shook her head. "She's always been good to us."

Ms. Van Lew's bravery and Momma's stories and wisdom led me to study at the Normal School and become a teacher. I was determined to pass along those lessons to as many students as I could. We deserved better. We deserved more. And we needed to do something about it ourselves.

Much like my students, Armstead knew that after school what awaited him was either to work as a sharecropper on someone's plantation or to take charge of his own fate and determine what he wanted to do for himself. His daddy was good with his hands and Armstead studied him intently as he repaired carriages, learning to build with little training at all. Papa, his granddaddy, worked meticulously with his hands, too. Papa's daddy had worked for the Jewish Germans who originally lived in the Ward and gradually moved farther north when the Civil War ended. His family had been freed before the Civil War started and were willed a piece of property from his former enslaver, Isaiah Isaacs. Isaacs was a very successful businessman and an immigrant, which gained him the respect of the Jewish community as a property owner and wealthy merchant. When he died in 1806, his will stated that his enslaved workers were to be manumitted and enjoy the privileges of free people. Afterward, a few other Jewish families followed his boldness and freed their enslaved servants as well.

✦co✦

One night on the porch, I was telling Armstead about my students and my hopes for them and their futures.

Armstead always gave me his full attention when I spoke. He'd gaze at me like no one else was around, wrap his strong arms around my shoulders, and pull me close to him.

"Maggie, you care deeply about these children, and so do I. If you know of any young men interested in carpentry, or brick masonry, I will be glad to take them under my wing and give them an apprenticeship and pay them."

A few days later, on a sultry summer night when the stars were bright and the fireflies and mosquitos were out, Armstead and I had a serious discussion, one I would never forget.

All our conversations had been meaningful. Except for the times when we joked and laughed without dealing with the seriousness of life.

"Maggie," he said, "we have been spending a lot of time together; all my free time has been with you."

"I hope you are not regretting it. I've enjoyed being with you." We both smirked.

"Each day, I find it more difficult to stay away. I think about you all the time," he kindly said, and I had to catch myself from blushing. Although what he said filled me with joy.

"I remember seeing you at my first Order meeting. You were someone that appealed to me from a distance," I said shyly. Our first encounter had been in a Sunday school class, though we hadn't properly met until the Order meeting.

"Whew, I am so happy we finally met that day. Lately, I've been doing a lot of thinking."

"About what?"

"Your interest in teaching, and how important the youth are to you."

I glanced over at him. "Now why would that bother you?"

"If we decided to take our friendship to another level, you would not be able to do the thing you love—you wouldn't be allowed to teach."

"Armstead, I will deal with that when I have to. I love children and will forever be one of their biggest supporters in whatever way seems good and fair in their lives."

"Have you ever considered children of your own?" he asked, gazing into my eyes.

"I absolutely want children one day. I would like to have at least a few of my own. What about you?"

"I want children, too. Maybe two or three."

"My love for children extends beyond the schoolyard. I enjoy working with the Juvenile Branch of the Independent Order of St. Luke. Educating and developing young entrepreneurs is one of the highlights of my day."

Armstead seemed content with my answer. He overflowed with admiration for me. He even let a wide smile flow across his face, his eyes glassy.

Then, without another word, he got up and knelt right in front of me on the front porch.

He took my hand, and a chill traveled throughout my body. Then he asked the question I'd been patiently waiting to hear: "Maggie Lena Mitchell, will you marry me?"

This didn't require any thought from me. Being around him had been the most comfortable I had ever felt.

"Yes, I will marry you!" The words flowed joyfully from my lips without any hesitation. My cheeks blushed pink.

CHAPTER 6

1886

ALTHOUGH I KNEW WHAT TO EXPECT, I didn't like it when the school-master said, "You need to pack your things and be out of here before there's a wedding. It's the law."

No matter how disturbing her words had been, it made me more deter-mined to fight for the rights of women and the laws that prevented women from having a career in teaching. As of September, when I would become a married woman, I would no longer be able to teach. I loved teaching and see-ing the bright eyes of the youth as they absorbed information like a sponge. It was a prestigious intellectual position, as most colored women were do-mestic workers and laundresses, like Momma had been. Women had limited educational choices. There were no industries in the South, so we were left with the jobs of picking up after the elegant and privileged white women. And in some instances, taking care of our husbands.

"Don't worry; we can afford it, Maggie," Armstead said as I poured my disappointment in the Virginia law out to him. And I knew he could support us because he was a prominent builder whom the entire Jackson Ward community sought out for quality service. And it was no secret he had purchased a large home right in the heart of Jackson Ward. But it wasn't about him being able to support us both.

"Armstead, you know I am not a housewife. I have work to do in the community."

"I have work to do, too," he responded, chuckling. "Are you concerned about the work you do at the Order?"

"No, Armstead. However, I would like to know what you expect of me once we're married. I know what I expect from you. I want you to continue to support my career and political goals in the community."

He cleared his throat. "I want whatever you want. I expect you to care as much for our family as you do your work. I hope this is not too much."

"Armstead," I said, "I will always be available for you and the family, but my work in the community is just beginning. There are businesses to form and people to care for. Family is my priority. But you must also remember that I take my service seriously."

"Maggie, I want you to be the woman I've fallen in love with. Of course I will support your work. And I've seen how you care for your dear mother. I have no doubt you can do both."

I heard him. His vision was the same as mine. And I didn't have any intention of becoming someone different once I took on his last name.

"Yes, I am committed to my job as secretary and to the Right Worthy division of the Order. The Right Worthy Grand Council was the leadership division of the Independent Order of St. Luke, and I supported them in my job as a secretary, a position that I had held since I was seventeen years old. It is a responsibility as well as a job. We all must continue to work for the improvement of the community."

I had been secretary to the Independent Order of St. Luke since I was seventeen years old. I had on occasion spent time with the True Reformers, another organization for us coloreds. Similar to the Order, the insurance and founding of colored businesses were at the forefront for the True Reformers, but my time with them was short-lived when I realized my ideals and goals lined up more perfectly with those of the Independent Order of St. Luke. The Order appeared to be more progressive, allowing women to play a role in their efforts and leadership. I loved working with this progressive fraternal organization. All their members were like-minded individuals, intelligent, energetic, and full of ideas. Somehow their visions were in sync with the development of savings and self-reliance within our community—practices I believed in and had committed my time to since I was old enough to participate. These were the basis of tangible improvements for the colored community. We just needed money.

"We will be married, Maggie," Armstead said, taking my hand in his. "And I'm looking forward to seeing what we'll build together."

❖⊂⊃❖

Armstead and I had long envisioned the moment in time when we could spend our nights together and be comfortably entangled in each other's arms. But first, we had a wedding to plan.

The hatmaker, dressmaker, and florist were all gearing up for our September 14, 1886, wedding. The dressmaker had measured me from top to bottom, measuring my waist one inch less than it should have been. "By September, you will fit into this dress nicely with a firm corset," she said with certainty.

"Ma'am, it will be too tight," I said, feeling the pinch of her measuring tape.

But she glanced up at me. "You will need to look your best on this day. Sometimes beauty is a little uncomfortable."

I wasn't a tiny person, and I often wished to forgo corsets altogether, but it was customary for a woman to wear them to create a strong foundation for her silhouette before putting on her top clothes. Still, the smaller measurements seemed extreme. When I got home from the dressmaker's shop on Leigh Street, I shared my concerns with Momma.

"I can make your dress," she said.

"Momma, you are probably the best seamstress I know, but you are going to be too busy helping me plan my wedding to be bothered with a dress."

She gave me a mischievous look, knowing I was making up a story. Still, my decision to use a dressmaker could free her up for other things.

"I can do both," she said smiling.

"Momma, you are going to need a new dress yourself."

"I've already chosen my fabric and it's ready to be put together."

My wedding had been a long time coming. At twenty-two years of age, I was almost at that point when people would give an unmarried woman the label of old maid. But I wanted to be sure that when I married, my marriage would last forever. And I was one to think things through thoroughly. Armstead had waited to be married as well. He was a fine man for sure, and one that many women had gravitated toward. There were other men in Jackson Ward, many as successful and maybe as handsome as Armstead. But none that I'd met or spoken to was as strong or open-minded as Armstead. He was the only man who not only understood me but matched my ambition and determination, and wanted to build on our goals together.

On September 14, the entire Jackson Ward community filled up the pews at the First African Baptist Church for our wedding. My dress was gorgeous. It was bleached white with buckled pleats all around and pearls sewn into the train and the veil. It was the most elegant dress I had ever seen, including the times as a child when I'd admired the clothes Mrs. Thalhimer had worn when we delivered laundry to her. The waistline was perfect, as the dressmaker had assured me. Armstead, handsome and poised, stood waiting for me at the end of the aisle, gazing at me as lovingly as I was looking at him. Momma stood to the side, tears sliding down her cheeks. In the middle of the crowd, there was only one white woman in attendance—Ms. Elizabeth Van Lew. As elegant as ever, she smiled at me as I made my way down the aisle.

Age had taken over Ms. Van Lew's face. Layers of fine lines covered the skin around her blue eyes. In conjunction with age, I knew some of the lines had to represent the many secrets and stories she'd held dear to her heart. She was still audaciously confident, standing straight up in the middle of all our relatives, friends, and neighbors. Being a woman of great conviction, she continued to do things that other white folks would never dare, and many despised her for it. Some boldly blurted out "Nigga lover." as she passed by, but she graciously ignored them. Seeing her among my friends was special but not unusual. She had sacrificed her wealthy life for the sake of my people and others in bondage.

When Ms. Van Lew was appointed to postmaster right after the war by President Ulysses S. Grant, she hired some coloreds to work in her office, defying all the Jim Crow attitudes. Over a cup of hot tea, rumor had it that Grant had told her, "You have sent me the most valuable information received during the Civil War and I honor you." "She's something else," Momma often would say, shaking her head, still baffled and awed by her bravery.

After the ceremony, we mingled with all the people who came to the wedding, including businessmen and women from all across Jackson Ward. Everyone was invited. We were a community sewn together by the threads of our struggles. And any reason to celebrate together was something to cherish.

After the ceremony, the ladies gathered all around me with questions I found peculiar and a bit private to answer. They were all finely dressed in long buckled dresses accentuated with Victorian and Edwardian hats.

Fannie rubbed her hands together as if hesitant, but persisted anyway in asking me, "Are you ready for tonight?" The other women around us giggled.

I smiled shyly.

Then the ultimate question came: "Will you be leaving the Independent Order of St. Luke? It takes up a lot of time. Your husband will probably want you home."

"Clearly you don't understand the relationship Armstead and I have," I said with passion in my voice, and had to pause before I continued. "Since I will no longer be teaching, I will be dedicating myself even more to the work that needs to be done at the Order. I plan on working to uplift the lives of us women and our community as a whole."

"There is no way any man would allow his wife to continue working as hard as you do, Maggie."

"Armstead isn't just any man. And I don't know about you ladies, but I intend to continue with the work I've started, and I hope you all will join me."

The reaction was subtle, as doubt clouded their expressions and one lady rolled her eyes.

Quickly the conversation changed as people rushed to the church basement to enjoy the ham biscuits and wedding cake.

It was such a grand day. The happiest day of my life.

The party continued over at the Virginian, where we danced into the night. Afterward, Armstead carried me over the threshold of his home—now ours. Waiting for the right man had certainly paid off. We were so tired we fell straight to sleep.

The following morning, I woke up in the muscular arms of the man I adored. When Armstead opened his brown eyes and stared into mine, I knew it was time. I had waited for this day since that sultry hot night he kissed me deeply and the beads of sweat slid down the sides of my face. I was a little timid, and my heartbeat had sped up rapidly. Yet, when he pulled me closer to him, I melted and laid my head on his bare chest.

When we emerged to prepare for work, Armstead cupped my face in one hand and smiled, saying, "Good morning, *Mrs. Walker*."

I blushed. I was no longer a Mitchell. I was now *Mrs*. Maggie Lena *Walker*. And it felt so good to hear.

"I hope the ladies at the Order won't bother you too much about our night today," he said with a wink.

I laughed out loud. "What night? We had our 'night' this morning."

He chuckled with me and reached for his Stetson. "A happy *day*, nonetheless."

CHAPTER 7

1886

I WENT TO WORK THE VERY NEXT DAY. I sat down at my desk and pulled out a pad of paper to begin to write down ideas on what we needed—work, funds, family. I literally had been pleading with folks in the community to come out and work with us. Although the loyal members who attended Order meetings on a regular basis answered the call, many of them were not willing to volunteer. One fellow simply said, "We done gave enough free work during slavery. I ain't doing nothing without getting a few greenbacks." His comments were unhelpful, to say the least. We needed volunteers for so many things, some major, some minor, from raising funds to filing and documentation. There was something for anybody to do, regardless of how much or how little time they had to give.

Our ongoing need for funding was a top priority. So, I turned to Mary Toliver. She had offered her services to us many times in the past. I prayed that her interest in volunteering had not faded over time. The duties involved pulling together a list of the colored families in Jackson Ward and other neighborhoods in close proximity. No one had taken her up on her offer because it was felt that it would take too much time to train her on the menial duties. Mary was a quiet, nervous type of person. And even more introverted since the death of her husband. People felt she was not cut out for the socially heavy tasks the Order might require, such as public speaking, leading meetings, and rallying people to donate. However, I knew from my teaching days that some people were more suited for the less visible tasks. I decided to stop by her home after work.

One knock, and the door swung open. Mary stood back and waited before saying anything. After I greeted her kindly, a smile rolled across her lips, and she relaxed.

"Come on in," she said. I strolled through the door and got straight to the point.

"The Order needs you, Mary. We need someone to help us get organized, and I know at one time you were interested in volunteering," I said, swinging my hands and even touching her shoulder as I spoke.

Mary blushed at my ask, her eyes lighting up as she said, "Thank you so much, Maggie, for giving me a chance." Although I had a few doubts myself about how much she could do, who in their good mind on this earth should turn down a volunteer? But people were peculiar that way.

"We've got a lot of work ahead of us. We'll need all the help we can get."

"I know and am willing to work with you on whatever you need me to do," she said, both of us still standing in her hallway.

Mary showed up the following day. She was early and eager to take on any task. We chatted about the Order's needs, and after a brief meeting, she started working.

In less than a day, Mary managed to put together a document of the residents she knew in Jackson Ward. Each afternoon, she'd leave early to stroll through the neighborhood to meet the old and new tenants. The list grew as more people migrated to Jackson Ward, some of whom we had never met. It didn't take long before Mary blossomed into an assertive lady, one who was focused and cared dearly about her job and how it would affect the community. I was glad to have her working with me.

We would meet in the mornings to analyze our outcomes from the day before. As Mary went door to door, I reviewed the data she brought back and came up with a plan to involve whole families in our transformation. The Independent Order of St. Luke was more than ready to grow.

Though I was excited about the work Mary and I were doing, I couldn't help thinking about how much I missed teaching, and wondered how I could incorporate it into the work I was doing for the Order. I pulled out my pad of paper again and proceeded to draft a plan that would include the Juvenile Branch of the Order. Some of the conversations with parents about their children's involvement in the community would be heated. Most of the progressive parents had the same belief—we wanted to instill the intricate possibilities of education and social service in our youth. But every now and again we'd run into someone who felt their children would not benefit from the Order and neither would they. If we could get them to buy into the concept of knowledge and dreams from a young age, we knew they would grow to be interested in the Order's work and in investing in the welfare of the neighborhood and their community.

"I wish I had children," Mary said solemnly. "I'd bring them here to learn." She sounded as if she was in pain.

Mary was not much older than I. She was a petite brown lady whom anyone would consider attractive. Mary's husband had been found murdered on the other side of Richmond. The neighborhood magpies rumored he had gone to visit a white woman and was killed by her brothers. Mary didn't believe any of that, she told me. "My husband went across town to look at a carriage he heard a white man had on sale. He didn't go after no white woman. She was the only one home when he got there. And they killed him." She spoke it with so much pain and conviction.

Mary's version was different from the version the Richmond Police Department reported. But everyone in Jackson Ward knew the bluecoats didn't care for coloreds. They had a reputation of corruption and deceit, as I knew firsthand. Her husband was seen talking to a white girl about a job. Her brothers beat him to death, and then bragged about it. "I bet no other niggas better come across them tracks for a white girl."

When I think about what happened to Mary's husband, my own daddy came to mind. How did he really die? No one could rely on the police to do their jobs. And Mary was pitiful after word about her husband went around. Some folks looked down their noses at Mary, believing the authorities, even though they had let our community down so many times. Mary told me Fannie had mumbled, "Now how can she walk around town knowing her husband was murdered for running after a white woman." Fannie could be a bit snooty, but she still caught some folks' ears even as others ignored her.

Now Mary needed someone who would be good to her and treat her with respect. And to fill the emptiness left from her husband's murder. "When my husband died," Mary said, "I was left with nothing to live for. You have given me something to do during the lonely days, and I am so grateful to you."

My heart ached for her. I wanted her to feel joy in her life. Women had so many burdens to bear.

That evening I went home and had a discussion with Armstead at the dinner table. Momma, Armstead, and I looked forward to this hour, when we could speak about our day and recap anything happening we needed to talk about.

"Honey, do you remember Mary Toliver?"

"Of course, you talk about her working with you at St. Luke."

"She's single."

"Right."

"I just wish she had someone like you in her life."

Armstead grinned. "Why don't we invite Mary over for dinner, and I will invite Otis. He is a good guy, but a little lonely, too. I think they might could spark up a friendship, at least."

I chuckled out loud. "You are wonderful."

Armstead just kept on eating. He loved my cooking and almost never left anything on his plate. Even after working all day, he would always offer to help me clean the kitchen. I wouldn't let him, of course. He had been using every muscle in his body to build homes and make repairs. The least I could do was to make him comfortable when he was home. Momma was right when she told me I had chosen the right man. He was always putting me first. And I loved entertaining guests, especially our neighbors. Having Mary and Otis join us for dinner would be an opportunity for me to showcase my fine cooking skills. Maybe I would roast a chicken with gravy and open a can of the string beans and potatoes Momma canned. Adding sliced tomato and corn bread, we would have a good meal.

"Let's invite them."

CHAPTER 8

1890

MOMMA STOOD WITH HER HANDS on her hips and her legs braced apart and, as if I were an irresponsible child, said, "You need to spend more time at home." When I didn't quickly respond, she added, "Lord, how I wish Willie could see you now." Then she muttered something to herself concerning his death. All I knew was that remembering that day still disturbed her.

"Momma, I'm home every evening when my husband is home. I cook most days, and Armstead is fine with the schedule I keep. I even make time to clean our home and help him with the books for the contracting company."

My answer seemed to perplex her. She peered at me with those dark eyes. "Now, I don't want you to get so busy that yous forget about your husband. You know family come first." She paused. Then her eyes became glassy. "You are one blessed chile, to have a man like Armstead. My Willie was a good man, too. We are both lucky women," she said and forced a giggle to conceal the anguish she still held in her heart from losing her husband too soon and never, ever believing what the Richmond police reported as happening. At

61

night I prayed she would put those thoughts aside and learn to live again. There was nothing she could do about Willie.

Things were coming together at the Independent Order of St. Luke. Mary and I had put together a list of potential members and we had scheduled continuous learning sessions for the Juvenile Branch of the Order.

Eagerly the children piled into the Juvenile Branch meeting room with ideas and plans of their own. Some of them were so innovative, we just couldn't believe our ears. We were amazed by their excitement; it was so contagious. As the years passed quickly and anticipation lit up their eyes, we couldn't wait to see their dreams manifested. We spent every hour they were in attendance discussing those ideas. In some cases, together we accessed strategies and ways in which we could accomplish all the things their young minds wanted to do. We put together business plans and came up with ways to involve the community. We made it a point to never tell them something was impossible. However, we did admit that in some cases a backup plan would be necessary.

"We don't want these children leaving with false expectations," Mary told me. She was concerned about building the children up only for them to be let down.

"I agree," I said. "But that's why we also come up with a backup plan—to level out and help set realistic expectations." One of the young boys said he wanted to be the president of the United States of America. Mary and I gasped at the idea, and quickly asked him to add multiple alternate goals to his list, starting with becoming an elected official in Richmond.

The community's hesitations and perception regarding Mary had definitely been a misunderstanding. She was smart and eager to do whatever was necessary for the children and for the advancement of the Order. She was a woman of few words but soaked up knowledge like a sponge. When she did speak, her opinions were well thought out and reasonable. I think being afraid to stand before an audience had added to the misperception. Nerves can and will get the best of us all. So, at times her thoughts would seem a bit muddled and indistinct. As she gained confidence in herself and her place in the community, though, her words flowed clearly, and no one could say anything else about her.

Not six months after Mary and Otis came to our home for dinner, they'd already formed an unbreakable bond. They were somewhat shy at first, but in an intimate setting like our parlor, they opened up to one another and something special happened. Otis, a very handsome man of nearly six feet in height, fell for Mary, a beautiful, petite woman. Otis talked about his job and Mary shared her desire for children with him. "But I've given up hope," she said to him, as if she was an old maid or beyond childbearing years.

"Please never give up hope," Otis urged her. Afterward, they couldn't stop talking, and their hesitant frowns turned into smiles. At work, Mary hummed as she worked and at times I wondered if she was thinking of Otis. Mary was blooming.

Four years later, I noticed a change in Mary. "Mary, you seem to be putting on weight, yet I don't see you eating much." She smiled at me shyly. Then she came over and grabbed my hands. "I'm with child," she said, smiling. "I can never find the words to thank you for all you've done to fill my life with so many blessings."

My smile matched hers as she spoke of Otis and their future child. Armstead often said that Otis wore his ears out talking about Mary. Now I understood why.

I couldn't help but worry for Mary, though. A child out of wedlock... My eyes drooped and my eyebrows furrowed as I thought on how to broach the topic with Mary in a delicate way. But it was as if she could read my thoughts.

"Don't worry, Maggie," Mary assured me. "Otis and I are married."

My heart rushed with excitement, and I had to sit down.

"You all right?" Mary asked me. "I'm so sorry I didn't tell you sooner, Maggie. It all happened so quickly!"

"Just feeling a little faint. I haven't had much to eat. And your good news—"

"That's how I knew I was with child!" Mary exclaimed, excited at the prospect of us being pregnant at the same time. "I started feeling faint and tired. Oh! Wouldn't it be wonderful?"

After Mary left that evening, I couldn't help thinking about Armstead and me. We had already been married for four years. Armstead had swung me off my feet just as Otis had Mary. He had been all I ever wanted and asked God for. Maybe it was time for the blessing of a child . . .

Two days later, I got so dizzy, I had to brace myself against the wall, papers scattering to the floor as I slid down. I caught hold of my mahogany desk just in time to prevent myself from fully tumbling along with them. I managed to pull myself up and sat in my desk chair, inhaling and gathering myself before leaving early for home.

Momma had warned me, "You are working a long time up at that place. And I'm afraid all of that is causing you to stop taking care of yourself." My momma, who had once been a midwife, was always asking leading questions. This time she declared with certainty, "You are pregnant, chile. Maybe you will slow down now."

I pressed a hand to my midsection. I was late, but I never thought I might be pregnant.

I sat down at the kitchen table and Momma took my hand.

"Momma, I'm a little scared. How will I feel carrying a baby?" I asked.

"Chile," she said, "each day you will feel like you are taking care of someone who is gonna be special in your life. And you's gonna protect it and care for it. It will be the best thing to ever happen to you." She rubbed my cheek with her hand.

Armstead shouted with joy when I told him the news. He picked me up and lifted me into the air, my dress swinging around in circles with me as he couldn't put me down. We grinned and shed a few tears of happiness. Armstead reveled in the idea of our future child.

"I've been praying for us every night," he said. "I hope it is a boy. I could use some help with these houses." He leaned back on the bed with a smile across his face. When I moved around the room, he stared at me, unable to keep his eyes off me.

"Girls are just as helpful. Besides, it would make me very happy to have a little girl. But having a healthy baby is the most important thing."

As Momma suggested, I did slow down the first few months of my pregnancy, and let Mary take over the lion's share of the work with the Juvenile Branch. They were all so inquisitive and eager to soak up any information I could possibly give them about the wealth of possibilities for their futures—something no one else was really talking to them about. The lessons we presented to them twice a week were making an impact on their behavior, too. They began to speak more positively about potentially pursuing entrepreneurship, and the short trips around town to the government offices inspired some to even think they could effect change in the statehouse and capitol.

There were now two pregnant women working hard at St. Luke's, and the Juvenile Branch was growing in size along with our waistlines. Now that Mary had a husband and a child on the way, she worried that she had volunteered for more of her time than she could spare anymore. Before Otis, she had needed something to occupy her days. And I could see that she enjoyed taking control, but the pregnancy was sapping most of her energy away. Her eyes would droop and sometimes she had to take spells of sitting to reenergize herself.

One day, Mary's soft voice drifted over from the other side of the room, where she was filing a paper away in our old wooden cabinet. "Maggie, I can't go out into the neighborhood any longer. It is too much for me."

"What's wrong?" I asked her. Mary stopped what she was doing and sat down in front of me. Her eyes were red as if she had been crying, and she lowered her head before she began to speak. There was an air of distress about her.

I asked, "Are you having problems?" According to the midwife, our due dates were only a month apart. She was around four months along and I was three months along, maybe a little more.

"Otis is worried about me. When I get home, I am too tired to fix dinner and I go to bed earlier than usual. This baby is taking all my energy," she said, placing her hands on her baby bump.

"I know what you mean," I said. "I am always sleepy, too. I find things to cook that will last a couple of days. All I do is add some hot corn bread straight from the oven and Armstead is fine. He loves my corn bread."

"My Otis is so protective of me. He hates it when I am tired and worn out. Now, you know, Maggie, strolling up and down the streets will wear you out. Some evenings, I am so exhausted I go straight to bed. And the people can be stubborn and resistant."

"I sure would hate to lose you, Mary. You have been so vital to the success of the Juvenile Branch. And as a secretary, you have been a savior to me."

I thought on it for a moment. Working outside with the wind and the sun beating down on you would drain anyone, let alone a pregnant woman. I could certainly find a way to lighten the load. My pregnancy had been good. I got tired at night, but never so much that I couldn't prepare dinner for my hardworking husband. And Armstead would rub my feet every evening, even though I had been sitting most of the day. He loved that I was pregnant and he couldn't stop touching me as if he was a little kid fascinated with a new toy. Each day my tummy grew, and I would put on the corset, but it did very little to rein in my belly. It just kept growing.

Mary said Otis was so gentle with her, he was afraid to make love for fear of hurting the child, so he only rubbed her back. The midwife had to assure him that everything was fine before they continued their lovemaking, which Mary said had been wonderful. Now he was worried about her standing on her feet too long. She was growing so big for a petite lady carrying only one baby. Maybe a little rest was what was needed.

"What if you did more office work, less walking?" I suggested. "Do you think you could put together the logs? I get so bored of all the paperwork sometimes, and I should get up and walk around more. We could split the street work more evenly."

"That may be a good compromise."

"Compromise?"

"I promised Otis I would quit and stay home," she said humbly. "Maybe I can do some of your paperwork from home? I'll talk to Otis, if you show me how to do some of that work. Although, Maggie, at times you are doing five things at once. I'm not sure I can keep up that pace!"

"I'll start you off slow and gradually add more if necessary."

"I want to see the midwife and have a discussion with Otis before I commit to the new plan. Sometimes Otis can be so stubborn when it comes to me. Deep inside, I believe he'd rather I not work at all."

"You have been working every weekday. If he agrees with what we've discussed, I think you can regain some of your energy back again, although pregnancy does take its toll on the body all the same." We guffawed. For a while, I was the only one able to amble up and down the cobblestones. Now Mary needed rest and, mentally, so did I. However, I was focused and would not let my pregnancy stop me from soliciting donations from the members in the community.

Mary and Otis were stricken when the midwife explained to them that Mary was actually carrying twins! They couldn't believe the good news, and neither could I. The chances of twins were nearly unimaginable. There was only one set of identical twins in Jackson Ward that we were aware of. The girls looked so much alike, we would often mistake one for the other. And they were mischievous, playing jokes on their teachers and the community. But their parents knew the difference, and when they were around, the girls were always on their best behavior.

Otis stood straight as an arrow. Normally a mild-mannered man, he garnered up more confidence than anyone knew existed when it came to Mary. With his chest out, he agreed that she could spend a few hours a day at the Order, "as long as she is not overworked."

"I can work the mornings," Mary explained, "and then you will have the rest of the day, Maggie."

I was pleased she could do a half day, as any help would do. Mary was cautious about her pregnancy as well. She had wanted children with her first husband, but it wasn't meant to be then. Now, she professed, God was making it all right.

As we continued to build up the list for the Independent Order of St. Luke, it seemed our hard work was still falling short of easing the financial burdens the Order continued to face. They were nearly bankrupt from all the insurance liabilities. People were continuously depending upon the fund to finance the medical attention required of the members and burials were increasing. Although there had been some deliverance from expenses, those funds were quickly running low. It felt as if we had been working in vain. Even though the Order was still struggling financially, we could see growth in the children's character and desires. They were inspired. And each of their families' involvement had increased because of their participation in the Juvenile Branch, whose association fund was doing well. But the rest was falling by the wayside.

Mary and I continued volunteering throughout our pregnancies. Mary got so big, she had to stay home most days because her ankles were swollen. I would stop by her house when I left work early and together we'd laugh and speak about the new task that would soon be ahead of us—raising children.

"Who would have ever thought we'd be knitting like ol' ladies?" I said to her while sitting in the parlor, untangling thread so we could knit blankets and baby coveralls.

"We have a new job to do now, and this one is forever." We giggled like little girls playing as we held up the blankets we were knitting for our babies. Sometimes the patterns were a bit off, but they were woven out of love. Momma was knitting the perfect blanket for my baby, so I didn't have to worry about the state of mine.

Thankfully, I was as healthy as an ox. My pregnancy did not prevent me from delivering the daily outcomes expected. I would knock on doors in the colored communities, inviting them to allow their children to participate in our Juvenile Branch, all the while convincing them to come to the Order's meetings and spend a little time learning what we were advocating for. Afterward, I would go over to the offices of the Independent Order of St. Luke and document my findings for the day.

"I can't do it no more, Maggie," Mary said one day, barely able to walk with the weight of two babies growing heavier inside her. We continued to spend time together making clothes for our babies, but Mary could no longer get up at dawn and work until noon. She had barely enough energy for her household tasks.

"I'll be back once these babies are born."

"Girl, we better get as much rest as possible, because from what I've been told, we will never be able to sleep late again. Well, until they are teens."

Chuckling and holding her belly, Mary said, "I've got two of 'em. Maybe, just maybe, one will help the other."

"Don't count on it. They will both want *all* your attention."

Mary's babies came two weeks early, but were normal in size. She had fraternal twins: a beautiful boy and girl. Although I was more than ready to deliver myself, and was tired at the end of the day, I still found time for Armstead and to cook dinner for us most nights. Momma always wanted to help me out.

Armstead said, "All Otis will talk about these days are his twins. He says they resemble him more than their momma, and that he did all the work." Then he reached over and rubbed my belly. "I can't wait for my little helper to be born."

"I hope it is a girl," I would respond. But somehow, I knew it was a boy. I had seen him in a dream. And the ol' folk often said God would send a sign. And he did: I saw a healthy little boy.

The night the baby came, pains shot through my body so strong, I cried out to Armstead, "Please help me!" But there was nothing he could do. He just stood there holding my shoulders, balancing me on the bed. Momma was a skilled midwife, and when I heard my child's first wail, I felt relieved. He was bright red, his skin flawless, and his little mouth the same shape as mine.

"That child is the spitting image of Armstead, and he has some lungs on him," Momma said.

He had cried out as soon as Momma had tapped his little behind, startling all of us. Delivering her own grandchild was a badge of honor. After washing him off, Momma wrapped him up in a blanket she'd knitted and handed him to me. Our little boy kept his eyes closed and snuggled close to my breast. It was only a few tries before he was nursing, his little lips suckling like a champ. Armstead and I both smiled at him.

"That's my boy," Armstead said as the baby suckled until he was full. I patted him as Momma instructed me. He burped and went off to sleep. We chose to name him Russell Eccles Talmadge Walker.

Momma frowned when she heard his name. I wasn't sure if it was out of surprise or pain.

"Is there a problem, Momma?" I asked her kindly.

She cupped her hands over her chin, slyly grinned, and said, "Well, I never hear you ever mention Eccles and then you name your first child after him."

"He was my father, even if he was not around."

"I just hope you will explain it to Russell when he is older. His grandfather came about in a time when colored girls and white boys together was something to keep as a secret. Mostly 'cause the colored girls were being raped. But we cared for each other, although it was at the wrong time."

"I think Russell will love his name."

"Me, too."

Mary stopped by a few days after Russell was born. I couldn't imagine her leaving twins at home with her mother-in-law, but she had.

"Who is feeding the babies?" I asked when she sat in the high-back chair in my bedroom. Mary appeared rested even with two babies nursing; it didn't seem normal.

"Child," Mary said to me, "I've got them on cow's milk already."

"How is that, Mary?"

"I just buy it from the farmer's market and add a bit of water to feed them.

Nursing worked for a while, but it is hard to feed two at a time. Besides, now Otis can enjoy giving them a warm bottle."

I frowned. "I can't believe you got Otis to agree to cow's milk."

"It wasn't easy, but once he saw he could feed the babies, he accepted it. Breastfeeding had me so exhausted."

As I witnessed my baby growing each day, I couldn't help staring down at him and stroking his curly tresses, wondering about his life. This perfect little one, born in a world where he would be considered a second-class citizen. His life was untarnished, still unmarred by the injustices, prejudices, and the differences. I glanced at the ceiling and said, "Lord God, what joy or renewed hope does he bring with his birth?" I looked upon my son once more and felt the warmth of love and hope.

CHAPTER 9

∽◦∽◦◦⟨•⟩◦◦∽◦∽

1891–1894

THE DAYS AT HOME with my precious Russell had drifted by fast, and my time with him was finally coming to an end. Going back to the Order was finally becoming real, and I would soon be getting back to the business in earnest.

My eyes closed quickly and heavily. Caring for a baby took a lot of energy, and at night I fell asleep with baby Russell still nursing at my breast. After I'd dozed off, Armstead would move him into the crib he'd made from oak wood and cotton-stuffed pillows.

Mornings were a challenge. I would awake a half hour early to start preparing Armstead's breakfast before he left for work, my eyelids only half-open. Thankfully, he wasn't hard to please—an egg, a biscuit, and a cup of coffee or tea, and he was ready to go. Momma had been living with us since we got married, and I always appreciated her help around the house. But, taking care of my husband was a sacred job that I'd promised God I would do.

"You act as if you don't need me," Momma said one morning as I filled the kettle up with water for Armstead's morning coffee.

"I do need you, Momma. But mornings are a good time for me and Russell to talk," I said, gazing down at his little round head. Momma rolled her eyes.

Going back to work at the Order had come quickly, and everyone needed my time. Caring for Russell had been the best job of them all, though. Before I left home, I loved staring at my baby boy, who was swaying comfortably in the rocking crib Armstead had so finely crafted for him. Russell stared up at me with those captivating hazel eyes, the same eyes as his daddy's, grinning.

All parents feel the same way, but our Russell really was a pretty baby, with features resembling those of Armstead and mine. I could already tell he was bright, and his complexion favored Armstead and Momma's reddish-brown hue. Armstead always gloated about Russell, and at times, I believe he and Otis had a verbal boxing match comparing their babies.

Having a baby around also aroused Armstead's sexual desires for me. Every chance he got, he would tap me on the bottom. Momma told me to wait for a least a month before allowing Armstead back into my arms, but as soon as the bleeding ceased, he was on me, and I just had to force him to wait.

"No, Armstead, it is too soon."

"Why can't I be with you?" he would ask pitifully, as if pleading could change my mind.

"Armstead, you ought to know better. You know it is too soon to make any moves in our bedroom. I've got to heal all the way, and besides, it is too soon to be with child again. Lord only knows what I would do with two babies."

He rolled over on his side, turning his muscular back toward me as if I had hurt his feelings. "I guess you don't know this, but Mary is pregnant again."

My mouth flew wide open, and I shook my head. "She couldn't be. I just spoke to her two days ago when she and her mother-in-law stopped by for a visit with Russell. She didn't mention a word about another baby. In fact, she was talking about finding time to volunteer."

"Russell is a month old. We can make love without getting pregnant. Where's that sponge you used to hide in the drawer in the bottom of the vanity?" he asked, as if he knew all my secrets.

I rolled my eyes. "You need to stay out of my things, Armstead Walker."

"I just want to be with my wife," he said.

"That day will come soon enough. I just want to make sure everything is healed first. Having a baby is hard work, but what do you men know about that?"

Six weeks later and sooner than expected, I was feeling back to my normal self. Momma had wrapped a linen sheet around my middle at night and during the day coaxed me to put a corset on and lace it real tight to pull my stomach back in shape. Sure enough, everything seemed to remember its original place. And even though I had delivered a baby less than three months before, I felt I'd had the necessary rest to go back to my work at the Order.

Armstead loved seeing my energy return. And even after a full day of working hard in construction, his hands sometimes blistered, he still had enough energy for making love. He would humbly ask, "Can I be with you tonight?"

When I said no, he would lightly kiss me good night and turn away from me. But every night, he would ask, as if he had to make up for lost time during my recovery from pregnancy. I was certainly drawn to him, but all women had a waiting period. When the time was right, I made sure to prepare and had already inserted the sponge with a little vinegar on it to be safe. I was not ready for another baby so soon. And Armstead was quite the romancer. He'd pour me a glass of port wine and watch me unwind. Then he would possess my body, and all I could do was moan.

When Russell was just two months old and finally sleeping through the night, I contemplated going back to work at the Order. Mary, on the other hand, was stuck at home with two little babies under one year of age and nearly three months pregnant. Her home was not in confusion, even though she had a lot to do. Her mother-in-law, just like my momma, loved the time she spent with her grandchildren. She assisted Mary and Otis, even cooking Otis's evening meals. I loved stopping by there with Russell in my arms, her home filled with the aroma of food on the stove and a freshly cleaned scent. We'd fold a quilt and lay the children together on the floor.

My momma, peculiar in many ways about her children, decided she would support us in the upbringing of Russell, saying she knew more about babies than most people. He was not to be spoiled and sitting around holding him was not going to work. Sometimes she'd simply take the baby out of our arms and lay him in the crib.

"He can cry. It is good for his lungs," she'd say, as if her word was final and most important. At times her ways would bother Armstead, yet he never said anything. But the squinting of his eyes told the story.

Russell was a curious baby, his almond-shaped eyes following me wherever I went. When I acknowledged him by smiling, his eyes remain fixated on me, watching my every move as if he was in a classroom learning. We could tell he was smart. He was observant. So, we prayed he would grow up with the same sense of community and life that we did.

Mr. William Forrester, the Right Worthy Grand Secretary of the Order, stopped by one evening to see us. He had come several times since I had been home, begging me to come back to work.

"Maggie," he said, "we need you back at St. Luke." I was quiet as he pleaded with me yet again. Although I had already decided to go back soon, Armstead pulled him aside.

Standing in the corner of the parlor, I listened. "Forrester," Armstead said, "you ought to be able to handle business until she is well enough to come back."

"Oh no," he said, pulling out a handkerchief and wiping the sweat from his brow. "I just miss Maggie and all she has been doing. Now, if you don't want her to come back, I will understand."

"You already know that Maggie is a woman with a mind of her own. She can do more in a day on her own than many people can with a slew of help in a week. Now, she's coming back, but I don't need you stopping by here every other day forcing your will on her as to when that will be."

"Armstead, believe me, you've got it all wrong," Mr. Forrester said. But Armstead was not one for debating. He only spoke after giving the subject much thought. I could tell by the way he paused before speaking. He looked Mr. Forrester right in the eyes, reading the expressions on his face.

"Can we agree on this matter? Maggie will be coming back, but you will not put any pressure on her to do so."

Momma stood by with her arms folded across her chest, listening intently, too. She brought a hand up to the side of her face in thought but didn't voice her opinion. Her eyes were fixed on Mr. Forrester as well. She knew I was independent and would go back to work at the Order, but she didn't like how often Mr. Forrester was coming by. He seemed anxious and at times confused.

Momma took me aside and said, "I don't think he's being honest about why they need you back or everything that's going on, and this is concerning for me and Armstead." Momma wanted to say something to Mr. Forrester directly, but as a woman, she'd always been encouraged to stay in her place and out of the way. When Armstead patted Mr. Forrester on the shoulder and sternly said, "Man, calm down," Mr. Forrester's disposition softened. He grabbed his hat and left. I could see the approval in Momma's dark eyes, and the subtle grin she indiscreetly attempted to hide.

Armstead had it handled. Mr. Forrester did not come back after that evening. And I went back to work when Russell was eight and a half weeks old.

❖❀❖

The tables and schedules we had set up for the Juvenile Branch, and the ledger with the listings of the children, addresses, and parents' names, were all in total disarray. It took me weeks to put things back in their proper place. I adjusted my schedule and cut back on the juvenile training to one night a week. It was all I could do. Mary and I worked ourselves ragged to get the Order in working shape again. But it was a short time before Mary's second pregnancy began to sap her energy, and she had to leave at Otis's request once more.

As time went by, I longed for Mary to come back. With three babies under two years old, she would hardly have enough time for Otis, who was attached to her like a child, let alone work at the Order. She adored the attention, but any woman with dreams also desired freedom, in my opinion.

A new pregnancy was inevitable for me, too, and I was so tired. With deep sadness, the baby didn't survive to his first birthday. Armstead cried when we lost our second child, only six months old when he returned to the arms of God. My heartache was so deep, I had to take a few weeks off from work. It was hard just to smile. The disappointment was written all over my face, and there was no way anyone could console me. Losing a child had to be the worst feeling in the world, and when I glanced at myself in the mirror, the dark circles and hollows around my eyes spoke to my pain. Armstead would hold me, and I would embrace him. Both of us were strong, and we could handle almost anything. But the death of a child was something we had never thought we would experience.

"Y'all are still young," Momma said. "You ain't the first woman to lose a baby. God saw fit to take him. Now you must try again."

Elizabeth Draper Mitchell was as strong as a horse, and it had to be the reason I had so much strength. After Daddy died, she didn't seem to be interested in finding love again. Men would approach her, but I believe fear of losing someone you love in that way again always seemed to steer her away from them. When Eccles and William were gone from her life, her sole focus became Johnnie and me. Now, Armstead and I loved having her in our home. When I gazed at her brown skin and the downward lines that had deepened around her beautiful dark eyes, I remembered the pain there had been and the stories still untold. In our time of grief, she quoted Scripture from an old worn-out Bible that her friend, and my namesake, Mrs. Maggie Lena, gave her: "For the Spirit God gave us does not make us timid, but gives us power, love, and self-discipline." Thanks to her fortitude, I was able to go back to work once more.

✤c✤

Though it had only been a few weeks this time, things at the Order were literally falling apart again.

"Maggie, I'm tired of this," Mr. Forrester said upon my return.

He stood beside my desk with a troubled face, eyes stressed from worry.

"We are expanding, sir. The Order's funds are growing and the Juvenile
Branch has more children than we can train."

"I'm thankful for all you've done with the youngins, but the adult division
is struggling. We owe more money than we ever have, and our total debt is
higher than three thousand dollars. I don't know how we can sustain ourselves." He sat in the chair beside my mahogany desk, which was set up across
the room from his. He then pulled out a handkerchief from his pants pocket
and wiped invisible sweat from his forehead. It was what he did whenever he
was nervous about anything. I supposed we all had our tics.

"Mary may come back to work one day a week and help us with the Juvenile Branch, and I could possibly assist you with a strategy to increase the
declining membership on the adult side." Luckily for Mr. Forrester, work
was my way of coping with the premature death of my child, whom we had
named after Armstead. Busywork took care of the idleness that the mind
needed to roam and linger on one's troubles. Being industrious was the only
option for me.

"Mary's husband is as stubborn as a mule. I don't think he will let her
come back. Not even for a few hours," Mr. Forrester said. "That man is like a
leech. He will latch on and never let go."

"Otis is not that stubborn, he's just protective. And besides, they have
three small children to care for."

Desperate to turn the conversation back to the Order's predicaments,
Mr. Forrester said, "We are getting deeper and deeper in debt, with no means
to repay the loans. We need some real help around here."

Mr. Forrester always depended upon me to give him advice and guidance, which seemed to be upside down in the way information tended to flow in the Independent Order of St. Luke. And he was leaning on me heavily now.

"I will stop by Mary's on the way home this evening," I told him. "Maybe Otis will agree to one evening a week. It will give Mary a break. Although, she will still have to work with children."

"She might need a break from Otis, too," Mr. Forrester said, chuckling. I smiled, knowing Mary loved being around Otis, no matter how possessive he was. She loved the attention, and so did he.

Mercifully, Mary and Otis both agreed that she could use a break from the house. Her mother-in-law frowned at the thought of being home alone with three little ones, so Otis said he would fill in for Mary to give her time to go.

From then on, I started writing down notes about the things we were doing at the Order. With enough information, we could properly inform the people about our works and what we were accomplishing. I knew it would make the members in Jackson Ward feel better. The more documented truth there was floating around, the less the gossipers would have to talk about. Besides, we could keep better records of how the money at the Independent Order of St. Luke was actually being spent.

CHAPTER 10

1894

"I'M SO HAPPY TO BE OUT of the house," Mary said, showing all her pearly white teeth and looking better than ever before. Although beautiful, she was a wisp of a thing before she'd had the babies. Now she'd filled out in all the important places and the brown buckled dress she was wearing enhanced her newfound curves. I'd never had that problem. Armstead complimented me on my curvy figure often. Above all else, Mary was happy.

Working with the Juvenile Branch was where she wanted to be. Getting to know the children all over again had been something she was looking forward to doing.

"I suppose there is a different group of children now," Mary said. "The ones who were here before are probably already thinking about how to implement their ideas and goals," she added, smiling.

"They still need encouragement," I said. "Unfortunately, some of the parents don't believe they can accomplish such lofty goals right here in Jackson Ward. We are self-sufficient in many ways, and we are thankfully putting our money back into our own pockets, by shopping in our own businesses, which is exactly what other folks seem to do to further their own."

"Whatever we do, the white man will never accept us as equals. Hell, they may not even let coloreds get a start," Mr. Forrester said.

"We can't concern ourselves with what white folks would 'let' us do," I responded quickly. "We have to focus on the changes we can bring about for ourselves, ignoring the opposition if at all possible." I knew Jim Crow existed. Who didn't? However, I refused to give any of my time and efforts to thinking on it. "If we believe we can do it, it will happen." It was so simple.

A few minutes later, Mr. Forrester was bent over searching through the file cabinet for documents another volunteer had misplaced.

"Where in hell did she put them papers?" he muttered in frustration.

We were silent as I continued handing papers and a journal to Mary, so she could catch up on what had happened while she was away.

When Forrester finally straightened up from his fruitless task, hands in his pockets and his jaws tight, he declared, "I would like the same things happening in the Juvenile Branch to spill over to the adult side. Our meetings are scarce these days. Folks are losing hope. I think they need some of that positive thinking you're always encouraging the kids to have about their futures."

His words resonated with me. It was true that some of the members of the Juvenile Branch had parents who also showed up consistently once a month on Wednesday nights, to support their children and to see what more they could do to help them along. But were they doing the same for themselves? Could we convince them that envisioning and enacting a better future for themselves would help their children, too?

Armstead had attended the Order meetings on the nights I couldn't after Russell was born. He would update me upon returning home, and once noted, "There's some confusion going on at the Independent Order of St. Luke. Whatever it is, I can't seem to put my finger on it." He could tell that something was wrong, but what exactly was happening remained a mystery. The Juvenile Branch was flourishing. And yet Mr. Forrester was always in a frenzy. If he would concentrate on the Order and stop his wandering eyes, as if he didn't have a wife, maybe he could get something done. It was those times when Mary and I both wanted to quit and go home, but our commitment to the community kept us there.

I kept detailed documents on everything we did and made sure the ledger of participants was updated daily. No matter what, I was going to see this through. I also wanted to make notes to keep the members informed of everything going on.

One evening, after Mary had left for home and I was done with the day's tasks, a well-dressed man came to visit. He was tall, around six feet like Mr. Forrester, and dark, with a certain sophistication that commanded attention. As a married woman, I was ashamed of the way I caught myself admiring his physique, and I couldn't help thinking that he was certainly a fine man. I suppose I understood Mr. Forrester's admiration of beauty, but nothing could distract me from my work at hand as a pretty woman seemed to do for him.

The man removed his Stetson when he entered the room and was greeted by Mr. Forrester, who asked him to please take a seat in the leather chair facing his desk. In such a small office, I couldn't help but overhear.

"I am not usually in this area, Mr. Forrester. I spend most of my time in Washington, D.C.," the man began.

"To what do we owe this visit to Richmond, then?" Mr. Forrester replied, pulling out his handkerchief and wiping his forehead nervously.

"It has come to my attention that the Order is facing some troubles." The man reached down into his satchel and pulled out a leather-bound notebook. He untied the sash around it and opened it, shifting closer to the desk in his chair. Mr. Forrester wiped his brow once again.

I opened my own journal again and pretended to be engrossed in my own task while they spoke. Rather than going home, I decided to take notes on the conversation and deduce for myself what had brought it on.

Stumbling, Mr. Forrester asked, "Whatever do you mean?"

"I'd like to show you what is really going on in the organization."

"All right," Mr. Forrester replied, his voice fading.

"Forrester, we are not growing at all in the Adult Branch. In fact, as you can see here, our membership numbers are declining. The Juvenile Branch is growing by leaps. We've got to increase our membership and fast."

Mr. Forrester answered, "Uh, right, okay."

"What is your team doing in terms of outreach?"

I watched as Mr. Forrester's bottom lip trembled. "We are doing just about everything," he humbly replied.

"We are an organization of progressive Negroes. We must keep this organization strong and functioning. We have seen other fraternal organizations fail for lack of participation and we can't let that happen here at St. Luke."

"I'll get right to it. We are already pulling together some people," he said, lying with a straight face, and then again wiped his head with the handkerchief.

"As the organization's accountant," the man stated, "I needed to bring these things to your attention. As you already know, we are in at least three thousand dollars' worth of debt and our assets number only around four hundred dollars. I have checked these figures repeatedly. I can't find any other funds and with membership declining ... Do you have the original list of members?" This man was seriously ferocious when it came to numbers, unlike the guy we had a year before. He was known for getting organizations back together.

Mr. Forrester started pulling out papers almost at random, shuffling them from page to page on his desk. "I can't seem to find it. Maggie, do you have the original list of members?"

Without hesitation, I quickly presented my journal to the accountant and turned to the pages with the names and addresses of the members, along with the dates of when they joined and the last time they had paid their dues. The man took the journal out of my hands and introduced himself.

"I am Mr. Theodore Adams, the outside accountant the Order pays to make sure their books are in order. I do it for several organizations, and they've asked me to alert them if we are not reaching our goals or are failing financially."

"Mrs. Maggie Walker," I replied. "It's a pleasure to meet you, sir."

He glanced down at the pages I'd marked, full of pertinent information. "You keep good notes. You're the one who works with our Juvenile Branch, yes?"

"Yes, sir."

"Keep up the good work. There is so much to do, and your numbers look very good in that area. Is there a section in this journal dedicated to juvenile memberships?"

I reached over his shoulder and turned the pages to the youth section. Mary and I had made sure we kept up with the students who had come through the training program. Included in those numbers were also the active members of the Juvenile Branch, those who came to the meetings and participated in the activities of the Order.

After he thumbed through the pages, he handed the journal back to me. I went back to my desk and my unofficial task of documenting Mr. Adams's visit and inquiries, but they lowered their voices for the next part of the conversation.

Before leaving, Mr. Adams walked over to me and said, "You are an asset to this organization, Mrs. Walker. You and your husband. Armstead donates to the membership fund often and always more than required. The Order appreciates you both so much."

"Thank you, sir," I replied.

Then Mr. Adams turned back to Mr. Forrester. "I will be checking again in the next few months."

"Naturally," Mr. Forrester responded, holding out his arm to let Mr. Adams pass as he escorted him to the door.

I put my journal away on the bookshelf and gathered my things to leave. Staying longer than normal would push my dinner hour even later.

When he returned, Mr. Forrester pulled out a flask and took a sip. Sinner's liquor, I called it, because it always appeared when something was wrong. When he saw me peering at him, he screwed the top back on the flask and stuck it into his pants pocket.

"We've got a lot of work to do," he said.

"Yes, sir," I said, leaving for the evening.

As I closed the door behind me, Mr. Forrester was still at his desk leaning over a few papers, appearing to ponder whatever the man had said to him.

CHAPTER 11

1897

"THESE PEOPLE HAVE some damn nerve!" Mr. Forrester yelled, slamming his hand down hard on the desk. His temperament flared quickly after reading through a stack of letters almost a foot tall.

All sorts of concerns and complaints were flooding his desk. One by one, he stuck his wooden letter opener through the edge of the envelope and swiped it open. He read each one of them. As he began to read, his facial expression dramatically changed. His jaw was tight and his brow was constantly creased. He took out the handkerchief and wiped imaginary sweat from his face twice. He'd had enough then. Mr. Forrester stood up and took all the letters of concern and tossed them in the wastebasket.

He peered over at me with a scowl on his face, hurling, "Maggie, you've got to do something. I need you to be more creative and come up with other ways to bring in more money to the Order."

I kept quiet as his verbal assault continued. Mr. Forrester didn't know I had secretly written a letter to W. E. B. Du Bois asking for help and was waiting for a response. I thought instead of how our efforts with the Juvenile

Branch were already bearing fruit. One of the members in the program had rented a small shop in Jackson Ward and was determined to be a successful carpenter. Armstead had taken him under his wing, teaching him as he built different projects throughout the community. However, the young man preferred working with wood, using a hammer and nails to fix and build structures from it, as it was much easier than mixing sand and water to create an entire building out of brick.

"Did you hear me, Maggie?" Mr. Forrester yelled, drawing my attention back to his outburst.

"Yes, I heard you, Mr. Forrester," I said and pulled out my notepad.

For sixteen long years, I had been working for the Order, not including the years I volunteered as a youth. At first, I'd started by running errands, then as a desk clerk, and once I began to demonstrate my leadership abilities, I was given more and more assignments. These days, members of the Order trusted me more than they did Mr. Forrester. Given the state of things every time I'd had to take a leave of absence, I could see why . . .

Mr. Forrester was furious at the apparent lack of progress being made. By his furrowed brow and his deep frown, I knew he was not going to take the blame.

"This place is not growing," he said loudly, slamming his fist on the table as his temper flared.

"The only increases I see are in the number of children running around here once a week," he added. What he was willfully ignoring was that with the increase of membership in the Juvenile Branch, curious parents wanted to know more about what was going on in the rest of the organization. However, Mr. Forrester was somewhat pessimistic and could not see how things were changing.

"Yes, sir, they are excited about what we are doing," I replied kindly.

Mr. Forrester shook his head. "But what good is it doing for the budget?" I couldn't help frowning at his response, but I remained quiet. Momma often said to me that some things didn't deserve a reaction. She was right, and with his frame of mind anything could set him off into a frenzy. Responding to his complaints was only going to make me say something disrespectful to him. Besides, it was time for some new blood to take over the business of running the Independent Order of St. Luke.

Mr. Forrester went on, blaming me—and Mary—for the decrease in funding, even though we were bringing in new members on a daily basis. We needed to work harder *or else*!

I wasn't sure what "or else" meant to him, but it certainly got my attention. I cleared my throat. "One of the reasons our participation is low, Mr. Forrester, is because of the lack of means to reach the people. It's difficult walking from place to place only to receive a no as an answer."

"Well, something needs to happen, and real soon," he replied sternly, peeking over his spectacles.

"Another reason participation is lacking is because folks around here don't really know what we are doing," I said. "If we keep them updated, and if they see themselves written about in a positive manner, maybe they'll want to contribute or participate more often."

Mr. Forrester's gaze seemed to bore a hole in me, but he remained quiet, waiting for me to explain further.

"We should start a newsletter," I said. "In it, we could share what's happening in the community. Some folks might want to highlight their businesses in the newsletter—and we could charge a fee for that. We can write about the people of Jackson Ward and maybe put a stop to some of the grumbling we hear about the Order. Folks are just not aware of all the good we do. This would be a great way to show them."

Mr. Forrester looked at me a beat longer, then rose from his chair. "Maggie, I'm sure this is something you can put together." Then he nodded and left the room.

Whether he liked my idea or not, Mr. Forrester left me with the burden of making it all happen. Being a mother while trying to keep the Order running left me exhausted. But there was no way I was going to let Mr. Forrester run it into the ground.

❖∞❖

At home, our family had grown. I now had two young boys to care for, and an unexpected ward. The blessing of a daughter came to us in a way I hadn't anticipated.

Margaret—Polly, as we fondly called her—was a distant cousin of Armstead's, a young girl around Russell's age who was left without doting parents in North Carolina. When Armstead and I heard of her abandonment, shortly after I'd returned to work after we'd lost baby Armstead, we went to North Carolina and brought her to live with us. She was the daughter I hadn't thought to wish for, and yet, I felt instantly that she belonged with us.

Then, in the summer of 1897, Armstead and I had welcomed another boy, Melvin. Armstead was elated, grinning whenever he glanced at our Melvin, who also resembled him. I loved my boys, of course, but I had always longed for a girl.

When I went back to work just a few months after Melvin's birth, Armstead was confused. "Maggie, you are giving our children to your mother to raise."

His comment roused me, but I was determined to not let it get the best of me.

"Armstead, we have had many conversations about how we would raise our children. And we have discussed my work at the Independent Order of St. Luke. You know both matter to me a great deal."

"I know, but we have three young children now, one of them barely a toddler. And the Order seems to be demanding more from you."

I shook my head. "Why are we talking about this again, Armstead? You know how important this work is to me. You've always known. I made this plain from the start."

"Yes, and I still admire that about you, but I didn't think your dedication to the cause would be at the expense of our family."

The Independent Order of St. Luke was taking up too much of my family time, he complained, but I was attached to it like an iron magnet. I hadn't given up on the Order being a force for positive change in our community, despite all the troubles that had plagued it in recent years, and I could envision that change just within reach now. The organization needed me more than ever in order to achieve it. Besides, Mary was not around much anymore since Otis insisted on her being home. Her few working days a week had been reduced to four or five hours a week. No one had known how possessive Otis would become. But after her first husband's roving eyes, Mary relished Otis's attentiveness. She enjoyed being cared for and considered the obsession something of great love. It seemed too much for me, and more problematic than love. But theirs was not my relationship.

✦◑✦

Armstead attended all the Order meetings, but the amount had increased and at times he'd scowl in frustration, declaring, "No one needs to meet this often." And yet, he insisted on going. "There is no way I'm going to leave you up there at night alone," he said. He came to the meetings and sat beside me, occasionally whispering to me about the amount of time spent on one subject.

One evening, I was preparing to turn in when I noticed Armstead sitting at the edge of the bed, gazing at me wordlessly. His eyes were serious, lacking any sign of his usual passion. Normally when he stared intently at me, he was expecting me to crawl into bed with him naked. However, I could see the concern in his eyes as I slipped my nightgown over my head and he kept on the long underwear that he frequently wore.

Once I was in bed and snuggled close in his arms, he said, "We need to talk, Maggie. I think it's time for you to stay home. Our children are growing up fast and I don't want them to miss their mother."

This was more resistance than I had ever received from Armstead. I had to think before I spoke because he had always given me the independence to make my own decisions about our family.

I looked him in the eyes and asked just as seriously, "Have I ever missed a meal with our family? Do I spend time in the evenings with the children? Have I ever ignored you or disappointed you in any way?"

He sucked in some air at my questions and with a pouted lip said, "No, but I want you here when I get home."

Mr. Forrester had me working so hard at the Order that at times the hands on the clock would go far beyond my supposed workday. For over a year, I'd been busy creating strategies to keep the Order from failing like so many of the other fraternal organizations across the country. Mary Prout had founded the Independent Order of St. Luke in 1867 in Baltimore, Maryland, and there was no way I planned on letting a formerly enslaved woman's organization fail. But Mr. Forrester's only plan seemed to be to make me work harder.

"Armstead, I understand your frustration. I know I promised that I would always make it home by five p.m.—"

"Maggie, you've got to either come home or tell Mr. Forrester to find someone else to help you. I want you to greet me when I come home from a long day of work. I love your momma, but she's not my wife."

I shook my head in disbelief. I slid closer to him in the bed and put my hand on his arm. "Now, Armstead, we have always worked together on everything. There is no need for you to get all worked up about me greeting you in the evenings. The only reason I have not been here when you arrive home is because of the additional work Mr. Forrester has me doing. You should know there is no one as important to me as you and our family. But the Order is failing for lack of leadership and I'm going to do all I can to restore it. It won't always be like this, and not for much longer now." Armstead pulled his hand away, but I grabbed it back and reminded him, "You know who I am and what I am doing. You have always supported me. What is really troubling you?"

He glanced over at me with those hazel eyes and said, "Maggie, maybe I am jealous."

I sighed. "Are you kidding, Armstead? You are the only man I want and need. And I will try to get home early at least twice a week to greet my handsome husband." He forced a superficial smile across his face that didn't meet his eyes, which were still very somber.

Being with a woman of strong character could weaken an already weak man. It takes a strong man to partner with a strong woman. Armstead had been my partner in all I did for the community and our family for more than thirteen years. Knowing he loved me kept me going most days, and all I would think about in my small window of idle time were him and our children.

"You know I love you, Armstead Walker, and you will always come first in my life."

I laid my head on his hairy chest and listened to his heart beating at the same rhythm as mine. Slowly, he pulled me closer into his arms. We made passionate love before drifting off to sleep.

✦◌✦

The next morning when I arrived at work prepared to make an effort to leave early, I found more chaos than usual. Things were happening in the neighborhood, important things that required my attention. The evidence was piling up around town. Policies were being implemented to keep coloreds off certain streetcar lines. The trolley concerns were happening all over, involving major cities across the Old Dominion, a nickname given to the state of Virginia. I knew things would happen all at the same time, but with my faith I knew I could change things.

Mr. Forrester's exit was coming. Each day he was more bitter when he realized people were no longer listening to him. "That damn Forrester needs to retire and find something else he can do," another customer said while Armstead was having his thick hair cut at the barber shop. "He ain't no manager and I'm tired of paying him a salary to do absolutely nothing for the Order."

"He's a hardworking man," Armstead responded. "He'll find a way to turn things around." But the awakening had already begun. Others waiting to be serviced homed in on the conversation like eagles.

"Hmph. He's had plenty of time to try to do so. Your Maggie seems to be the only one over there with any sense. Too bad she's a woman."

Armstead chuckled and asked, "And who is it that runs your household? And ran it when you were a child? Tell me it's you or that it was your father, and I'll call you a liar. A man would be lost without the mother or wife who runs his home, make no mistake."

"I didn't mean to be disrespectful, Armstead. I just wish we could find a man with her strength and determination."

"You're right that the Order would be lost without Maggie. *Because* she is a woman, not despite it." He then added, "If it wasn't for Maggie, that place would not be able to provide any assistance to this neighborhood. My wife is doing all she can to take care of you all. Afterward, she comes home and takes care of me and our children."

"I'm sorry," the man said, looking astonished at Armstead's response. The barber, who had cut Armstead's hair for as long as I've known him, said, applying thick suds to Armstead's face, "Maggie is some kind of woman. No offense, Armstead, but she is a helluva woman. I wish I had married a woman with the beauty and confidence she has."

The men in the barbershop were silent, all of them listening motionless.

That evening when I brought up the subject again, Armstead simply said, "I worry about you and your safety. What you are doing has everyone watching you like a hawk, including those white men. And they are not interested in Jackson Ward becoming anything more. They like it when we are down and dependent upon them. I just couldn't stand it if anything happened to you."

"Did something happen, honey?"

"I just heard one of the activists across town was beaten so bad his family could hardly recognize him. I will not allow that to happen to you."

"I promise, I will leave for home at a decent hour."

But soon after, Mr. Forrester took the podium at one of the Order's weekly meetings and solemnly stated, "I am stepping down as the Right Worthy Grand Secretary of the Order."

Everyone seemed startled by the announcement and multiple conversations broke out across the room about what this could mean. Then Mr. Forrester glanced over at Armstead and me before taking a seat again, leaving the crowd confused and in disarray.

That night in 1899, I became the Right Worthy Grand Secretary of the Independent Order of St. Luke.

CHAPTER 12

1899–1901

I SETTLED QUICKLY INTO my new role as Right Worthy Grand Secretary. Then suddenly I realized the immensity of the responsibility. Questions floated around in my head as I sat at the large desk Mr. Forrester used to occupy. Now I was feeling the thrill of being able to enact the real changes I'd envisioned ever since I first learned of the Order as a child.

I had just received a note from W. E. B. Du Bois concerning the newspaper I wanted to start to attract the attention of the community and others. W. E. B. agreed it would be an effective way of getting the word out. It would also serve as our eyes and ears within and for the community.

Although I had W. E. B.'s blessing, I still felt a bit at a loss. So, I took out my pad of paper and began to write two more letters.

The first was to Booker T. Washington, a dominant leader in the African American community. He had once been enslaved himself and had the trust of the Black elite and his contemporaries. He was even sought out by presidents of the United States. He had heard about me through my work with the Independent Order of St. Luke, and we'd been able to form a connection.

Whenever I was perplexed by something, I would consult him. He was not shy about giving advice.

The second letter was to Mary McLeod Bethune. She was a little younger than me, but she had done quite a bit of mobilizing, and I considered her a friend. So I sent a letter to her asking for advice as I took on a leadership role in the heart of the Confederacy.

I needed their care and attention as I developed a proposal for the Order. I also valued their opinions on what the best decisions and acts would be for Jackson Ward moving forward.

I was given the nickname the "race woman" by some. Though it wasn't meant as a compliment, I didn't care at all. I knew God above was watching out for me. I didn't believe in losing sleep over other people's insanity. When General William Tecumseh Sherman gave forty acres and an army mule to colored folks after the war in 1865, it wasn't long before delirium set in and President Andrew Johnson, over a glass of scotch, retracted the land that General Oliver Otis Howard had disbursed to the formerly enslaved and returned the property to the enslavers. I was fully aware of the destructive nature of the white man and mindful of ways in which he segregated us coloreds from whites. I felt that the only way to handle it was for coloreds to create their own wealth and I sought the attention of some of the most powerful coloreds in the United States. Mary McLeod Bethune and W. E. B. Du Bois often responded to my concerns. Booker T. Washington had been to my home, and we'd shared ideas on the improvement of our situation. I knew I couldn't do it alone.

From the moment I was elected, I threw myself even deeper into the task of turning things around for the Independent Order of St. Luke and building it into the organization that our community truly deserved. But first, I needed to bring our mission to them, and ask more folks to become members and trust that we would do our utmost to help them improve their lot.

Our fraternal order was not going away without a fight. For that, Armstead and I, and even Momma and the boys, took to the road going not just door to door but city to city throughout the state—Lynchburg, Newport News, Alexandria, Roanoke, and even into West Virginia. But after two years, and a few uncomfortable encounters, I thought to myself, there just had to be a better way to spread the word about what the Order was doing and how they could join in our efforts. I'd been thinking on it for some time, organizing my thoughts in a new journal before presenting to the other members, when I finally shared my proposal.

I remembered how our travels had been and pondered especially on the kindest of the colored landowners we'd encountered, all of them eager to give us a place to stay. But when we stopped at poet Anne Spencer's home in Lynchburg, she had pulled out the fine china and served us a feast fit for a Thanksgiving meal.

"Y'all doing the good of the world," she repeated several times during our conversation. Upon leaving, I wondered if she would write a poem about us and our travels. She was a member of a civil rights movement, and an important member of the colored intellectuals who often spent her free time with Du Bois and others who fought for what they wanted to see in the colored community, or sought to create it themselves. Spending even that brief time with her was inspiring.

It took some hard praying and faith, but with the inspiration and ideas from Du Bois, Bethune, and Washington, I was ready to present to the members of the Order. We relied on all the media sources to get the word out about our accomplishments. The *Richmond Planet* was the first Black-owned and -run newspaper to let folk know what we had accomplished so far and planned to do.

In 1901, I had laid out my step-by-step plan for our community's economic empowerment to a full room. Folks came from everywhere to hear my proposal for the establishment of a bank, a department store, and a newspaper—all to be run under the banner of St. Luke. The room broke out into several conversations and chatter. Almost everyone seemed enthralled by the plan, yet there were a few doubters in the crowd who challenged my proposal.

"Why do you feel you can do this when Mr. Forrester could not?" one man shouted from the crowd.

"I can't speak for him, only myself. I have consulted with great thinkers and politicians from here to New York City. I have asked for their ideas and blessings. This is a big endeavor, but isn't this what we want?"

The same man who had asked the question stood up and clapped, and a wave of applause joined him and took over the room. I knew there was some doubt, but it seemed not enough to worry about.

I got to work right away putting together the first issue of the *St. Luke Herald.* With little effort, folks were eager to invest in a newspaper for us and about us. Even Mr. Thomas smiled at the thought of making a small return on the money he'd invested in the Order. It wasn't long before word traveled of the Independent Order of St. Luke's business matters and that, under my leadership, we were no longer in financial distress. Folks came willingly from across the States to offer their money then. One lady offered all she had been saving to the Order.

"I just believe in Maggie Lena Walker," she said, handing the money to me directly with a smile. Her declaration concerned me a bit, because I couldn't guarantee her a large return on her life's savings, and yet she had so much faith in me.

"I will do all I can, Mrs. Sadie, but we don't make promises here." Mrs. Sadie was a frugal little lady who lived alone. She was a laundress for a wealthy family who still lived in Shockoe Bottom, a place most coloreds knew as "Hell." Before the Civil War was declared a victory for the Union, it had been a place for slave trading. Mrs. Sadie had a sharp memory, though, and could recite all the things her mother had told her about the Bottom, yet she would go there daily to do laundry for the wealthy who refused to leave the old history behind.

"You done give the peoples around here a reason to save. A reason to hope for the future," Mrs. Sadie told me. I made a promise to myself that I would take special care of her deposit. Mrs. Sadie was a mainstay of the community.

"I'm proud of what you've done 'round here, Maggie," she said with a grin that revealed all the pain and hard work she'd had to endure while she'd been enslaved. She was old now, with deep creases surrounding her eyes, her teeth brown and ragged, yet she was eager to contribute to a community she called home. Jackson Ward was a place for all coloreds who believed in progress. After the war ended, Mrs. Sadie had continued as a laundress, but now owned her own laundry establishment, servicing everyone. She had raised her children with the same work ethic, and now her son ran her business. When she left, I put her money in the vault we kept in the office—a makeshift box we kept locked and hidden until our bank could be built. I added her to the journal I kept, put a check beside her name, and vowed that I would add a profit to it, even if it came from my own satchel.

CHAPTER 13

1902

AFTER A RESTLESS YEAR in 1901, the slow progress happening in Jackson Ward kept me up at night. I was exhausted from canvassing the maze of streets, visiting anyone who would listen, and afterward going home to care for the children. Momma would cry for me to be more settled, "You are a mammy now. Your family should be first. Women have to pull back sometimes." I heard her and would hug her tightly every time she urged me to slow down, but I was too tired to utter a word. On the other hand, Momma was constantly reminding me of Ms. Elizabeth Van Lew and her various acts of bravery in service to the Union and our community. So, I believed she had mixed feelings. Some days she wanted me out making a difference in the world, and other times she felt it was too much. I shook my head and said, "It will be all right, Momma. I will be all right," and held my hand up to calm her. "Just don't worry." She just stared at me with those dark mysterious eyes.

At night, I would fall asleep with my legs squeezed tight together in hopes that Armstead did not want to run his fingers up and down my body, especially between my thick thighs. At times I would be awake and dared not flicker my eyes.

I sprayed a lavender scent in the air each night, as it was meant to have a calming effect, yet my restlessness over building Jackson Ward into a self-sufficient community always clouded my thoughts, depriving me from the deep rest I so needed. And as Armstead whispered gently in my ear, "It is also your duty to please your man," I wanted to turn over and unlock the spirit in me that was rising.

"I will always be yours," I said as my eyes became heavy and I drifted off to sleep. When I would awaken the next morning, he would still be under the covers, head and all.

Momma always worried about the stress I was under, and begged me to slow down. "You need to slow down, girl. Nothing happens overnight. Only when God show up in the sky will things change." So, at night, I gazed up at the stars in the heavens, searching for His sign.

I got the sign one night when I saw a shooting star cross over us, and the next day the sky burst open and rain poured down all around us. When it ended, a rainbow curved over our house. I just knew it was a sign that God was ready. I had already signed up thousands of new members at the Order of St. Luke.

"Now, Maggie, I didn't think you's gonna double my money. I just trusted you 'cause of all you do in the community," Mrs. Sadie said when I stopped by her laundry, where she was darning a wool sweater for one of her patrons. When I told her about the success of her investment, her weathered eyes lit up. Even the indentations around them seemed to flatten.

"Mrs. Sadie, it ain't too hard when we all come together. I just wish others believed in the progress of this Ward like you do."

"I knows what it is like to work without getting paid," she said. "Before I started my laundress business, I worked for them white peoples. Look at my hands: they's tough as a leather strap from washing clothes on a washboard and scrubbing them until my knuckles were raw, without a dime of money.

But things started to change after the Civil War. I was a little girl with hands like a man. Now I get paid to do it for the same folks who used to spit on me and look down on me. I'm in good shape now and my chi'ren will have their own money."

Tears welled up in the corners of her eyes and she took a handkerchief to wipe them. Moments like this inspired me to keep working, knowing that the efforts of the Order were making a difference. I wanted people like Mrs. Sadie to feel good in her own neighborhood. To feel free and without doubt.

After I handed her the return on her money, she counted it and took it into her weathered hands and stuck it into her bosom, a safe storage like a bank.

I was determined to make our community self-sufficient. We needed to be able to compete with white folks, and I was not going to settle without a bank. Besides, our travels and investments had been successful. Within two years and miles of travel, the Order's funds had begun paying out death benefits, which encouraged eager business owners and members to submit monthly dues on time and with a certain degree of caring. Now we needed more. We had more than 1,500 new members, including Sara Satterfield, a white woman who felt she wanted to contribute to the "colored people's fund," as she called it.

Sara was from the Bottom, a place similar to where the low-country coloreds lived when they came to Richmond, either as a free or enslaved person. Although Sara was white, her conscience bothered her. She had been one of those angry people who was a Confederate deep in her heart, but she admired me. I didn't like her and when I would see her in passing, I'd roll my eyes unintentionally at her. I just couldn't control it. One day she stopped me as I was walking through Jackson Ward. "Maggie Lena Walker." She called out my whole name from behind the spectacles she wore down on the tip of her pointy nose. At first I ignored her. I had heard brutal stories about how her family had treated Negroes and frankly, I didn't like her at all. When she called my name again, I forced myself to answer, "Yes, ma'am."

"I hear you are a leader around here." I stared beyond her at a little boy with a runny nose, shining shoes like a professional in front of the cobbler shop. He was barely seven years old, but he had a skill already. There was a rhythm to each slap of the cloth across the man's shoe.

"What can I do for you, Ms. Sara?" I asked as politely as I could, although I wondered why she was even in Jackson Ward.

Peeking over the top of her spectacles, she replied, "I came down here to pick up some laundry I dropped off at Mrs. Sadie's place. But I hear from my workers that you are some sort of hero around here." She glanced around at the folks going in and out of businesses. Most of them were new to offering their own service. Armstead and I had made sure that anyone seeking to open a business was partnered with someone seasoned, which encouraged them to have faith in their God-given abilities. The hard work was all too evident, and even Ms. Sara was impressed.

I put my hands on my hips and bit my bottom lip. I had work to do, and very little time to share my goals with her. She was not our friend, just someone with a reputation of oppression. She had Black servants in her home, yet she'd chosen to support the businesses of Jackson Ward. It was too baffling for my understanding. And just the scent of the rosewater perfume she had on was making me sick to my stomach.

"You don't have to look at me with such an evil eye," she said.

"I apologize if that is what you think. I'm just very busy and have a whole lot to get done, Ms. Sara. I've got a lot on my mind." I knew my actions were not pleasing to many white people. However, she was in my neighborhood, and I forgot for a brief moment that I would not be treated as an equal.

She pushed her spectacles up her nose and swept loose strands of her gray hair back into the bun she had it in because the wind was whirling up and blowing all of us around a bit. "I think we might get a little rain, wouldn't you say, Maggie?"

I glanced up to the sky and the low-hanging clouds. "It may come sooner than I can get everything I want done." My words did nothing for her. Instead she reached down into her satchel and pulled out a sizable number of green-backs. I turned my head to prevent any misconceptions of me staring at her money. It was rumored that colored folks had been murdered for staring at white folks' money. But then she tried to hand it to me.

I threw my hands up. "Oh no, Ms. Sara, I can't take your money."

"You take everybody else's money around here to manage the Order and to subsidize the burial of the dead, right?" Ms. Sara said. She had learned all of this from the colored people she hired, no doubt.

"Yes, ma'am," I replied, reluctant to even consider her money as some-thing for coloreds after the time I heard she beat one of her Black servants with a leather strap so hard he nearly died. Momma said they had to use dirt and oil to fill in the gashes in that man's skin. My understanding was Ms. Sara stood unmoved while one of her men did it. She was nobody's friend in Jack-son Ward.

She obviously read my thoughts by the expression on my face.

"I know what you've heard about the Satterfields. Hell, that is who we are. We done a lot of things we shouldn't have to y'all darkies." Just the mention of the word *darkie* sent a chill through me. It was at that moment I wanted to choke her skinny red neck. Instead I stared at her as she attempted to hand me a wad of money again.

I inhaled deeply before speaking: "Ms. Sara, we don't need your help. After what you've done to us coloreds, even after being freed we were tor-mented. Isn't that enough?"

"Hush, gal," she said, but I couldn't stop.

"You hate us, Ms. Sara. You hate us 'darkies,' as you say." Several people were standing close, listening to me speak. One of the men gestured by put-ting his hand over his mouth begging me to be quiet, but I couldn't. It was time she knew how she had treated people, and the audacity was making me boil inside.

"Let me explain myself," she demanded.

I could hardly breathe through my nose because I was so upset. I just inhaled as much air as my lungs could hold and released it to calm myself. I was almost as white as she was with anger, and my cheeks flushed pink with pain. Just knowing how my momma said she allowed that man to be beaten clouded my vision. I finally slowed my heart rate down enough to listen to what she had to say. Besides, my actions could have gotten me locked up, but I was not afraid, not in the least. I would go to jail for what I believed in, even die.

"I was raised to hate coloreds," she said. "My parents and even my grandparents didn't care much for Negroes. Tom Rice had given a great minstrel show as Jim Crow, and that helped shape their mind-set."

While Jim Crow was a fictional character, to white folks he was a true embodiment of us coloreds. Tom would don blackface makeup to depict a character with absolutely no education, disgracing and embarrassing coloreds who knew they were smarter than the minstrel he portrayed. But the racist white folks loved him, and they were even crazy enough to believe the nonsense he portrayed about us. They applauded his despicable act, which exemplified and exacerbated the discord of the Reconstruction era. It completely set society back after the courts had overturned the "separate but equal" doctrine. Even the British joined in with the charades.

But I would not allow Jim Crow to define us.

"I have watched Mrs. Sadie for years as she took care of our clothes and made sure everything was perfect for me," Ms. Sara said. "I'm getting old now and I know many coloreds are good people. I'm sorry for my ways, and that is why I come down here to shop. This is the least I can do for all the pain my family has caused."

"Why didn't you speak up and stop what was going on?" I asked.

"You see, ignorance comes in all colors and forms. My family is British and has hated Negroes and Jews for generations. I just want to do better now." By the time she stopped talking, a crowd had gathered around us. "I just want to contribute to the Order. Use the money however you see fit. It is time coloreds had something of their own."

"Ms. Sara, there's a whole lot of people standing around with one ear in our conversation. You want to help us, and although we can use your money, it just seems too hypocritical to even consider taking it from you."

A man standing in the background interrupted. "Take the money, Maggie. We probably helped to get it for her. Take the money. All she owns is thanks to enslaved workers," he yelled.

Another man said solemnly, "That's right, Ms. Sara, you owe us."

A woman even spoke up: "Ms. Sara, you are a mean old lady." I couldn't believe the ruckus of those surrounding us who were listening in on our private conversation.

I was building allies with the white racists around. I was meeting with them one by one who had a problem supporting colored folks. All of them were grounded in their strong beliefs. I needed them to back off, and give us the support we needed so we could build our empire. In my mind, Ms. Sara could be one of them if she really wanted to help us.

So, instead of taking her money at that time, I decided a meeting with her would be better suited to our efforts. No man could do anything without the assistance of the enemy. It was a fact I knew very well.

Ms. Sara invited me to her home for our talk. I welcomed the offer even though the men standing around insisted, "She's no good, Maggie. She's just nosy, and after all we have built . . ."

"Let's give her a chance," I urged, trying to calm the crowd.

Mr. Walter rolled his eyes up in his head. "Well, you can try."

The meeting with Ms. Sara didn't go as smoothly as expected. Her motives proved to be just words spit out for the occasion. I informed her of how much we appreciated her concerns and donations, but that we wanted to do it ourselves.

"Well, don't say I didn't try to help y'all." Then, to herself, she mumbled, "How the hell do them darkies think they can become better without us white people?" To me she said, "I will give you this money if you allow me to have input on the progress in Jackson Ward."

It was clear to me that Ms. Sara just wanted to exert control in the Jackson Ward community.

"No, thank you, Ms. Sara. We are just fine doing it on our own."

Her face flushed. "There is no way you can be truly successful without our help. Mrs. Sadie understands that. And she knows how to treat us white folks."

Mrs. Sadie was smarter than Ms. Sara suspected. She was building a legacy to leave her children, with hard-earned coin and not with "help" from folks like Ms. Sara.

Afterward, I overheard Mr. Walter say to the other men around, "Maggie's as white as Sara is anyhow." His comments made my blood boil. I was not going to apologize for who I was or how I looked. I was my momma's child and my daddy was not the white man who fathered me, but the man who had raised me. I had been told before that my complexion was an advantage with white people. I was everything but a colored woman to some, and unladylike above all else. I didn't pay any mind to those comments at all. Too bad all they could see was the lightness of my skin, and not the fact I had been and was treated as inhumanely as any of the darker-complexioned Negroes. But, at times, my complexion did work in my favor. Some white people appeared to have a softer heart to coloreds as light as me. I took no satisfaction in that—I was still colored—but I did take full advantage of it for Order business.

The governor had become somewhat of an ally. He would open his door to me, and I'd walk into his spacious but hideous office and sit poised and without leaning in his imported leather chair, made by the best furniture maker in the country. Many bad decisions had been made in that room. With his deep blue eyes, he gazed at me attentively and listened as I began to talk. I was careful to refrain from maintaining eye contact with him for too long. Men like him were insecure and worried about position and power, and I didn't want him to believe I was exerting too much over him. I had spent many hours working on my approach. He was racist and prejudiced, but of course he didn't acknowledge or recognize it. He was not the typical southern Democrat, who hated Negroes vocally and on sight. Ms. Sara was nothing compared to him.

I had requested a meeting with the governor in writing. Though he had ignored my requests each time, it wasn't long before he invited me to his office himself. I walked in with my shoulders squared and placed each foot firmly on the hardwood floor so he could hear me coming. Governor James Hoge Tyler knew of me and was aware of my reputation. I could tell he was not at all impressed with the confidence I exuded when I walked into his office.

"Maggie Lena Walker," he said.

"Yes, sir," I answered, standing straight as an arrow with authoritative poise.

"You may sit," he directed. I nodded and took a seat.

"I hear you are some kind of rebel around these parts," he said as he stroked his thick beard.

"No, sir, I am the opposite," I replied in as humble, yet confident, a tone as I could.

"Mrs. Walker, I invited you to my office, but there is nothing we need to talk about."

"Oh, but there is, sir."

He glared at me with cold eyes, as if what I had to say was of little importance. "What do you want? I do not relish receiving a Negro in my office."

"Governor, have you ever needed help with something and the only person you could get the answers from was someone you didn't care for?"

"Yes, I have. What is your point?"

"As a free colored woman, I need your leadership and advice."

He pulled his chair up to his desk and finally turned his full attention toward me. "You, a colored woman, are asking me for help?"

"Yes, sir. You see, us colored folk just want to stay out of your way. We want to remain in our places."

"Negroes don't have a place, not even in this room."

"I know, and I am ashamed of this fact, but am so grateful for your generosity in accepting my request for an audience with you and in hearing me out now."

With each word uttered, his face softened.

"Governor Tyler, we need your help with the downtown business owners, who are threatening our existence every day."

"What do you expect me to do about it, Mrs. Walker?"

"We coloreds just want to mind our business and stay away from any conflict. We are attempting to stay out of the way of the Confederates and others who deem us a threat. I thought you might help."

"I'll tell you what. I will give it some thought, and you come back to me in a month or so and let me know how things are working out."

I smiled at his answer. I had expected him to flat-out say no and see me to the door. It was enough for me, since I believed in working with people, including prejudiced ones, to get results.

It wasn't long before things began to change. People noticed less police brutality and the residents of Jackson Ward continued working to build their community.

✦co✦

On March 29, 1902, the Independent Order of St. Luke published the first issue of its newspaper, the *St. Luke Herald*. It was the perfect way to reach beyond Jackson Ward and into the surrounding states. We had members who lived as far away as Boston. The hiring of the staff had been arduous, but the results turned out marvelous. Ultimately, I hired around thirty women, all eager to get to work in our offices.

In Richmond, oftentimes colored women could only find menial jobs as washerwomen, servants, or factory hands. The jobs I was creating and offering them were positions imbued with dignity. In building three new businesses, we needed people for all positions. We hired folks, mainly colored women, as bookkeepers, clerks, typists, and stenographers, and promised to train all of them in their given field. Our employment strategy drew the attention of folks from as far away as Maryland. The *Baltimore Afro-American* interviewed me for their paper. "It was a novel and instructive sight," I told them, "and the deeds that I had accomplished ought to afford encouragement and inspiration to every Negro in the land." I was proud of what we were accomplishing and hoped it would serve as an example to all colored folks across the nation.

Whatever I have done in this life has been because I love women. I love to be surrounded by them. Love to hear them talk all at once. Love to listen to their trials and troubles. Love to help them. And the great love I bear for our Negro women, hemmed in and circumscribed with every imaginable obstacle in our way, blocked and held down by the fears and prejudices of whites—ridiculed and sneered at by the intelligent Blacks. Let us all advance.

✦co✦

At dinner with my family, I brought a copy of the first issue of our newspaper. I held it up so Momma and the children could see, then laid it down on the table and encouraged my youngest son, five-year-old Melvin, to read a sentence. I had been working on his reading for a long time, and he enjoyed reading and learning new words. Included in the issue was the total amount of death claims we'd fulfilled. Melvin read it without any assistance.

"Isn't he too young to read about these things?"

I shook my head. "No, ma'am. Isn't this what I've been working toward all these years? Teaching colored youth to care about their community, to want to invest in themselves and in their future, for the betterment of us all? This is what it is about, Momma."

She pursed her lips but didn't argue. "As long as this chile eats his dinner," she said, wiping her hands on her apron and moving the paper to the side of Melvin's plate, so he could finish eating.

Russell, now almost twelve years old, pulled the paper in front of him. "Momma, you increased the burial fund just like you promised."

Armstead patted him on the shoulder. "That's right, my boy. That's right." Then he glanced over at me and smiled lovingly.

One day as I was getting ready to leave the office, a lady came through the door. Her hair was matted to her head. She was clean; however, her clothes were worn. She hesitated before speaking.

"Mrs. Walker? Some folks say you might could help me," she said, standing before me with dreary eyes.

"Have a seat," I said, pointing to the chair facing my desk.

"Mrs. Walker, I am not a member of the Order, but I am in desperate need of some help."

"We are here for everybody."

"My husband, Henry, died on Sunday, Mrs. Walker. He just dropped down and died. There wasn't anything I could do for him. Tell me, how am I supposed to pay to bury him? I can't even afford to feed my two chillun. I never shoulda left South Carolina. That's where I had my people. Poor as we were, we were never hungry."

Tears welled up in her eyes, and I watched as she struggled to gain her composure, wiping the teardrops with the back of her hand as she spoke. As she continued with her story, I could see the stress on her face, her worried, dark-set eyes, and frown. After hearing about her needs, I knew we had to help.

"Tell me your name."

"My name is Sally. Sally Washington."

"Well, Sally, the Order can help you with the burial expenses. I want you to talk to Mr. Walter, the undertaker, and tell him to call me tomorrow." She nodded her head.

"Thank you, Mrs. Walker. When I get up on my feet, I'm going to join the Order."

"Do you have a job?" I asked.

"I work downtown for some people cleaning, but it just ain't enough."

I reached in my satchel and found a few dollar bills. I handed them to her.

"Now, stop by the market on the way home and buy some food," I instructed. Sally became overwhelmed and tears streamed down her face. As she left my office, I could see the burdens lift up off of her chest.

The *St. Luke Herald* had a purpose, and it was my responsibility to let the people know the status of our community, and how, if we stuck together, we could make a difference.

With input from W. E. B., I had spent two years organizing a newspaper for the community. The *St. Luke Herald* was my way of keeping the community informed of everything happening around Jackson Ward and with the Independent Order of St. Luke. I called it my trumpet to sound the news.

In the paper, we included details on the current status of benefits collected, benefits requested, stories on new and progressing businesses in Jackson Ward, and which of them were looking to hire new workers. We added anything we felt would enhance the current lifestyles of the coloreds in our community. It would provide the means for organizing and proof of progress that we needed for our community to truly begin to thrive.

CHAPTER 14

1902–1903

BY ANY MEASURE, the *St. Luke Herald* was a success in the community. All throughout the neighborhood everyone was talking about the newspaper. Some even stopped me as I walked to work and boldly requested to be featured in a future edition. With the circulation of the *St. Luke Herald*, the community began to trust the Order and their efforts more, and to entrust them with their hard-earned money. But to help them grow their nickels more effectively into dollars, we needed a bank of our own.

That evening's meeting of the Independent Order of St. Luke took place in one of the rooms of our recently constructed St. Luke Hall. With all the projects we had in development, we'd outgrown the First African Baptist Church. Armstead and his company had constructed a grand building for the Order to serve as our main headquarters. It contained meeting rooms, the offices for the *St. Luke Herald*, and a printing press for the paper in the basement. Our sights were now set on opening a bank in St. Luke Hall as well.

"Good evening," I said, calling the meeting to order. "There are a few important items on tonight's agenda. First of all, the creation of our very own bank." A murmur ran through the audience before they quieted once more. "A year ago, I proposed that we create three key businesses to expand our reach and what was possible for us to do for the residents and business owners of Jackson Ward. We've accomplished the first. The *St. Luke Herald* has done what we hoped and more, communicating the progress and goings-on of our community and our organization to the Order's membership while also bringing more folks across Richmond, the state of Virginia, and neighboring states into the fold."

The assembled members broke out into applause.

"The time has come," I continued, "to invest more fully in our own. First, we need a savings bank. Let us put our moneys together; let us use our moneys: let us put our money out at usury among ourselves, and reap the benefit ourselves. Let us have a bank that will take the nickels and turn them into dollars. The pennies, dimes, and dollars of one individual may be few, indeed, but the combined dimes and dollars of a thousand individuals change the weak word *few* into the powerful word *many*. To do so, we will use the extra funds collected from our members and others around the state to open our own bank." The room roared in awe at finally being so close to achieving this goal. Thunderous applause took over the room.

❖╾❖

The process of establishing our own bank from the ground up had not been easy. I had spent difficult hours with Mr. John Branch, the president of a conservative bank downtown who didn't cater to the small deposits we made into their fund. He had been stubborn at first, afraid to get involved with anything or anyone who was fighting for the betterment of Negroes. He had embraced the nasty accusations of Jim Crow and felt we were animals with little intelligence.

The day I met him, he talked down to me as if I were ignorant. "Y'all coloreds are trying to take on too much with a bank," he said, sitting high behind a wooden desk in a high-back chair. His bluntness made it so much easier to gauge him and predict the outcome of our meeting.

"Mr. John Branch, you are one of the most respected bankers in town. Your bank is an example for all the other banks around and I would like to know what it takes to do your job."

He chuckled like I was tickling him, but I did not smile.

"What have I said, sir, that brings you so much joy?"

"Maggie Walker, you have always been a boisterous colored gal. And now you are certainly taking it to another level of intolerable."

I humbly pleaded, "Now, Mr. John Branch, I am only trying to improve the community I live in. I know that what I am asking may seem far-fetched for a man of your station. I have already spoken to the colored bankers, and they simply cannot give me all the necessary information I need."

Just the comparison of his banking skills to those of the colored bankers inflamed him. Not one white man cared for being compared to a colored man, someone they felt was illiterate and stupid, no matter how accomplished he might be.

"What do you need from me, Maggie?" he said, running his hands down his mixed gray beard.

I took a moment to gather my thoughts. "I would like to shadow you; become your apprentice of sorts. I could follow you during your workdays and watch how you handle the business of running a bank."

"Now, it wouldn't reflect well on me to have a colored woman following me around. Besides, my wife don't like me fooling around with the help."

I wanted to scream, but instead I pulled out my handkerchief and dried a nervous sweat from the bridge of my nose.

"Are you all right?" Mr. John Branch asked.

"Yes, sir, I'm fine."

"Well, I might be able to find some time for you. You are smarter than most of them niggas, who claim to be bankers." I flinched at his casual use of the n-word. "I will agree to train you one day a week. That's the best I can offer." Relief washed over me that he had finally relented to teach me. I wasn't going to let Mr. John Branch's racism keep me from achieving my goals. Who knew, he might even become an ally by the end. But I wouldn't let his name-calling distract me from the ultimate goal of our mentorship agreement. Calling us niggas wouldn't change the fact that we colored folks were smart and capable and would find a way out from under the thumbs of racist white men like him.

❖CƆ❖

After several months of meetings with Mr. John Branch and the other bankers, I felt confident that the St. Luke Penny Savings Bank would be manifested as only God could do. At the next Order meeting leading up to the bank's opening, I sought to ease any final fears or doubts among the members.

"As we prepare to open the doors of the St. Luke Penny Savings Bank this week, we are already hard at work on creating our own department store. We are tired of spending our money in places that will not even allow us to come through the front door without being treated like criminals nor let us try on the items they display. We are going to have our own place of business." The members applauded in agreement. "Between the *St. Luke Herald* and the St. Luke Penny Savings Bank, we have created at least thirty new jobs for our women and men. The future St. Luke Emporium will give us the opportunity to create even more jobs. Our community will be able to apply for these positions free from discrimination, and in so doing, we'll be supporting our own with our own money." Smiles lit up nearly every face in the room.

Before finishing, I added, "We are stepping into a new era with God on our side. We have knocked on your doors numerous times and gathered funds for years. This is all possible thanks to your support. This is *your* accomplishment, not mine!"

The room shook with excitement. There were questions, though.

One of the undertakers stood up, dressed in their famous drab black. "Now, I must admit, Maggie Walker, you've done some great things around here, but how in hell are you figuring on running a bank?"

A few others glanced at each other as if he had asked the very same question that was on their minds.

"Well, I've been having meetings with our governor and Mr. John Branch, who owns the bank downtown. And I've learned how to set up things for the benefit of our community. We even have the governor's approval."

One of the men yelled, "So you've been down there telling our business to the white man?"

The room went silent.

"No, I have not been telling our business to anyone, but I must mention and remind you that there is nothing we can do without them. And there is nothing they can do without us."

"Explain yourself!" he hurled back at me.

"I am determined to make our bank successful. I promise you, I have done everything in my power to learn how to set one up and how to secure it against the snakes. It is never a sin to learn from someone who doesn't look like you. Have any of you run or operated a bank? If so, please allow me some of your time."

No one else said or volunteered anything.

"Will the white people be using our bank?"

"This bank is for the residents of Jackson Ward, and Negroes from neighboring towns or states who want to feel their money is safe."

There was a smattering of applause at that and the doubters seemed to calm down.

"Remember this," I continued. "If we are to have a successful department store in the future, we are going to have to work with white vendors. At least to start. They are the ones who supply some of the merchandise you ladies and men cannot find in Jackson Ward. Having strong partnerships with them will be our first step toward success. And of course, we want to stock products from our own businesses right here in Jackson Ward."

Armstead stood up first, clapping with all his might.

The Order had eight thousand members at the time, and that number was growing each day. Before I ceded the dais to the treasurer for his financial report, I closed with, "Some of you call me 'the race woman.' I am proud to serve you. If we can enhance our knowledge and improve our financial situations in this segregated era of willful discrimination, then we are using the talents Christ has provided for us. So, I am a 'race woman.' A woman who is proud to be colored."

There was more thunderous applause, and I nodded in gratitude and appreciation at the members before stepping down from the dais. As the Good Book said, "For unto everyone that hath shall be given, and he shall have abundance."

⟡

It was chilly on November 2, 1903, the wind whirling around our feet and snow flurries floating through the air, but it didn't keep the people with furs, hats, and scarves wrapped tight around their necks away. Everyone in Jackson Ward and from across the States stood outside the building, waiting for the St. Luke Penny Savings Bank to open its doors. Fannie stood close to the entryway with her nose in the air, but with a gentle smile across her lips. All the entrepreneurs and residents of Jackson Ward were prepared to brave the chilly temperature for the long-awaited grand opening.

The crowd roared with thunderous applause when I stood on a stool above the eager group and said, "Now we have our own bank!" Armstead stood right at my side, bracing the stool so I would not tilt over. If there was an award given for the most supportive husband, he'd win without any doubt.

"It's about time, everyone." The enthusiastic crowd responded with cheers and applause. I couldn't help applauding myself in agreement. For me, it was about economic action to uplift the community by coupling hard work with fulfilling the responsibilities of righteous Christian morality. When I saw the undertakers and their wives up front and full of joy, my heart thumped faster. I always believed marriage was a partnership, and seeing both husbands and wives in the crowd made me very happy. Together they had partnered in the decision to support the St. Luke Penny Savings Bank. Mary and Otis also stood among the crowd, along with their four children. It was a pleasure seeing Mary out of the home. I'd scarcely seen her with all I had to do for the Order and since Otis had decided women should remain in the home while the men worked. His attitude bothered me, as he was putting his foot on the God-given talent promised to all, including women.

Armstead had spoken to Otis about his ways many times at my request. "Give Mary a little air to breathe," he had implored. But Otis simply said, "She loves it like this." He was clueless when it came to acknowledging his controlling ways and at times Mary glowed with happiness. However, her eyes appeared worn and stressed from taking care of all those children without a break.

I felt a woman should be able to choose her own vocation, just as a man does. Let her go into business, let her make money, let her become independent, if possible. When she marries, she would bring something into the partnership besides clothes and her warm body. It would be an equally vested union in marriage.

The St. Luke Penny Savings Bank would be different than other banks. It would be a place where women and men were welcomed to work. Women were constantly reminded they were only suited for jobs in the home, cooking over hot stoves all day, cleaning, and raising the children. All the while men spent their evenings puffing on pipes and watching the smoke dissipate into thin air, while discussing all their so-called accomplishments of the day. Mostly the conversations were insubstantial and lacked clear successes. Yet, I felt a man with a job was very powerful. Especially if he denied his wife the same right to have one.

Mr. John Mitchell Jr. had printed a story in the *Richmond Planet* about the grand opening a week prior that resonated with me greatly. He wrote, "Maggie Lena Walker must be thanked for doing something no other woman has ever thought about. She's made all our lives easier."

As we opened the solid wood doors of the Penny Savings Bank wide,

crowds poured inside, lining up and eager to make a deposit. I knew it was
my love for my community that inspired me to make sacrifices for the economic development of my people. I smiled at Armstead, who had his arm
around my waist, and his chest stuck out with pride. But not long after we
opened our doors, tensions around the public transportation system began
to worsen throughout Richmond. Something would have to be done.

CHAPTER 15

1904

THE TRAIN CAME TO a screeching halt. W. E. B. Du Bois stepped off the southbound train, as I stood smiling to greet him. Intelligence and confidence exuded from his tan face and curious brown eyes as he stepped down from the colored platform car. He was a northerner and along with him came a sophistication alike to many of the wealthy around town. It was a blessing to be his hostess for dinner at least, since the president of the *Richmond Planet*, John Mitchell Jr., had already decided W. E. B. would spend the night in his home. Any amiable time with Mr. Mitchell aided me in my quest to build our economically sufficient community. And any time with W. E. B. Du Bois was as valuable as the bank I planned on opening.

Thirteen former slaves had created the *Richmond Planet* long before I'd put together the *St. Luke Herald* and it had a circulation of 4,200 weekly subscribers. When Edwin Randolph stepped down as editor of the *Richmond Planet*, John Mitchell, the paper's new editor, was vital to molding the opinions of Negroes in the city, state, and nation. The *Herald*, on the other hand, was still limited to informing the members of the Independent Order of

St. Luke of what we were doing in the community to increase and progress our economic equality.

Most of the coloreds in Jackson Ward valued the intelligence of W. E. B. Du Bois. He was always creating visions of Negroes growing in places we had never gone before. He was also traveling across the seas, speaking to Africans and others about the equality of the Negro. However, there were a few people who called him uppity and self-indulgent. "That man is just for the advancement of himself and the separation of the have and have-nots," Mr. Walter had complained. "That 'talented tenth' mess is just a way to separate us," Mr. Walter said when I told him that W. E. B. would be coming to town. He shook his head, said, "Y'all fall for just about anything," and threw his arms up in the air. And even though I believed there was some truth in his opinion, W. E. B. strongly believed in equity when it involved money. I decided it was best not to comment, at that time. Mr. Walter was always aware of what was going on, and as stubborn as a bull when you were trying to debate with him.

A lot was happening in the Confederate South. My good friend Mary McLeod Bethune was also experiencing some concerns in Florida. So, I had invited Mary to town to discuss her concerns as well. Our dinner table would be full of pontifications and strong stands. We had plenty to discuss.

Mary had arrived a day before W. E. B., dressed in black as she usually was. She loved to accentuate her attire with a broach or a string of pearls, but black was certainly her favorite color. She also carried a satchel in which she kept a journal and her notes about what she was doing in Florida. Mary was an educator and a good friend. Although I was older than she was by more than ten years, we shared similar passions. Anything I could do to help her, or she could do for me, was something special. Armstead would attend our gatherings as well; he was often the voice of reason when the strong minds got a little loud.

Momma, Mary, and I kept bumping into each other in the kitchen. I'd cooked a roasted chicken with string beans and potatoes, and they were helping me with other fixins. Sometimes we'd sing hymns as we cooked. Mary had a beautiful voice, and we'd often sing "Precious Lord" together as tears welled up in Mary's eyes.

Momma had spent the entire day before making one of her famous pound cakes. She needed the extra time to sift the flour. The more it was sifted, the lighter the pound cake would become, and all the flavors of almond, black walnut, vanilla, and butter would culminate into something no one dared to resist. "There's no way Du Bois is going to leave town without having some of my cake," she declared.

"I know, Momma. You are going to make the man positively fat."

Mr. Mitchell was also invited, since Du Bois was resting his head at his home. He wouldn't have missed it even if we had tried to exclude him. He was a strong advocate for better services for Negroes, and his newspaper was the source to read about what was truly happening in the country. There was so much to converse about. While progress was being made for some, too many coloreds were being overlooked.

After that evening's Order meeting, Mary and I walked ahead of the men to our home, which was just around the corner from St. Luke Hall. When we arrived, Momma had already started heating up our dinner for the night. Booker T. Washington, who had come in on a late train, had gone straight to our home from the station and was now helping Momma set the table.

Our finest embroidered white tablecloth was on the table, along with the silverware Momma had polished. Having Mary Bethune, W. E. B., and Booker together for dinner was an honor. Mr. Mitchell loved to eat at our home, and we often had him there even uninvited. But this time the dinner would also include a funeral parlor owner, welder, and restaurant owner. We wanted the leaders and entrepreneurs of the community to join us for the night's discussions.

As soon as hands were washed, Armstead blessed the table. He enjoyed giving thanks for all we had, though at times he could be a little long-winded. He was a man who not only provided for me and our children, but was also grateful for us.

Everyone appeared to enjoy the food, and conversations flowed easily while we ate. Polly was giving the boys orders as I would; my mini-me in the home. Russell and Melvin needed a bit of taming, and Polly helped me with that. Momma treated them like she did Johnnie, as if they were her little princes. She'd make them chocolate candy and allowed them to play outside longer than I would. But Polly was sure to remind them of the promise they made to Momma and Daddy. She was mature for her thirteen years in a way Russell wasn't yet.

"Maggie, I must say you have really done a good job with the membership over at the Order," W. E. B. said.

"It's so impressive," Mary agreed. "But not surprising given that you're the one running things."

"Maggie works night and day to help this community thrive," Armstead added.

"And so do you," I said, covering his hand with mine. "Without your support, I could not get so much done."

Armstead gave me the barest hint of a smile; praise never did much for him. For him, everything was his duty. Momma loved him as if she had birthed him herself. He was another son she'd always wanted and the kind of man she swore she'd prayed for me to marry.

The children ate quickly and then Momma ushered them out. She explained to them as they helped clear the table, "It's time for y'all to go to bed. The grown folks are talking." Russell stood around watching everything and listening. Normally, Armstead and I discussed our day in front of the children, but tonight we had guests.

"Russell, go on to your room," Momma said, and he ran up the stairs.

Over long-stemmed glasses of port wine, we began to stir up a few things.

"I've had conversations with James Gamble of Procter & Gamble concerning the funding of my new school. He has not committed yet to anything, but I think we are onto a true investor. I could use a visit from you down in Florida, W. E. B.," Mary said.

He sipped at his glass of wine and said, "I will do all I can to bring people in for a fund-raiser for your school, Mary."

"That's enough for now," Mary said. "I have baked pies and cakes and sold whatever we can to build up a fund for the school I plan on opening. Our people need access to a good education, and you know how hard it is to motivate some folk. It's like pulling teeth, I tell you."

"I can come down there, too, if necessary," I told her. When it came to civil rights for colored folk, all of us did whatever we could.

"There are some concerns around here you ought to be aware of as well." The table hushed before I continued. "Our transit system is failing us. Now, nothing grave has happened so far, but everyone is complaining about having to give up the seats they paid for with their hard-earned money to white riders."

The Virginia Passenger and Power Company was forcing coloreds to give up their seats to the whites who wanted one. Though word of all of this had started in 1902, the situation hadn't improved, and it seemed primed to get worse.

States across the nation were practicing the separate-but-equal rule of justice. Even after paying equal fares, they were told to give up their seats to white riders at any time. The conductors were also given the authority to seat white folk in the front of the trolley and coloreds in the back.

When news spread of this happening in Richmond, Mr. Mitchell called a meeting, inviting me, W. E. B. Du Bois, Booker T. Washington, and Mary McLeod Bethune to attend. He said it was time for all the decision makers to discuss the matter. This Jim Crow separatism was an issue that wasn't going away anytime soon.

Seated around my large mahogany dinner table at my home were the main freedom and justice leaders of the nation. Others in the community were also in attendance, and those without seats stood around the table, up against the walls lined with framed newspaper articles.

Mary was the first to speak. "We are not going back. This transportation issue is happening all around the South, and we cannot let it stand any longer. Our money is worth just as much as theirs."

Heads nodded throughout the room. I spoke next.

"I've been hearing this was coming for some time now. I think I mentioned it to John, and we both agreed that we need to do something about this. Rumors started down in Louisiana in 1902. It's been two years now. It's gone on long enough."

Booker added, "I read in a white newspaper on the train that they're saying segregation was as necessary as it is natural. They said it was some sort of safeguard for white people. This kind of language is despicable, and I for one find it disturbing. We must counter all this backwardness before it continues to threaten to undo all the hard-won progress we've made."

Mr. Mitchell spoke up then: "If they will not treat us fairly, then we will refuse to pay money for their services."

I added, "Why are we paying them for service, when they don't even want us on their transportation? We are the bulk of the riders on the Virginia Passenger and Power Company's streetcars. We are providing the funding that keeps them running. We coloreds have more power here than we realize."

"I understand exactly what you are saying, Maggie," Mr. Mitchell replied.

W. E. B. finally interjected. "We can boycott them. See how they fare without our hard-earned moneys. We don't need them."

"God's given us feet to walk and the distance from Jackson Ward to the heart of downtown isn't that far," Mary commented.

I projected loud and clear, "It is time to put a call out to our community and let them know that we are going to fight this mistreatment and how. We are not going to allow them to rob us blind, take our money, and then make us stand." The people standing around the room applauded ferociously.

Mr. Mitchell immediately took out his journal and began writing.

"I'll print a story about it in the *Planet*. It's the easiest way to make people aware of what is happening and how we plan on dealing with it."

"I will put this information in the *Herald* as well," I added. "We will all come together and see what kind of effect we can really have on *their* financial security."

All those sitting around the table were in complete agreement. The community members in attendance also cheered on our decisions.

"Eventually, things are going to get ugly," W. E. B. said. "If I was you, I'd be bracing myself for when this becomes uncontrollable."

"It seems every time we take a step forward, something else rises up against us," Mary said.

"I refuse to allow any white man or anyone else to take my God-given power away from me," I said. "I might have to change my approach, but I will figure out a way to secure economic empowerment for Negroes. We have got to continue to fight for rights intelligently and see if we can right the wrongs of the past."

"We are going to watch this train issue like a hawk," Armstead said.

"We are making strides across the country," W. E. B. said. "We are getting educated and doing some things no one ever felt we could handle. My travels have taken me to places where coloreds have united to actively challenge the perceptions and impressions that Jim Crow has given white folks about us, and things are changing. Remember how the Jewish people came together; well, we can try to do the same. We've got to focus on making a change and not on the resistance of others to that change."

"When you come to Florida," Mary said, still furiously taking notes, "I would like you to repeat that. We need to believe we can make a difference."

"We are all in this together, Mary. I just wish everyone could see the vision," I said.

"They will," she said, confident without any doubt that her plan of opening a school would flourish.

"You've got a lot of things going on, Maggie. How do you plan on doing it all in the next few years?" W. E. B. asked me.

"I tend to look toward God for advice, and then Armstead," I answered. "I don't necessarily always understand how all this is going to come together. But with hard work and determination, it is going to happen. Besides, our community is ready for a change." I held my chin in my hand, as I often did when I was pondering over ideas.

W. E. B. turned to Armstead. "You've got yourself a woman who thinks like a man."

A subtle frown creeped across Armstead's face and a wrinkle appeared between his eyebrows. Armstead clearly didn't take too kindly to his comment. "She's a *woman* with a vision," he replied, staring straight into W. E. B.'s eyes. "She's not a pushover and it is the reason I believe she's going to be the one who is going to enact real change in Richmond."

W. E. B. didn't have a response to that. The one thing we both felt was necessary was to have a clear vision and treat everybody with respect, regardless of gender. And use the Bible to battle discrimination as readily as possible.

For the rest of the night, Mary told us about the disturbances in Florida, the need for education, and the lack of participation from the community. "Fear has everyone in an uproar, but what on earth can a little knowledge hurt?" she asked.

"Mary, I will be there in two months. I'll help you bring the community together," W. E. B. promised.

"What date exactly can I expect you?" Mary asked, ready to make note of it in her journal. W. E. B. gave her a date and she diligently wrote it down. "I'll hold you to that," Mary said.

"I'm sure you'll remind me about it soon," W. E. B. said.

"We can help too, if you need us, Mary," I told her. Armstead nodded. Most of the night, Mr. Mitchell just listened and jotted down notes in a leather-bound journal he carried with him everywhere. He was a journalist, and at times we had to remind him that some of our conversations shouldn't be shared in the *Richmond Planet*.

"Mitchell, what's on your mind?" W. E. B. asked him.

He shook his head and replied, "We got so much to do, and it is my job to give the people the right information and possibly convince them to come together for the general wealth and advancement of colored folk."

Most folks had already gone home for the night. The candlesticks had burned all the way down before we got up to leave the dining room table. There were a few slices of cake left and the bottle of port wine had been empty for hours. But there was still much more to discuss.

W. E. B. loved this type of dialogue, and he relished being around intellectuals. Education was as important to him as it was to Mary, Mitchell, Armstead, and me. He had already caused an uproar against benightment of colored people in Paris, displaying Negroes in a positive way with more than 353 photos. He was determined to dispute the Jim Crow that lingered like a ghost in the minds of intelligent white folks.

CHAPTER 16

1904

OUR SIGNS WERE HELD HIGH and waved with each gust of wind. "I would rather walk than be mistreated," one read. The streets were lined with workers walking, some moving at a fast pace and others barely shuffling along, but none of them yielding to the streetcars. There were signs everywhere along the transit system route, too.

We had published our rallying call in an April 1904 issue of the *Herald*, and John Mitchell Jr.—who'd spearheaded the effort—printed a headline in the *Planet* concerning the streetcar company's unjust treatment of coloreds and diligently opened the eyes of the community. I also asked members of the Independent Order of St. Luke to spread the word all around Richmond and across the state.

As word of a potential boycott spread across Richmond, people planned to travel on foot. We even devised a scheme to get anyone who could not work due to the lack of transportation a job in one of our local businesses. We were determined to put an end to all the nonsense happening around us, which was threatening to drag us back into a history that we were trying not only to forget but to move on from for good.

Our grassroots efforts included canvassing the neighborhood like we'd once done when asking folks to join the Order. I knocked on doors, bringing my children with me, and handed out pamphlets with information answering any questions they might have about the boycott. We brought together women and men in the community to do whatever they could. Mrs. Sadie, who was elderly, was concerned about her business.

"I use that streetcar to make laundry deliveries whenever it is necessary. I have a client across town, and she ain't gonna like me missing my delivery of her laundry."

"Mrs. Sadie, this is for the betterment of all of us. If we do nothing to stop them, then these people will think it is all right to pull us backward."

She gazed at me with weathered eyes. "I'm too old for this fighting with white folk. They's gonna win this war, too." I could see the discomfort and defeat in her eyes. She had been giving them all her attention for years, working her arthritic hands until they were raw, and still it was never enough. However, our dignity was being challenged once again. First enslavement, then freedom, and now Jim Crow laws—its own form of enslaving us colored folks. How much more could we be expected to handle?

After we learned how serious the actions of the Virginia Passenger and Power Company were going to be, we were forced to take a stand against the "separate but equal" practice. It had started in Louisiana and for the life of me, I thought maybe those of French heritage would fight alongside us, but of course they did not. And when Mississippi quickly followed in the separatism, it was no surprise, either. Virginia authorized the policy, but left it up to the streetcar companies to decide how they would handle it. So, Richmond's Virginia Passenger and Power Company decided to act accordingly.

I ran into constant opposition from coloreds who felt the boycott of the transit system was not necessary. As Mrs. Sadie had commented, "Standing is not a problem for a short time. It is better than walking. And besides, I am too old to walk . . . Done did enough of that in my day."

Her argument was noted, and Armstead and I decided that if a ride was what she needed, we would kindly provide it for her.

"Mrs. Sadie, we will take you to deliver your cleanings and bring you home. We must present a united front for this to turn in our favor."

"Well, I guess that will work." She looked puzzled yet relieved. "Now, I don't want to be late."

There were others in the colored areas of town who simply said, "No, I am not going to do it. I don't mind standing." I shook my head in disgust, knowing things would never change for them as long as they feared their own advancement.

"You pay the same money as whites do and yet you are willing to give up your seat?" I asked.

Mr. Harris, who wasn't a resident of Jackson Ward, stared me straight in the eyes and said, "I don't have an automobile or a horse and buggy to get around town in. All I have are these hands to work with, and I ain't gonna give up my job for no boycott."

"Mr. Harris—" I began, but he closed the door right in my face.

Nothing was going to stop us from making it happen. Mostly coloreds used public transportation and I knew that if we continued with a boycott, it would hurt white pockets. We contributed to the economy in every form, and without coloreds doing the manual labor and using the streetcars to get to work, things would shut down sooner than later, and some businesses would also suffer.

One of the merchants who sold fabric in Jackson Ward was a lady whom I adored and loved for the quality of work she produced. She had designed my wedding dress. I knew she was progressive and cared about the community, yet she glared and insulted me from across the room.

"You can get away with most of your antics because you are bright and almost white. When the racist sees you, they see themselves and give in to some of your demands. Maggie Walker, you have an advantage over everyone else around here, being half-white and all. Stop asking the rest of us to put ourselves in harm's way." Her twangy southern accent irritated my ears, but I listened.

"Thank you for letting me know how you really feel, but I'm as colored as you are."

"You's white to me," she said with no hesitation.

After she finished her declaration, I turned and walked out of her shop. The last thing I wanted to do was defend my character or ways of getting things done to her. Most people didn't understand what needed to be done when faced with adversity. At times, my mind would be haunted with the ghost of Ms. Elizabeth Van Lew and her courage. She had to fight with her own people, too. And how could they forget the enslaved colored folks still working out in the tobacco fields from sunup to sundown without being paid a single penny? Fear was always the enemy.

Mr. Mitchell continued to push for a boycott. He visited me often in the Order offices at St. Luke Hall.

"I am going to make sure these people know we exist," he declared before even taking a seat.

"I think they already do," I answered, closing the journal in which I'd documented the day's activities.

"Maggie, we must flood the headlines with information concerning the boycott. We must also argue with those who are opposed to what we are doing. The more we communicate, the better."

"Our numbers are increasing," I said. "People *are* walking to work, but we need more to join our efforts. The *Herald* is going out to everyone on our circulation list. We are letting them know that this is crucial for our survival. Keeping such dangerous power as this in the hands of hotheaded and domineering white men will certainly only bring about trouble for our community."

"What does Armstead think about all of this?"

"You know Armstead," I said. "He is a warrior; the strongest man I know. But he wants us to have peace where we live. Just last night he was saying that he would like me to be a little less involved in this. But John, I am fully committed to economic equality and justice for colored folks. I could not have asked for a more understanding husband. He is the reason I can do so much."

"He's a lucky man."

"No, John. I'm a lucky lady." He chuckled.

The next day, I wrote copy and instructed my printer to get it out as soon as he could get it on press. After checking it for any errors, I printed and distributed it to our readers.

We had been working to mobilize people for months and there were fewer people on the streetcars. Some were putting their feet on the cobblestones; others were packed together in a buggy or a few cars. The more information the *Richmond Planet* and the *St. Luke Herald* put out concerning our rights, the more people joined the boycott.

The newly elected mayor of Richmond, Carlton McCarthy, also paid me a visit. Uninvited and without warning, he knocked on my office door at St. Luke Hall. My assistant tried to alert me, but he walked in right behind her without an invitation. When I saw the white Democrat standing in front of me, I felt heat rising around my neck.

"What can I do for you, Mr. Mayor?" I asked tightly without offering him a seat. He took the liberty of sitting down in front of my desk anyway and removed the Stetson he was wearing.

"Mrs. Walker, I hear you are organizing the boycott in this city, and I am here to warn you about this type of thing."

I frowned at his tone. "Sir," I said, "all we are asking for is equal rights. And from my point of view, this is justice."

His face flushed at my response.

"Come now," he said, "y'all can ride the trolley wherever it goes in the city. We are just asking you all to sit in the back of the streetcar. That is the best we can do for you coloreds."

"Mr. Mayor, we pay the same fares as any white person to ride the trolleys, and we want access to the same seating as them, too."

In his agitation, he reached inside his jacket pocket, pulled out a white handkerchief, and wiped it over his face. I leaned in closer to him. I could tell my closeness was bothering the Confederate soldier in him, which was his claim to fame in Richmond.

"Mrs. Walker, I know you want things to be equal, but colored people are not equal to the white man. And never will be." His profound statements were of no value to me.

"Mr. Mayor, we *are* equals. We bleed red, as you do. We are more alike than different. We work and pay our bills, as does the white community. We are major contributors to this society, and riding and paying for transit is our right."

He stood up then, clearly upset. "I was warned about how stubborn you are."

"I'm just determined, sir. But if someone desires not to ride your streetcar system, it is their decision to make."

He pointed a finger at me. "I know you are encouraging this defiance from them niggas."

I stood up from my desk. "What is the real problem, sir?" I asked, staring him down, unblinking. He was no taller than I was, but his threats had rattled me, and I was angry. Realizing that he'd put me on guard even more, his tone of voice relaxed from the harsh tongue-lashing of a moment before.

"Money is being lost. You are taking money right out of the transit system's pocket," he said without moving or flinching. His blue eyes attempted to project concern and compassion, yet I could see right through him.

I sat back down. "I am sorry to hear that. But when you pay for a seat on the trolley, you should be able to sit wherever there's an empty seat and not be forced to move. You are asking us colored folks to pay the same fare as a white person, but then making us stand up if a white person desires our seat. Also, sir, what good does separating us do?"

He responded sharply, "We are not interested in sitting close to any colored people. We want you all to sit in the back of the car and be happy we are allowing you to ride at all!" He put his Stetson hat back on his head and turned toward the door. "Remember, we *do not* want coloreds and whites together."

As he walked out the door, I turned back to the blank page in front of me and wrote the headline for the next issue of the newspaper: "*Let's shut them down now.*"

✦ᴄ✦

Our efforts continued all through the spring and into the summer. The warm, sultry weather made it easier to walk to work without weathering the Virginia chill. Each week, more and more people joined the boycott and were seen walking side by side to work. The streetcars would pass them as they traveled downtown, and most times the cars were completely empty.

At times, the walking workers would shout when the streetcar came by. It was their way of voicing their disappointment without causing a disturbance of any kind. Even the people on the streetcars waved, and some got off at the next stop to continue on foot with the walkers.

"Negro Haters" was the name John Mitchell Jr. called the streetcar law enforcers. Many of the white people were also disturbed enough about the law that they decided to walk instead of ride the trolley. John Meyer, a white carpenter, refused to sit at the front of the streetcar. He sat in the colored section and was arrested. A colored lady from New York was arrested and fined twenty-five dollars for saying "To hell with Jim Crow laws." The Virginia Passenger and Power Company was receiving messages from all over. And the white people who stood against the law were with us to the end.

By July 1904, the Passenger and Power Streetcar Company filed for bankruptcy and was auctioned that December. In the matter of a few months, our determination had shut down the streetcar company completely.

At the next meeting of the Independent Order of St. Luke, I stood up and reminded the members about the power of their money, and to never forget it. The crowd cheered when Mr. Mitchell came to the podium for having spearheaded it all. For my part, I could only marvel at the economic and political power we had when we could all come together.

CHAPTER 17

1905

MOMMA CALLED ME from the kitchen. "Chile, where are you?" I had just sat down and lifted my legs into Armstead's lap. And like always, he rubbed my feet through my nylon stockings. Even in comforts, walking everywhere was still difficult on the cobblestone sidewalks. My feet would ache from the pounding. But there was something special about walking around Jackson Ward, with the expansion of new businesses and how proud the people were of our small community. How the sounds of the voices chatting and even the smell of fish frying on Fridays invigorated me.

After the mobilization and the daily work of the Order, my feet and back hurt. Armstead was so attentive, and at times I knew he was neglected, although I loved him with my whole heart. So I made my moments with him and the children count. Before I sat down for the evening, I kneaded my hands into his shoulders, and he leaned back with eyes closed so I could massage away the stress from his day of building and constructing the new developments around Jackson Ward.

Both of us were workaholics. Neither of us took real vacations. Most of

us Negroes didn't have places to go anyhow. There were a few places on the
East Coast where we congregated. A beach in Maryland where Frederick
Douglass's son frequented and had purchased land. The other places were
a distance away. So, on occasions, Armstead and I would steal an evening,
while Momma watched the children, and we'd ride out into the colored sec-
tions across town, lay down a blanket in a park, and have a meal.

"Maggie Lena Walker, did you hear me calling you? Don't make me come
looking for you," Momma yelled again from the kitchen.

"I'm coming!" I hurled back. And then I put my feet down on the bare
floor and walked barefoot into the kitchen.

Momma was always busy herself. She had not had a suitor since Daddy
died. Her joy seemed to come from taking care of her grandchildren, and
Armstead. I knew Johnnie could see how much she gloated over Armstead,
but it never seemed to bother him.

"Sit down, Maggie."

I took a seat and waited.

"I'm a little worried."

"What are you worried about?" I asked, only now seeing fear in her dark
eyes.

"At times I wish I had never shared my experiences at the Van Lew mansion with you. There's some things I should have kept to myself."

I frowned because I didn't understand where the conversation was going.
It was already dark outside, and it was beyond the time in which she turned
in for bed. The Van Lew mansion had nothing to do with me.

She went to the cast-iron stove and poured herself some hot water and
added some sarsaparilla to it.

"You want some?" she asked.

"No, ma'am." I hated the taste of sarsaparilla, but she swore by its healing
power. Said it was good for the arthritis she had in her hands and knees. She
thought it would help me, too, since I was always walking through Second
Street in Jackson Ward. I left my car at home most times and walked, as it was

easier to mingle with the members of the community by walking alongside them. "Momma, what is going on with you? Are you feeling all right?"

"Ain't nothing wrong with me. I just thought I needed to give you a little 'vice."

"Let me tell Armstead I will be upstairs in a minute. I don't want him waiting up for me."

"I'll be waiting for you right here," she said, her dark eyes serious with worried thoughts.

I went into the parlor and kissed Armstead lightly on the lips. He opened his eyes. "Go on upstairs, I'll be there in a few minutes. Momma wants to talk to me. The children are all tucked in bed."

When I came back into the kitchen, Momma was sipping her second cup of tea and had one steaming for me to drink.

"Maggie, it is all right to be 'volved in the community, but I am afraid them white boys may come for you. They killed my Willie, and I still don't know why. I don't want them to mess with you," she said, shaking her head.

"Momma, you've always told me that my faith will take me places, and I still believe in this. God is watching over all of us, and I will be fine."

"Chile, these white folk ain't changed. They done killed people for just gazing in their direction."

"You are right, Momma, but I believe this is my calling. I can't stop defending our people."

"You know shutting down the Passenger and Power Company hit them in their pockets. They hate it when we mess with their money."

"Momma, the Jim Crow laws will always run our lives if we fear them." She sipped her tea. "Are you scared?"

"No," I answered, "because God is with me in all that I do."

"I just want you to be careful."

"I know you do, Momma," I said, and hugged her neck.

"I try to keep the mayor and the city members informed about our concerns, even if they believe in separatism," I added.

She sighed. "I wonder where you get your courage from. Did it come from your real father, or the stories I told you as a child about Ms. Elizabeth Van Lew? Sometimes I tend to forget about my people and how they were strong-minded and brave. Some of them stood up to the white man, too. They's shot down, but God knows they did what was right."

"Momma, it comes from you. You struggled all your earlier years without ever complaining. Being a laundress is not easy, but you did it and you did it well."

She chuckled and said, "Chile, it was just something I had to do."

I smiled. "This is something I have to do. And I'm not done. I am working on the emporium now, so we can finally have a place to shop and try on clothes without being treated like thieves or undesirables."

"Be careful, chile. You are all I got in this world. Your brother sometimes forgets I even exist."

"Oh, Momma. You've got your grandkids and Armstead, too."

"Yes, I suppose you are right. When is the emporium going to open anyway? I need me a new hat for church."

"Hopefully real soon. I'm getting sleepy."

"That's the sarsaparilla," she said knowingly. "It is a healer."

Momma finished her cup and turned off the lantern, and we both went upstairs to bed.

✦◗◖✦

Mr. John Branch, the president of the bank downtown, was known as a segregationist, yet against all odds, he and I had become friends. I included him in my business decisions, and he was a part of my plan, no matter how much he pretended to hate colored people.

"You care too much for them damn folks," he'd tell me, forgetting that they were *my* people. He knew I was mixed, and I never tried to pass as a white person. So, when he allowed his rhetoric and racism to spill from his lips, I muted myself from any thoughts that would prevent me from doing my job.

While the streetcar boycotts carried on, I had been meeting with Mayor McCarthy and other businessmen downtown. I sensed that Mayor McCarthy had developed a begrudging respect for me, though I knew admitting it would be a sign of weakness to him.

"Maggie, whether we agree with you or not, I know you're going to do it anyway," Mayor McCarthy said. "The question remains to be seen whether the emporium will stay open."

"Yes, sir, we are hard at work on it now. I would like to invite you to the grand opening." I handed him an invitation printed on the finest paper. He looked at it and promptly put it in the wooden wastebasket beside his desk.

"Now why would I attend the 'grand' opening of a colored store? There are plenty of quality department stores right here in downtown Richmond. What could your store offer that theirs don't already have? It'll be a cold day in hell when you catch *me* in a colored store!" He raised his voice toward the end, with his unusual southern drawl, more like that of someone from Georgia.

"I just wanted to extend the invitation," I reiterated to him. "To see for yourself what our conversations and my plans have led to."

When I asked him to come by, I knew he would perceive it as an insult. By involving him, I hoped he would call off the lynch mob who was totally against the advancement of colored folk. The threats were growing by the day. And some of the people in the colored community were afraid at the idea of shopping in the emporium.

"Mrs. Maggie, I'm sure you believe that you're doing a great thing for coloreds by opening this store, but I cannot be seen endorsing it. White folks are going to get mad and shut you down at the first opportunity, and they'll punish me for supporting you in this little experiment. I can't have that."

I smiled politely at him and held my tongue, confident in my faith that we would no longer accept being treated like second-class citizens. Boycotting the Passenger and Power Company's streetcars had created a more ruthless and crueler group of racists lashing out against colored folks, even though they were in the wrong.

But when anyone is afraid for their safety, they will attack more viciously, and I'd had my share of words with colored folks who'd turned on me as evilly as any white person. Fannie simply told me one evening as an Order meeting was ending, "The only reason you are accepted by that racist mayor is because you are damn near white yourself. Most of us aren't so lucky!"

Although it was possible, I couldn't help but boil up inside when comments like that were volleyed against me. I had been through hell, too. And I was doing all of this for them, for *us*. Beads of sweat would form on my nose and I would take deep breaths just to keep from lashing out at the comments. To the white businessmen, I was just another nigga, even though my birth father resembled them perfectly. And often the abuse from white folks was so routine and ordinary, I didn't even share it with my family. For fear of Armstead approaching them and being killed, I held a lot of the nastiness inside. Once, one of the large prosperous downtown businesses sent a big white man to my office. Although we rarely allowed strangers in, he had been pushy like the mayor and walked right past my assistant.

He was dressed in the finest menswear. He wore a dark top hat, which he removed upon entering. I didn't recognize him. He was tall, slim, and maybe in his fifties.

"What can I do for you?" I asked from behind my desk.

Politely, he asked if he could sit down. After he was seated, he glanced around at my Italian bookcase and my paisley high-back chairs and sighed. After a glance, he began to speak.

"You don't know me, Maggie Lena Walker, but our paths have crossed." I frowned, knowing I had never met him even once. I tended to remember most people I encountered.

"Do you mind explaining what you mean?" I pried.

"Let's just say, I knew your father. We were in the war together."

His reference to my birth father piqued my curiosity. "So, to what do I owe this visit? Did he send you to speak to me?"

"No, not exactly. But I do come with a proposal and I hope you will consider it."

I knew my father was no longer on this earth. I had attended his funeral from a distance. I had watched from behind a large headstone as they laid his body to rest at the Hollywood Cemetery, looking over the James River. I didn't get to know him, but from time to time since then, I had stopped by his grave for a visit. I had never told Momma or Armstead about these excursions; it was my secret. I had a few things I wanted to say to my father, concerning neglect and entitlement. "Mr. Cuthbert, wasn't I deserving of the things white children had?" I implored of his grave. He couldn't answer me, but I said yes for him. An afterthought came to me reminding me he had sent me a beautiful dress for my graduation. In the Richmond I lived in, there was not much he could do. A colored woman and a white man seen together were looked down upon, and with a child even worse.

I leaned back in my high-back leather chair and tried to figure out who this man was. Was he at the grave site that sultry summer day, when there was no air stirring, just flies and mosquitos?

"Who are you?" I asked.

"My last name is Cuthbert."

I adjusted in my seat as I felt the agitation building inside me at hearing my father's last name. Was this man a relative of mine? Should he mean something to me?

"What do you want, Mr. Cuthbert?"

He put his hand inside his coat and pulled out an envelope with a string around it.

"I represent the downtown merchants, and we would like to offer you ten thousand dollars to back off the opening of the St. Luke Emporium on Broad Street."

"Now, sir, why would I consider doing a thing like that? The community has been waiting for something of their own for a long time. We are not welcomed in your stores. We come in through the side doors and we are treated without any respect at all. Your dressing rooms are not available to us, and neither is your return policy. We need our own services. What harm could our emporium bring to you and the other downtown merchants?"

He swung the envelope in front of me. "This is a lot of money. You would be a rich woman."

"And I would cheat my people out of an opportunity to be treated like human beings."

"If you consider this offer," he said, "we can see about letting y'all coloreds in the front door. I don't think the merchants are ready to offer return policies and dressing rooms to you people."

"Sir, I don't know who you were to my father, but go back downtown and tell them I wouldn't take their money under any circumstances."

"You might regret this."

"Then I will live with my regret. Please find your way out."

As he was leaving, I wondered again who he was to me. Was he my uncle or even my cousin? I had never actually seen my birth father or any one of his relatives. I could tell he was sent because of his last name, yet it didn't disrupt the plans I already had in place. Did they feel I would succumb to a family member? Albeit one I had no real connection to.

On Wednesday night, when the Juvenile Branch met, all three of my children were in attendance—Polly and Russell, now fifteen years old, and Melvin, all of eight. Each one of them was eager to hear what was needed to make an impact in the community, something that had been instilled in them since they were old enough to understand. Seeing the passion in their eyes did something to me. They were the future, and I wanted the best for them. I started by telling them the exciting news. "The St. Luke Penny Savings Bank is where you all will place your pennies and nickels. Remember, pennies saved turn into dollars."

The children sat quietly, some smiling from cheek to cheek, others still thinking about what I had said. "Do you all realize that now your parents and grandparents could make a deposit in the bank and watch your money grow?"

One of the bright young men raised his hand. "Mrs. Maggie," he said, "will putting the money we earn working and from chores in the bank help free us from the white man?"

He was an inquisitive and smart young man who often asked questions about freedom. "Well, yes, it will. And with the money you save, you can open your own businesses across the city, in another town, or even in another state. You can pay yourselves and achieve what I call economic equality."

"So, if we save and keep our money and watch it grow, we can go to college, and open our own business?"

"You see"—I had their full attention—"the white man keeps us dependent upon him for a home, food, and other goods. Our best defense is to affect the pockets of the segregationists who value capitalism over humanity. Always support each other and do not let the white folks turn you against one another."

My confidence in our progress had white and colored men alike afraid of me. Speaking in barbershops and shoeshine parlors about how I was "unladylike" didn't disrupt my goals. Progress was being made all around Jackson Ward. All the naysayers knew it.

✦◦✦

My meeting with the downtown vendors went well. They agreed to provide me with the same service as the high-end stores downtown, like Thalhimers and Miller & Rhoads. At times, I had to wait and watch to locate who the supplier for a particular item was. Other times it was easy, as a store clerk would tell me without hesitation. It was a long and arduous process, and all the members of the Order of St. Luke provided information and contacts to services. With the bank's success, many of the merchants offered their products willingly.

Hiring people for the store was an easy job. Women from Jackson Ward and other places in the city stood in line to apply. Some came from as far away as New Jersey looking for a job in our store. Most of them were willing to do anything to find their independence.

The emporium would offer clothing, hats, and dry goods imported from New York City. And just like I had for the bank opening, I staffed it with colored folks—mostly women—a store for our community run by those who were part of the community.

On April 10, 1905, when the St. Luke Emporium cracked open its doors with custom-made, brown-skinned mannequins in the windows and three floors filled with all the things we had depended upon the white merchants to provide, people were ecstatic. Some of them even cried at now having a department store of our very own.

Broad Street was transformed. There was a place just for us, and we no longer had to endure the insults of inhumanity from white folks in their stores. Yet all day, there were white people standing on the other side of the cobblestone street with menace and jealousy on their faces. At times they would yell "Don't go in there!" as folks came by to shop in our department store.

❖c❖

Darkness has a way of creeping up on you. As the orange sun sank below the horizon and the day went from dusk to dark, I realized I had lost track of time and quickly took my small Colt pistol from behind the counter and slid it into my satchel before locking the front door of the St. Luke Emporium. I could never be too careful.

The day had been a busy one, and my legs were tired. When the doors had opened at 9:00 a.m., Gladys Johnson had been the first woman to walk in, a bit tentatively. She'd put a hand to her head, overwhelmed by the amount of merchandise we had, amazement written all over her face.

She stopped in her tracks at the front of the store and stood for a long minute, glancing from left to right, taking in the newness, her face going from perplexed to joyful.

"This has got to be a day to celebrate in Jackson Ward," she mumbled to herself.

Now Thalhimers and Miller & Rhoads were not the only places to buy quality goods.

"Show me around," Gladys said, taking hold of my arm, and I gladly escorted her through, stopping at each counter to show her the merchandise and point out the different departments. Her eyes lit up at the sight of the women's clothing, the custom-colored mannequins draped in the latest fashions. She strolled silently and slowly, running her plump hands around the edges of each glass counter as if this were her first time in a department store.

"This is good," Gladys murmured, picking up a pair of dress gloves. She admired them a moment and slid them on before placing them back where she'd found them. "I think I will look around some mo.'" Letting go of my arm, she continued through the store, examining everything she could touch. I had a few fine pieces of jewelry locked in a case and she stopped to gaze down at them, smiling.

Fannie Tweedy came in right behind Gladys, her nose turned up as if she had caught the stench of chickens in a coop. But her big brown eyes danced when she glanced up at the ceiling and saw the lighting fixture. Her scowl softened, and the indentations in her forehead smoothed out a little. I'd ordered the chandelier from a secondhand store in Manhattan. It was similar to the one in the center of Thalhimers and just as prominent. Armstead had repaired it, replacing the pendeloques and polishing the brass up like new, and it sparkled and gleamed from above. Suddenly a smile swept across Fannie's face. I could sense her approval. She had never expected to find anything as nice here.

Fannie came from one of the wealthier families in Jackson Ward, undertakers with a reputation for servicing only colored people of means. She was dressed in a fine cloche hat she'd bought at Thalhimers and held a silk satchel close to her torso as if she expected someone to grab it from her. She was a snob through and through. Most people, including those with money, avoided her.

But the emporium seemed to have stopped her dead in her tracks. Nothing she'd found on her famed shopping trips to New York could outdo our inventory. We provided the same quality and care—for less. It had cost us, but we could afford it. The St. Luke Penny Savings Bank had become a magnet for those wanting to invest their money, and Armstead and I were doing well.

With many of the women who lived in Richmond's Jackson Ward visiting the store, I listened as attentively as possible to get feedback on what we had accomplished here. Women trying on tailored suits, silk dresses, and cloches twirled in circles in front of the floor-length beveled mirror, obviously feeling good about the new look.

"My God," Ester Butler said, "this dress is so much cheaper than the one at Miller & Rhoads, and it fits me like a glove. And you know we aren't allowed to try on clothes over there." Ester turned toward me. "Maggie, I could cry, I am so happy," she said. I stuck my chest out with pride, smiling, knowing that the St. Luke Emporium was needed and appreciated.

I walked over to Fannie, who was holding up a bolero blouse and a pleated skirt to match. She saw me gazing at her, turned halfway toward me, and smiled. Her expression shocked me—she never seemed to be happy about much.

"You know, it is all right to watch me, Maggie. I know you seek my approval, unlike those white lady clerks at Thalhimers who follow me around like I'm going to take something without paying."

"Fannie, of course your opinion is important to me," I said. "You are the most fashionable woman around here, and I hope we live up to your standards." I gave a grand smile of my own.

"You've made the women around here happy," she said, turning to face me fully. "Look around. Everyone is so glad we have something of our own and dressing rooms where we're allowed to try on things before buying them."

At other emporiums downtown, coloreds couldn't even return clothes that didn't fit; for them, all sales to colored folks were final. Here customers were being waited on by colored clerks, spending their own money in their own community. And we enjoyed treating our customers well.

"I'm glad this suits you," I said, secretly overjoyed by her response. Because no matter how uppity she acted, she had a certain degree of influence over the residents of Jackson Ward.

"Yes, it does, and there are no white lady clerks following me around like little puppy dogs, sniffing at my coattail. I feel free to roam as I choose."

This was a journey of tireless nights and days. Before we'd started, I had spoken about my plans to all the important connections I had, including the mayor. His reaction was not pleasant.

"We don't need any more stores. We already have too many. What on earth could you offer that the other stores don't?"

I had cringed at his response, but I was no pushover, and I wasn't afraid of white officials. "We just need our own, Mr. Mayor."

Putting the store together had been a work of great labor and immense rewards. I had spent hours bartering with the local vendors, at times begging them to put their goods in the store, knowing they faced serious opposition from white shopkeepers. This followed years of exhausting meetings with our residents, encouraging them to begin to become homeowners and entrepreneurs, to dream big.

The St. Luke Penny Savings Bank had opened first. Once we owned the bank, we used colored money to finance the emporium. Money was power. In the end, no one could prevent me from opening our store. We were fifteen thousand Negroes strong in Jackson Ward, running our own businesses, making and spending our own money in spite of the Confederate effort to reverse any progress we had made after the Union won the war. I got the emporium up and running by building a community of supporters that in the end included our racist conservative mayor.

❖◁▷❖

As I locked up for the night, the Colt securely in my purse, an unwelcome sensation washed over me. I felt warier than usual, but I shook off the worry and kept moving. As I turned toward where my car was parked, I paused in front of the store window for a moment, admiring the display, still visible in the darkness.

Earlier in the day, hours before opening, I had meticulously arranged the mannequins and filled the space around them with some of the pretty pieces of furniture and decorative items also for sale in the store. I knew that the display was attractive; I felt satisfied with my work. I inhaled and smiled, taking pride not only in the day's efforts but also in my persistence. My efforts to establish a department store had succeeded in making a real difference to everyone who resided in the neighborhood.

Jackson Ward was a place where coloreds felt secure. Its cobblestone walkways led north from downtown through rows of magnolia trees, toward gardens fragrant with sweet bluebells. Delicate wrought-iron gates surrounded Italianate town houses. If you lived here or passed through, you couldn't help but notice the elegance of Jackson Ward's residents.

With an unmistakable sense of propriety and belonging, these folks could sniff the aroma of fine dining from their own restaurants, deposit money into their own banks, and attend their own theater and clubs, dressed in outfits that rivaled those of Virginia's wealthier white residents. Jackson Ward was a sight to see and a pleasurable place to call home. We coloreds considered it a privilege and a blessing to live among such beauty after our mommas and papas had been enslaved. I had heard some folks call it the "Black Wall Street" of the South. This little corner of Richmond was a treasured enclave. Yes, it had been a long day and I was tired, yet I knew my customers left satisfied.

As I glanced down the sidewalk, a chill shuddered through my body. In the darkness, I could see silhouettes of people standing near a street lantern on the cobblestone sidewalk ahead of me. When I got closer, there stood three bearded men. One was taller than the others; all of them stood together with their arms crossed in front of them. My chest heaved as I struggled to control my breathing. I pulled my clutch close and felt for my pistol, slowly removing it and putting it in my dress pocket just in case I needed to use it.

I kept one hand in my pocket with my clutch wrapped around my wrist. These were sinister-looking white men, and their menacing stares told me that they were waiting for me. Fear and doubt washed over me, but I squared my shoulders, took another deep breath of the fresh night air, and continued toward them. As I moved closer and we met face-to-face, suddenly the men blocked my way on the sidewalk. When I attempted to go around them, they encircled me, and I found myself caught in the middle and could feel their anger. The largest of the three easily towered over me. He moved close and shoved his body up against mine.

One of the men, dressed in ordinary business attire, with a bowler hat and a jacket, improbably had a tooth missing, surely a sign that he'd gotten into or started his fair share of fights. Keeping my hand on the pistol in my pocket, I stared him dead in the eye.

"Now what can I do for you gentlemen?" I asked, feeling my heart pounding under my ribs.

One of the men chuckled and leaned back as if I had cracked a joke or was a Ringling Bros. clown. The man who had pushed against me retreated, and he and the third, whose beard was so thick it disguised his face, stiffened.

"Excuse me. I need to get home. Is there something wrong?" I asked, trying to keep my composure.

"We're here to give you a message," said the heavily bearded man. "You're going to have to close down your store. Or else."

I pulled air into my lungs again and forced a grin on my face, feeling the fear that had been building suddenly begin to subside. Beyond the men, I saw the shadow of someone else, a man I knew from the neighborhood, approaching fast, swinging his arms over his head to catch my attention. I glanced at him and subtly moved my hand to indicate that he should keep away. The man stopped but bent down and picked up a large stick. He remained in place, at a distance but close enough to overhear much of the conversation, and to act if necessary.

"The St. Luke Emporium is a place where everyone is welcome to shop," I said. "We sell many of the same things you can find at Thalhimers or Miller & Rhoads, only they're less expensive, one of the advantages of not being located downtown. If you want to stop by during business hours, I will personally help you find what you need."

"What we need, Maggie Walker, is for you to close up shop. You are stealing business from the merchants downtown," one of the men said, his tone threatening.

I shook my head. "No, sir, we're not stealing anything. We are just trying to serve our community. People feel comfortable shopping here because most of us coloreds aren't welcome downtown."

The tall man finally spoke, his breath coming in sour exhalations. "*We* are going to shut your colored ass down. Who do you think you are, anyways?"

I paused before responding. This was something I had been dealing with my entire life, and I recognized the threat for what it was: yet another attempt to intimidate me and make me go away. A few years earlier I might have crumbled, but not now.

I took two steps back from the man, whose breath was putrid at close range.

"Now, sir, as I said, the St. Luke Emporium is for everybody, including you. Tell your bosses downtown that we don't want no trouble. This store is needed in our community." I sighed. "And tell them, too, that if they want to kill me over a colored department store, then they can. But I'm not closing down just because they are unhappy with me."

"Your ass will regret this, Maggie Walker," said the man with the missing tooth, staring me in the eyes. I gripped the pistol in my pocket tighter.

I refused to blink.

Having said my piece, I backed out of the circle of men and walked right around them into the street. They didn't move, just stood in place staring me down like I was scum, but I knew better.

The neighbor who had been watching from a distance abruptly walked over with the stick still in his hand.

"Mrs. Maggie, you should never be out this late, especially alone. Those men are dangerous," he whispered.

I nodded in agreement, but quietly assured him that everything was all right. Then, more loudly, for the three men to hear, I said, "When you believe in the work you do, nothing, not even fear, can stop you."

I took out a handkerchief from my satchel and wiped the sweat trickling down the sides of my face. My nerves were rattled, and my hands shook as I steadied myself. Together my neighbor and I walked to my shiny new blue Packard, and I offered him a ride home.

We drove right past the men still lurking on the sidewalk. I waved to them as if they didn't matter, though I knew this was just the beginning. Dropping my neighbor off at his home, I headed in the direction of my house. I knew that my family was waiting for me to make dinner. Although it was late, I decided to roast a chicken and make my favorite milk gravy, something special to put a cap on this memorable day.

CHAPTER 18

1905–1911

DEPOSITS WERE COMING IN from across the state of Virginia and from other states as far up the East Coast as Canada and west into Illinois. The St. Luke Penny Savings Bank was progressing faster than any of the members had expected, and the staff struggled to keep up with the pace. On opening day, a total of eight thousand dollars were deposited, from folks coming from all over and standing in line for hours to be serviced. To handle the influx of money coming into the bank, I hired more employees, all people of color.

The burial fund was increasing as we signed up more members to the Independent Order of St. Luke. We were expanding our economic base beyond burial services, the bank, and the department store; we were now able to offer insurance to the members for medical needs. What was once simple was now becoming more complex. We had to make sure our books and money served the people just as promised.

❖co❖

For as much as we grew in status, I required my staff to give back. I held a monthly meeting to discuss these expectations.

161

My first meeting had been rocky. When we gathered for a short meeting after hours in the bank's conference room, there were plenty of questions to answer, and what was supposed to be a short discussion became a heated argument for some.

"Mrs. Walker," one of the clerks nervously asked, her hands shaking like a leaf as she spoke, "why is it that you are so hard on us? We work hard, but the minute we are late to work, you are riding our back like a shadow. You don't seem to understand."

I cleared my throat before answering, "Young lady, we are a professional organization. The bank opens at nine a.m. and I require you to be here early enough to set up and prepare for the customers coming through the door." The other clerks lowered their heads.

"Can you at least give us a little bit of time?" she added. I thought I had already answered that question, but obviously I didn't give her what was expected.

"The customers are here at nine a.m. and they expect us to provide them with good and prompt service. If we are not in the bank and in place, then we are doing them a disservice and likely to lose their business and their trust in us."

She sighed and sat down.

Another one stood up and placed her hands on her hips.

"Mrs. Maggie, why are you requiring us to do service in the community? You are asking us to volunteer at church and in the civic organizations in addition to our work hours. This kind of request has nothing to do with banking."

I paused before answering her because what she said seemed to be elementary in the realm of professionals. "Remember, the Bible says, 'When much is given, much is required of you.' This is the expectation of God. You are paid well, and it does not harm you to give back to your community. Besides, without this community and their support, the bank would be non-existent."

"I understand," she said, "but sometimes I have things to do of my own."

"I'm not asking for all your free time. Just cut out a little time to be given back to your community."

"I can find time," she said, and some of the others grumbled in agreement.

"I have firm and high expectations for each of you," I continued. "This is why I ask what I do of you. It is no more than what I expect from myself and my own family. You should be supporting and looking out for one another. It's only together that we may all grow and build a brighter future for the community."

The first two years of opening each business were intense. Women and men had to be trained in accounting, office management, and bookkeeping, and changing the mind-set from domestic worker to office worker was a task. Coloreds had to reprogram their thoughts toward higher expectations. I ensured they were all paid well for the services they rendered.

It wasn't long before things started to change, and the clerks didn't require as much training. They had become a community within a community, working together like a real team.

⟡·⟐·⟡

At the next Order meeting, I reported on the increase in membership and the amount of money we were taking in daily, to which the members broke out in thunderous applause. After the meeting ended and Armstead and I were preparing to leave, Mr. Walter and his wife, Annabelle, walked toward us.

"I hear there are going to be problems soon from the state," Mr. Walter said without hesitation.

"What sort of problems, Mr. Walter?" I asked. Mr. Walter was a man of many words and he always had his ear to the ground. Even though he annoyed a lot of people with his questions and concerns, he always knew pertinent information before any of the rest of us did. He used his connections well, which had allowed him to profit. I figured he had a close friend in the government, and that they had shared information with him.

"We are doing well, but I hear the governor is going to try to regulate our insurance and the associations of the fraternal orders," he said, sounding somewhat annoyed.

"We have our books together, if that is what you mean?"

"No, I just wanted to warn you about the rumors going on around us."

"I know about the insurance being scrutinized and the disassociation the state wants us to consider. However, I dare not do anything until I am approached."

"Maggie, you will need to make sure we can still be paid for our services. The undertakers are the first to lose money whenever there is a problem with the insurance." The undertakers were always concerned about their money, but all of us would one day die. Their business was the least of our worries, since there would be no shortage of need for them. However, insurance was important to us all in life. Medical care was costly.

"Mr. Walter, thank you for the news concerning our insurance. I will look into it."

"You are welcome, Maggie. I know we can always count on you."

I nodded my head and we all strolled to the door to go home.

A week had not passed before the news broke out about insurance companies being associated with fraternal orders. Mr. Walter was right. John Mitchell Jr. rapidly printed a headline about it in the *Planet*, and the newspaper spawned concern faster than word of mouth would have. It was like someone in government had decided we needed to be stopped before our growth had even reached the entire community. And we needed to get ahead of them.

⊰⊱

The financial panic of 1907 and the recession that followed led to highs and lows for the Order in 1908. New York suffered the first worldwide financial crisis of the twentieth century. It transformed a recession into the most severe economic contraction in history. It led to a monetary reform and ultimately the creation of the Federal Reserve System. It changed how New

York clearing house bankers perceived the value of a central bank because the panic took hold mainly among trust companies, institutions outside their membership.

Though I had increased Order membership, the recession that followed the previous year's worldwide financial crisis exposed the mismanagement of colored and white businesses. We kept concise books at the Order but came under scrutiny when the state of Virginia ordered audits of the insurance companies and banks associated with fraternal organizations. They promptly decided to require businesses to disassociate themselves from fraternal orders, but the St. Luke Penny Savings Bank was housed in the same building as the St. Luke Emporium, after being moved from St. Luke Hall to 112 Broad Street in October 1905. In November 1911, although we were thriving, we packed up our things and moved the St. Luke Penny Savings Bank to the corner of First and Marshall Streets.

"Maggie, this is going to get bigger," Armstead warned me at the dinner table on Sunday, while we supped on Momma's chicken gravy and the green beans she'd canned last summer with potatoes and the biscuits I'd rolled out for our evening meal. All our children sat around us, on their best behavior at the kitchen table. We always discussed serious concerns in their presence. I wanted them to pay close attention to the work their parents were doing, as one day my expectation was for them to take over where we left off and accomplish so much more.

"Armstead, we have done about all we can do to keep the state off our backs. Satisfying the state's requirements is why I come home so late at night sometimes. I know a Negro establishment is going to be scrutinized twice as much as a white one."

Armstead wiped his chin. "This is not a colored battle," he said. "Everyone is being watched. I just want you to be prepared for what's to come."

"I suppose we are in for some changes," I said. "We've made so much progress and I would hate to feel that we will fall backward on anything."

"Jim Crow has got to these people," Momma said. "They's in a frenzy, and there is no telling what they are capable of doing. We shut down the streetcar company, and you'd done added membership to the Order up at the church. White people is the devil." She bowed her head, shaking, then added, "We done been beat, killed, raped, choked, worked like a bull."

Momma was always good-spirited. She loved her church friends and family. But if anything piqued a nerve or a reminder of Daddy's departure from this life, she would often remind us that she felt the white man killed him. It was never proved or investigated, although we understood the policemen had lied. And there was nothing to be done about it. Armstead and I worked hard to ensure that our children and the community would not have to suffer the same way Momma had when Daddy was taken from her. Economic equity was the answer. We had to create the kind of wealth where we would be accepted at the bargaining table. Armstead's reputation often preceded him when it came to getting things done. He was a successful businessman and through his white contacts was the only colored man allowed to work at the postal service. Armstead was thrilled to have gotten a coveted position as a mail carrier, but was also always hard at work as a contractor with his brother at the Walker family's company.

"We are doing our very best to stay the course. Just know, Maggie, we are always going to face scrutiny. The white businesses will not have the same degree of worry." I heard every word he said. Still, I felt the St. Luke Penny Savings Bank would survive.

"Armstead, Mr. John Branch has given me the best advice possible to anyone operating a business, especially a bank. And even though he don't like Negroes, he respects the fact that I will endure scrutiny and racial discrimination in order to advance my people. I just don't think God has brought me this far to leave me now."

"Amen, chile," Momma uttered. "We are going to continue to pray because God can handle all things. But don't you ever forget, you's colored, and most of them don't like us, let alone want to allow us to succeed."

"Maggie, don't have so much faith in the white businessmen or Mr. John

Branch. He may have agreed to teach you, but he is not on your side," Armstead urged, always worried that I was too trusting of people.

"Is anyone on our side, Armstead? We are sometimes fighting a battle and our people are against us. We have to trust someone, even if they happen to be a white racist segregationist."

"You've said a word, chile," Momma said. "But listen to yo' husband."

"I don't trust too many people," I said. "I see every day what the selfish decisions of the white man has done. And half of us call out the name of Jim Crow, not knowing he was just a stage show. White people have allowed an uneducated performer to turn their thoughts into criminal acts against us." I glanced up in the air. "No man is bigger than the God I serve. Not Jim Crow, not anyone. I will not succumb to threats or even money. I know if we consider our economic condition, we can continue to advance despite the current financial crisis."

"Maggie, I never thought your head would be so hard," Momma said.

"You taught me to dream, and I will always dream and work for the betterment of our community."

I looked over at my youngest son, who had his fingers in his ears. "Get your fingers out of your ears, right now," I told him. He did and gobbled down his food, then audaciously asked to leave the table.

I knew that at times our conversations were overwhelming for the children, but I wanted them to always be aware of what was happening in our world. Knowledge was the key to solving our troubles.

❖❀❖

Later in the same year, a week after our family discussion, we found out that the True Reformers Bank and other fraternal banks were failing. They had been set up incorrectly and didn't have enough support or capital in reserve to sustain themselves. We prayed for John Mitchell Jr. and the bank he had invested so much time into.

At night, I prayed and thanked God for all the advice that Mr. John

Branch had shared with me, even though I had to walk behind him like a dog. The knowledge was invaluable. The St. Luke insurance business remained in compliance in every state and grew. Meanwhile, white and colored banks alike were failing in light of the increased pressure to comply with the proper certifications and documents required by the banking industry.

Mr. John Branch was available throughout the audits. He told me, "I knew you'd get through all of it, Maggie."

"How did you know, sir?" I asked.

"Because, despite my rudeness, you are brilliant and hardworking, and always willing to endure whatever hardships present themselves in order to get a positive outcome for your people. You are exceptional, Maggie Lena Walker," he said, and I smirked, knowing it took a lot for him to admit any of that to me.

✦co✦

By the beginning of 1911, I had transitioned the St. Luke Penny Savings Bank into an independent corporation, which had deposits worth more than $100,000 by the end of the year. Colored business grew and prospered despite the financial disasters all around. Yet there was always more work to be done.

Armstead said, "Darlin', you must slow down. You've put everyone else's well-being before your own health." At times I felt tired and worn. I gazed in the mirror and saw the marks of hard work and exhaustion around my eyes. Jackson Ward was growing, and I felt like a washrag at times. Armstead would love on me from head to toe, and afterward I would feel revived. Yet the next day, the work would begin all over again.

CHAPTER 19

1911

RUMOR HAD IT, some folks were aiming to close the emporium.

"Mrs. Maggie, our shipment didn't come in today, and Mrs. Fannie is requesting the new pantaloons. We were expected to have them in stock by now. We heard the upscale stores like Thalhimers and Miller & Rhoads are selling them, and they are flying off their shelves." I couldn't help but feel as if someone were trying to sabotage our business.

I had spent countless hours making sure we had quality merchandise for sale in our emporium. In Jackson Ward, Fannie was not only the community aristocrat; she was also the best-dressed woman around. Most women wanted whatever she wore, and if pantaloons were what she wanted, we should be selling them.

What my saleslady said bothered me. "I'm going over to the distributor's office today to find out what is going on," I said. Aside from Fannie, I had a flair for fashion myself. I enjoyed finery as well, down to the shoes I wore.

"Please do and make it quick. I don't think Mrs. Fannie is going to like it if she comes back and they are not on display. She is threatening to go shopping at Miller & Rhoads instead because she's been told they carry them," my top saleslady warned me, anxious and worried.

Fannie could do that to anyone; she knew how to get her way. The pantaloons were a new look for women. They were loose-fitting yet somewhat revealing wide-legged trousers made of chemise that draped a woman who wanted or dared to show her silhouette. Women like Fannie would pay top prices for them, and I wanted them to purchase them from our emporium.

"Mrs. Maggie, some of the other things we ordered haven't come in, either. The hobble skirts and lampshade tops are also out of stock. We ordered them from another business, and they assured us they would have some to us in multiple sizes. Do you know what's going on?"

We all wanted our clients to be satisfied, but if we continued to go without merchandise, the magpies would get word and spread it across Jackson Ward, and John Mitchell Jr. would certainly print it in the *Planet* as well. News was news.

John used to print solely about civil rights and justice, but since we'd opened the emporium, fashion and shopping had occasionally made the headlines in his paper. Oftentimes it was good for business, drawing in people from everywhere to shop at our store. Buying colored meant something to coloreds across the state and as far away as the news traveled, and his newspaper had a very large distribution base. It not only helped the emporium, but also helped us to bring in more customers to our bank and insurance office.

"Carrie-Sue, give me a chance to look into it. We are going to find our merchandise. Just tell Fannie I am working on her behalf. She will be happy to hear that it's specifically for her. She always expects to be the center of attention."

The next morning, I got dressed and headed over to the distributor's warehouse on Tobacco Row. It was hard to find someone who was willing to talk to me, but I finally found a man who seemed to be in charge. At least he carried himself in that manner.

"Sir, my name is Maggie Walker and I'm trying to find out what happened to the merchandise we purchased."

He quickly replied, "I don't know what you want."

"I just want to know where our supply of the following items is." I handed him a list of the things we expected from them.

He took the list from my hand and gazed down at it without saying anything. He suddenly went still.

"You all right, sir?" I asked.

"Just know you are not going to receive any of the things listed here from us," he said, scanning the document with his eyes.

"What do you mean?"

"Well, ma'am, we have been advised to slow down deliveries to that location." Just then, I noticed some unhappy white men starting to close in around me. Everyone seemed to be protective of the information he had barely mentioned.

One of the bearded men in ragged clothes spat, "You don't have to tell that nigga nothing."

The one holding my list looked at him cluelessly. "I thought she was a white woman."

I stood still, listening to one of the most unintelligent conversations I had ever heard. "She ain't white, I tell you. She's the colored woman who owns the emporium."

Neither of them cared that I was still there, hearing every word.

"Where is your boss?" I asked, provoking an affronted glare from both of them.

"I'll go get him," the one with my list said, and he scurried inside the warehouse, closing the door behind him. The other one didn't say a word to me but stood with his arms folded across his chest and an authoritative grimace on his face while guarding the entrance into the warehouse as if I were a criminal.

His friend returned in less than ten minutes with the tall man who had tried to pay me not to open the emporium six years ago. Cuthbert was his name.

As a greeting to me he said, "I told you not to open that emporium, Maggie Walker, but you insisted."

"And that is my right," I answered, while the other two stood around without blinking, listening to every word I said.

"You are lucky I knew your damn daddy. If not, you would have been tossed in the James River just like Willie Mitchell." How did he know my father? Was he involved in Daddy's murder? I knew in that moment that Daddy's death was always on Momma's mind. It didn't matter, because neither of them would ever own up to it. Nothing would be done anyway, since Daddy was colored. Using his death to threaten me was as destructive as they came. It certainly proved a point. One that colored lives have no value even so many years later. I put my hands down in my dress pocket and held on to my Colt pistol the entire time he was talking.

I didn't take his idle threats lightly. Beads of sweat were forming on my nose. "If you are going to withhold my merchandise, then I need to know why. We have been doing business with you for years."

He frowned at my comment.

"Your emporium is taking money away from Thalhimers and Miller & Rhoads, the finest department stores in town, and they are not going to let you and them uppity niggas in Jackson Ward destroy their businesses. I warned you about this a long time ago," he said, unyielding.

"So now you are going to try to shut me down?" I asked, staring straight into his cold blue eyes. Cuthbert gazed back at me without blinking. He was serious, and my instincts told me he would do anything to prevent my emporium from prospering. We had been doing well, and it was rumored that at least a 15 percent downslide in customer shopping was affecting the bottom-line profits of the major stores. There was no way they would allow our store to continue with the growth we had been experiencing.

"We will," he said. "Some of your patrons are already returning to the right stores because you are no longer able to fulfill their needs. Eventually, your store will be completely empty. There will be absolutely nothing left for you to sell."

I stood, helpless, listening to their threats and accusations. I was not finished with them. I would fight to the end if necessary. As I turned to walk
away from them, Cuthbert hurled at my back, "Remember, you are not white.
You are colored. Know your place and stay there, Maggie Lena Walker. I
warned you once before. Now I'm getting tired of telling you."

I turned around and said, "This is as much my place as yours, and the
Bible has made it very clear. If you could read it, you would understand that
I am not going anywhere. God created all men as equals."

He yelled back as I spun to walk off again, "You are not a man, Maggie
Lena Walker, even though you think and act like one. You are just a woman."

I kept on walking. I knew who I was and neither Cuthbert nor anyone
else was going to make me feel any different. But his comment about my
daddy, Willie, lingered and concerned me. What did he know about him and
how he had died? Besides, the name Cuthbert bothered me, too. Was he my
birth father's brother or one of his family members who was as racist as was
to be expected in the Jim Crow South? I wasn't sure who he was, but I knew
eventually I'd find out.

I didn't go home, or to the bank or the emporium. I went directly to the
Virginia State Capitol. It was time to speak to someone with some authority.

❖CƆ❖

William Hodges Mann was elected governor of the state in 1910. I knew he
would at least listen to me. I got into my car and drove down Broad Street
and up to the Capitol. I had been there many times before, but every visit
was different. At times I had to beg to enter the governor's office, and other
times some generous guard would notice me and allow me to go in without
a struggle.

The governor was available most of the time, especially for the citizens of
Richmond. If a dignitary was visiting or in town, I would be asked to come back.

When his assistant saw me, she rolled her eyes. "What do you want now,
Maggie Walker?" she asked at the sight of me.

"I was wondering if I could have a few minutes of Governor Mann's time?"

I waited for her to offer me a seat, but she did not. Instead she left me standing right in front of her desk and came back in ten minutes.

"The governor is in a meeting. He can't see you at this moment. You need to come back."

"Thank you," I said and left.

I ended up at the Thalhimers building, waiting on Mr. William Thalhimer in the same fashion. I was astounded when I was allowed to come up to his office on the top floor. The saleslady who directed me to his office also followed me there and didn't leave until after his assistant acknowledged her.

He invited me inside the spacious room with high ceilings and office furniture more beautiful than anything I'd ever laid my eyes on.

"What can I do for you, Mrs. Walker?"

"May I sit down?" I asked.

He glanced up at me from behind his spectacles and told me to have a seat. I sat down in front of his desk.

"Mr. Thalhimer, I have an emporium down the street. And I've been informed that you are trying to shut me down. That you do not want it there."

He cleared his throat. "Mrs. Walker, you need to find a way to take care of your own business. It is not our responsibility to worry about the St. Luke Emporium."

"We are running it as efficiently as we can, but it is getting more difficult when our mutual suppliers refuse to deliver my orders to our store."

"What do I have to do with your operations?" he said in a seemingly concerned tone, though he now propped a foot up on his desk.

"The vendors are afraid you will stop using them and put them out of business if they continue to deliver products to me. Is there any way you can work with our merchandisers?"

"This is business. My profits have taken a hit since you opened your emporium, and we have served Richmond well for seventy years. We cannot allow you to continue to affect our bottom line."

Isn't competition good? I thought to myself.

The visit had been fruitless. He was just as racist as the rest of them, and would only respect other white competitors, like Miller & Rhoads. "Thank you for your time, Mr. Thalhimer."

As I left, I searched for my handkerchief to wipe the beads of sweat dripping down the side of my face. It wasn't hot outside, but I was boiling on the inside. That was it. This matter would have to be settled by our customers. Did they want the emporium? Would they continue to support us? And how much of this could they stand before they would return to shopping at the other stores? First, I would need to remind them of their loyalty to the Jackson Ward community. We weren't going down without a fight.

❖⌘❖

Immediately I called for a meeting at the Order headquarters. John Mitchell Jr. put out a call to action to the community. The *St. Luke Herald* reached out to all our subscribers.

When we finally convened, obscenities were hurled at me as I stood at the podium.

"I thought you promised us a store of our own in our neighborhood. But what good is it if the shelves are empty?" someone asked.

Another deep voice said, "We can't find anything these days. What is going on, Mrs. Walker?"

Armstead stood up and shouted over the crowd, "Now, listen here! My wife has worked day and night for the Jackson Ward community, and this is the treatment you give her?" He paused while the voices around him quieted before continuing: "Without her tireless efforts, most of you would not own a business or have enough money to shop with. What is wrong with you people?"

"We just want to know, will you be restocking the emporium?" Fannie said.

I sat still with my head held high as the insults subsided. When all the shouts of disappointment dwindled, I stood up and cleared my throat.

"Let me start by reminding you that we have been in business for more than six years now. We have made your life easier, and I have worked my fingers to the bone to make sure the emporium represents us. We have brown-hued mannequins, and our prices are competitive to those at Thalhimers. We have provided every service you are able to get in the other places. Besides the emporium, we have our own bank and insurance companies. And some of you sell your own products in the emporium. We have so much to be grateful for."

The outbursts started again after that.

"Then why are we hearing threats of the emporium shutting down?" said a man from the back of the room.

"We are at the mercy of the merchandisers. Most of the high fashion is sent by train from New York and distributed to the stores by several companies in Richmond. They have decided to stop serving us due to the profit loss of the other stores. We are doing well, but colored money is needed to sustain their businesses, too, and it has been a challenge to convince them to provide their services to us. And many of you have given up and are already shopping at Thalhimers and Miller & Rhoads again. Your loyalty is the only way we can continue to compete with them. Where's your heart?"

Shouts were coming from all sides.

"When will you have the merchandise?"

"Why can't we get service from somewhere else?"

"Some of the things I need, I can't wait until you fix this relationship to get them. I am an avid shopper and I need access to the items I want," Fannie hurled unapologetically.

"Me, too," someone else said.

I paused and took a deep breath. It bothered me that no one understood the economics behind the lack of supplies and merchandise. They didn't know how critical they were to the economy. Instead of fighting with me for the emporium, they had chosen to turn away from us at the first sign of a boycott from suppliers and threats made to our first and only department store's survival.

"Maggie, you have done your best," Mr. Walter stood up and said. "You've offered folks employment and helped people like my wife do the things they love. The bank is in good shape, and the way you finance businesses is more than we can ask for. But them white men ain't gonna let us continue. I hear Thalhimer has threatened every vendor in town, not just the emporium. We can't keep our businesses running like this, either. He is too powerful."

I bit my lip and shook my head. Mr. Walter had said it all. They didn't have the capacity to hold off from shopping at Thalhimers and the other stores until they felt it in their operating budget. Until Mr. Thalhimer would not have a choice but to release the vendors.

"Thank you, Mr. Walter, for explaining our current predicament. We can't even go directly to the sources. The store owners have congregated together against us, and even the manufactures in New York will not go against them. They've formed a consortium against us, and we don't have enough money or support to fight them. Neither the governor nor the mayor is willing to speak on our behalf."

The room was quiet. All conversation ceased. The faces before me were contorted with concern. I fought back tears myself, because I hated to lose, to disappoint. We had worked so hard to build a business and an environment where coloreds were treated like human beings and not as enslaved or second-class citizens. But, as in most cases, even the people I had worked so hard to help had turned against me. I had done all of this for them. And now . . . we had to close our department store. I suppose our boycott of the Virginia Passenger and Power Company streetcars had provoked more backlash than I'd expected.

"Just remember, some of this is your responsibility as well. You've chosen to shop in a place where you are mistreated, rather than stand against them and not enter their doors. There should never be anything more important than humanity to you, but you've made your choice."

CHAPTER 20

THE DAY OF THE FINAL SALE, tears welled up in my eyes. I had put many hours into the opening of an emporium where we could shop with dignity. And it was a great place, and as elegant as the other department stores. The Jackson Ward community loved the fact that we had a store that offered everything they needed in one location, in their community. Now with our final sale, colored folks were buying everything, including the brown-hued mannequins.

After the emporium closed, I put more energy into the bank, advancing our economic growth for the establishment of more businesses. Jackson Ward was developing more varieties of businesses than ever before. Some women were still feeling the exclusion from quality jobs, many still being housewives, and some were angry from losing their job at the emporium. All of it bothered me.

The postman delivered a letter to us declaring that Mary McLeod Bethune was on her way, and he smiled when I told him the good news.

Mary came to Richmond shortly after the emporium closed, and not a moment too soon. She arrived by train, wearing her usual black. I met her at the station, and we embraced each other with a spirit of love. Then we got into my automobile and traveled down Broad Street right by the shuttered emporium. As we passed it, noticing the windows boarded up, both of our eyes welled with tears, but neither would allow one tear to roll down our cheeks. We went straight to my house, where Momma had prepared a meal of fried corn, turnip greens, corn bread, and ham, with a sugar cake for dessert.

It had been a while since we had been together, and after enjoying our meal until we were fit to burst, we stayed up for hours in the parlor talking like young girls in a college dormitory.

"Maggie, you've got to come to Florida soon," she said, patting me on the shoulder.

I grinned. "Mary, ever since you and Du Bois left almost eight years ago, I have been losing sleep. These white people are so deliberate in their actions. They are trying to reverse all the progress we've made, and it is calling me to address the same issues all over again. Some days I am just too tired to fight the same battles time and time again. But I promise you, I am going to show up one day and surprise you."

"You know, Du Bois surprised me and made a trip to Florida. I didn't know if he would find the time, but he did. He was working on the Niagara Movement while he was assisting me with ideas, and he'd gathered up some real powerful activists. At least all of us want the same thing: equal rights for Negroes."

"I received a letter from Du Bois not long ago," I said, "and he simply told me white people are jealous of us being smart and entrepreneurial in response to what was going on with the emporium. He already knew. But, just like me, he was hoping we could find some unyielding vendors and turn it all around."

Mary shook her head. "Racism is an everyday battle for us, but I believe we are doing the work to make things better."

It had been at least two years since I had been to Florida. My family loved the beach and Mary made sure we had a good time when we visited. But Florida was much more outwardly prejudiced than folks were in Virginia, even though we were in the heart of the Confederacy.

Mary took a sip of the table wine and said, "Our fight is never over. We will be fighting for the rest of our lives. At times I want to give up, but I can't. I wake up thinking about how coloreds and women are being treated. I will always search for ways to help us. When I opened the Literary and Industrial Training School, after our last visit in 1904, I didn't know if we would have any girls in the school. But we opened with thirty girls on the roster. Little Albert, my boy, was also one of my students. It was a sight for sore eyes when they marched behind me into the schoolhouse," she said, setting down her glass and throwing her feet up on my davenport as if she were at home. She was one of the smartest women I knew. She had made writing pencils herself from charred wood and ink from elderberries. Who would have believed she could accomplish all she had with just $1.50 and a vision. And she was still working for the betterment of women.

I chuckled, knowing her quest was also mine.

"Women have endured more stresses than men for centuries," I said, shaking my head. "We have taken the pressure like the mortar Armstead mixes to build and keep them bricks together. We stand in the burdens of time. As you have said, we will continue to fight no matter what."

What I said seemed to remind Mary of something that truly upset her. "You know what bothers me the most? The so-called Equal Suffrage League. White women fighting for the right to vote; meanwhile they always forget about us Negro women. We have the same concerns they do and more. Our voices deserve to be heard just as much as theirs."

She had hit a bull's-eye with that statement.

"That's why we have our own suffrage movement, Mary. We are all women, but racist white women will always feel their plight is different from ours. It is, I suppose, since we've had to deal not only with rape, abuse, and the negative treatment of women, but also the threat of enslavement, being lynched, or killed just because of the color of our skin. The load we bear seems much heavier by comparison."

"Don't forget, they handle things different from us, too."

"Ain't that the truth," I said.

"They also seem to be fighting only for middle-class women with land. Most of us don't own land, and we're definitely not middle class. Even though there are certain plights that all women have in common."

"You've said that right."

Mary took another sip. "You know we have some things we need to talk about that are not as serious." She paused to make sure Polly was out of ear-shot. "Lord, your little Polly is full-grown and every bit as assertive and com-manding as you are." It was true. Somehow I'd blinked and she and Russell were now twenty-one years old.

"Now, you know I don't tell anyone what to do in this house," I said.

Mary chuckled. "You tell everybody what to do, even Armstead."

"Girl, keep your voice down. If Armstead even felt I was telling him what to do, he would summon me out of this house. That man is the strength around here. But you are right, I let him *think* he is in total control."

Mary chuckled and said, "Maggie, you are who you are. Besides, that man loves you with all his heart."

"And so are you, Mary Bethune." We both took a sip of wine and giggled.

Mary and I always enjoyed our time together.

Then Mary added, "You know, I wonder if W. E. B. ever gets tired of us calling on him."

"He always answered us."

"Now that is the truth. If he felt anyone was wasting his time, he would certainly say it."

We talked until our eyes drooped from either exhaustion or wine. For me, it was the red wine. We lost track of time and when we glanced up at the clock, it was already one in the morning.

The following morning at breakfast, Mary and I sat joyfully beside one another, strategizing over coffee about meeting with the Virginia Equal Suffrage League, knowing how blind they were to the plights of Negro women.

As Armstead bent down to kiss me good-bye for the day, he said, "Now, can I count on you two to stay out of trouble?"

Mary answered, "Of course you can. We don't get into trouble. We do what needs to be done for the greater good." He glanced at her in admiration and smiled.

Momma said, "They are always up to something, and I just pray they come home safely."

Momma was getting old, and she didn't like the things going on around her. She was also still mourning Daddy after all these years. At times, I wondered if she ever thought about my birth father, Eccles. He never married and neither did she after Daddy's death. But when I mentioned my encounter with Cuthbert, I noticed that she was distraught by the incident and more than a little upset by the name. Time heals most wounds, but there are always those that are even harder to get past, especially when you have no means of gaining closure.

Mary and I left the house shortly after Armstead to head to the office of Richmond's Equal Suffrage League, at 802 East Broad Street. Melvin, now fourteen, walked out with us, and we gave him guidance about his schoolwork and studies. Mary was great with children; she knew how to discipline and speak to them without any frustrations. It was something I could work on. She had been around children her entire life. Her mother had birthed seventeen children and she was number fifteen. I think some of her success came from being around a family of siblings. She had been working her entire life and was a professionally trained educator. She was a willing activist for women and wouldn't allow anything to interrupt her goals for education and industrial learning.

Russell worked at the bank, learning all he could to take over for me. He had followed in Armstead's and my footsteps, attending the Richmond Normal School. And for some odd reason, Polly loved being home with Momma, doing the chores that had been traditionally assigned to women for centuries. I would have never believed this was what she wanted to do, but children will learn who they are as they get older.

The women greeted us kindly at the door, but we were later informed by one of the members and a major mobilizer that Negroes were not allowed to partner or form with them.

"I know y'all have your concerns, just like we do," one of the women said, "but y'all are different."

I glanced over at Mary. She shook her head at me but remained silent.

We listened intently to all the reasons we were not suited for their organization, among them that women who joined their organization were required to be educated and to have documented reasons for being part of the movement. There was nothing for us to do but smile and nod in the face of their ignorance. On the way home, Mary said, "She is so clueless. We are the same in more ways than she is willing to admit. None of us—white, colored, or otherwise—have any real rights. We are a part of the suffragist movement, too. We've endured as much and more than them, but they'll never understand that because none of them are colored."

There were rarely times when I was at a loss for words, but this was one of them. When women turned against women, it felt as if someone were pulling my soul right out of my heart. It was upsetting, to say the least, to be excluded from efforts and events, like the march on Washington, D.C., that white women were organizing.

"Eventually they will see that there is value and strength in numbers. The more there are of us standing side by side on the battlefield, the better the outcome," Mary said, gesturing wildly with her hands, as she was still frazzled about our encounter.

"No woman could do anything without a man's approval," she continued.

"They obviously didn't realize they were also enslaved to society and to the men that ran the country. And when you don't realize you are enslaved, it is hard to accomplish freedom. We need each other. All women should come together."

"I couldn't have said it better myself. Mary, if they won't include us in theirs, we should organize a march of our own. We would bring together colored women from all over and make a statement that we matter as well."

"Believe me," Mary said, "there are colored women all over mobilizing as we speak. This movement is not just for the Equal Suffrage League, the Daughters of the American Revolution, or other white women–led groups trying to keep us out. They will be happy to make sure that those women know this is for all of us."

As I pulled up in front of my home, I said, "We will go to D.C. and we will rally for the same attention they are."

Mary stayed with us for two weeks. Her sisterhood and presence were like a vacation to me. She was a woman with goals and aspirations, and we never felt any animosity or jealousy between us. We were true sisters and friends.

During her visit, the children, though grown now, felt like they'd been given a special treat. Mary played checkers and word games with them each night. Her spending time with me after the closing of the emporium gave me the strength I needed to start the fight again.

After everyone had gone to bed in the house, I told Armstead about our day.

"You are a strong woman, Maggie. You are brilliant, and so brave. You have a singular vision, misunderstood and disregarded by so many, and yet you persevere. If any woman deserves to march on the nation's capital and claim what is rightfully theirs, it's my hardworking and exhausted wife," Armstead whispered as he kneaded my aching body, kissing me, relaxing me, and helping ease me to sleep.

CHAPTER 21

1913–1914

THE 1913 WOMAN SUFFRAGE PROCESSION was a big success in Washington, D.C., but it lacked the interest of colored women. Millicent Garrett Fawcett, their leader, said they were campaigning for middle-class, property-owning women, thus leaving out women without money or property to their name. Negro women were never considered at all. However, in Washington, D.C., a newly formed sorority, Delta Sigma Theta, was not so easy to deter from involvement. They were called renegades only because they wanted to see justice for women and improve the communities in which they lived across the country. Just as we had our suffrage march in Richmond, the Deltas joined in with the white women in the Woman Suffrage Procession and declared they were worthy of the same rights as white women. As expected, they were not welcomed, but they were determined to take a stand all the same. So, when the twenty-two Negro women joined the march, all the newspapers reported it and said it aided in the advancement of the initial cause. The twenty-two members of the Delta Sigma Theta sorority strutted right down Pennsylvania Avenue to the nation's capital along with more than five thousand white women and 250,000 spectators of this parade of women.

I printed it on the front page of the *St. Luke Herald* for all to see.

"You can't go on printing this kind of information, Maggie," John Mitchell Jr. warned me with fear in his eyes. He stood in front of my desk and audaciously threw the latest issue of the *Herald* down upon it, the paper making a slapping sound as it hit.

I glowered as I gazed up at him. "I most certainly can and *did*," I said, raising my voice. Then I searched his face for any indication of lunacy. Absolutely no one had ever thrown down my own paper in front of me with such force.

He pulled up a chair and sat down. I knew he had to be out of his mind. We both printed the news. His outrage was completely uncalled for.

My assistant was aware I didn't like surprise visitors, but like most men, they ignored her and walked right past her without giving her the decency of an official introduction. At times John could be a difficult man and hard to contain anyway, especially when he had something stirring in his mind. He was as determined as they came.

He came in just as I was winding down from a day at the bank and gathering the paperwork I would need to carry with me to the headquarters of the Independent Order of St. Luke, where more stacks of paperwork sat waiting for me to sign and file. Frankly, I didn't have time for his visit.

"Maggie," he said, "you are going to make these segregationists mad. You just printed a story about Negro women and their lack of inclusion in the suffrage movement. You know this is just going to make a lot of people angry."

The *Herald* had been reaching people across the state of Virginia and as far north as Canada for more than a decade. Sharing information through our paper had helped our community grow. Communication was the reason our bank was still standing when others had failed, and St. Luke's insurance company continued to expand because we printed our economic and political statuses and shared them with the public. There was no way I was going to allow those women to exclude us from equality and be silent. John was lashing out in fear.

I stood up and adjusted my wide-brimmed hat in the round mirror with a wood-carved frame on the wall. "Colored women have rights, too. And I will not just stand aside and let the 'ladies' of the Equal Suffrage League leave us out of the conversation."

"How does Armstead deal with you?" he spat back, his tone deliberately condescending.

"Armstead is more than aware of what I am doing. I discuss most things with him. And believe it or not, John, he always loves and supports me. Why you need me to tell you this, I don't know. You've known us for long enough," I shot back at him, my face flushed with rage.

John frowned and shook his head, seemingly baffled by what I'd said. "Maggie, we can't have everyone in Richmond angry with us. I believe we lost the emporium because we were responsible for closing down the streetcar system."

I turned to growl back. "It was the vendors and the other store owners who made us shut down the emporium. They felt we were taking too much from their pockets. This should be an indication of how important the Negro money is to the U.S. economy. We have power in our pockets, and we should utilize this information with every breath we take."

With that, John seemed to deflate a bit, though his voice was still tinged with anger. "I'm getting tired of all this fighting, but I'll be damned if I allow a woman to outdo me. I can hang in here a few more years . . . The *Planet* will start printing about suffrage as well. We must be united in all our efforts. The white man knows us better than we know ourselves. We can't let him detect any weakness or division."

He should have come to this conclusion on his own, without needing to argue with me first. It was the fact that he was in competition with a woman that seemed to always get to him. He could never let me do anything without his consent or copying my acts. Afterward, he took a step back and his face and neck muscles relaxed.

"I am an optimistic woman working hard to try to level things for all of us," I said. "Our men and women have suffered for way too long. We are going to have to continue informing the people, no matter who it might upset. Mr. Walter can't be the only person who knows what is going on around us."

"How does Walter know so much?" he asked doubtfully, as if he didn't believe Mr. Walter knew anyone of consequence.

"He has friends in high places," I said, waving the question away. "John, we all should be able to cross the color line and have relationships with everyone. Ms. Elizabeth Van Lew, God rest her soul, risked her relationships and fortune for the betterment of us coloreds. The least we can do is fight for ourselves. I am not afraid of any man, John. The good Lord watches over me at all times. I am His and His alone. The Bible asks us to speak the truth and let righteousness be our guide. I am doing just that," I proclaimed and scooped up my things from my desk.

"You are no ordinary woman, Maggie Walker. You are daring and different, and fearsome."

I sighed. "Listen, I am not unique by any means. There are more women like me fighting for the same cause. Mary Bethune, to name one," I said, looking him right in the eyes, for Mary was a friend of his, too. "And you must know of Ida Wells, being a journalist like her. We honor who we are, and we take pride and joy in helping people who resemble us in the least. There are women like us all across the United States. You just haven't acknowledged us all."

Defeated, he said, "I believe you have done more than all those women put together, Maggie. Even with setbacks like the emporium closing, you continue to fight."

I glanced down at my hands. The hands of an office worker, with no indications of hard labor because all my work had been in strategizing and planning for every possible outcome of whatever move we were intent on making. I had always sought the assistance of people in the government, because, after all, we all needed protection, and we really needed each other.

"Isn't that what we should all do?" I asked.

"I suppose you are right. We all have an obligation to pull someone along and through. Jackson Ward has seen tremendous growth, and I plan on doing whatever I can to help continue that, Maggie."

I tilted my head and grinned. He had finally gotten it.

We had no choice. We could either continue in a Jim Crow state of mind or change the narrative to point the arrow in the right direction.

John picked up the copy of the *St. Luke Herald* that he'd thrown onto my desk, apologized for his outburst and for interrupting my work, and promised to do his best to heal the disease that seemed to continue to spread throughout the country, no matter how hard we tried to beat it back—racism.

After he left, in the stillness of the office, I sat back down for a minute, the adrenaline from our debate leaving my body. I propped my head up on my hand and thought about George Washington Carver and his determination to train students on skills, and how W. E. B. Du Bois had felt higher education was the secret to success. And then there was a lady up north people sometimes thought was me, Madam C. J. Walker, who had become a millionaire by selling beauty products to her own people. There were opportunities for us, especially if we would pull together and support our own resources. Our freedom was within us. "So a man thinketh, so he does it."

Sorting through the documents on my desk, I thought about my dear friend Mary and how helpful she had been to the Order, especially the Juvenile Branch. Mary and Otis's children had become self-sufficient, and I could use her at the office. Aside from Mary McLeod Bethune, she was my only real friend.

❖co❖

Although I continued to mobilize women, pull them together, and make them aware of the issues that plagued us, it took me almost a year after the march to hold a meeting in my home. In February 1914, I invited several women in Jackson Ward who I thought had some influence. Fannie was the first to arrive to my home.

"Oh, I never knew you lived so lavishly, Maggie," she said. As usual, she locked her inquisitive eyes on my chandelier and then surveyed each room like a hound dog. When she asked to see my bedroom, I told her it was my sacred place, and only Armstead and I were allowed there. She sighed but relented.

"Thank you," I said to her. What was she expecting?

A few minutes later Mary, Edith, Sarah, and two others came through the door, all on time.

We gathered in my parlor. Armstead had aligned a few of the dining room chairs around the wall, so everyone could sit.

Momma had prepared mini ham biscuits and lemonade for us to sample while we had our meeting.

After everyone had taken a biscuit and either a cup of hot tea or a glass of lemonade, we sat down.

"Ladies," I said, "I'm so glad you were able to make it."

"Lord, Maggie, what have you got on your mind this time?" Fannie asked and threw her hand in the air.

Mary, who was almost always quiet and soft-spoken, said, "Can you please just let her talk?" I was amazed. The most she ever talked about was her children and their schooling, and she never raised her voice. Fannie had that effect on most people. She knew how to vex you.

"As you already know," I said, "we are not making as much progress as we could be with our causes. We have got to join organizations like the National Association for the Advancement of Colored People and the National Association of Colored Women's Clubs."

"I'm part of the Jackson Ward Women's Club," Fannie chimed in.

"Fannie, she is talking about organizations that will help advance our causes. The Women's Club doesn't advance anything except your social calendar," Edith said.

"How dare you!" Fannie huffed.

Edith rolled her eyes and turned away from Fannie.

"Calm down, ladies," I said. "We are here to speak about the things we need and must do to get the respect needed as it pertains to jobs, education, and even voting rights. The NAACP has been here whenever there are racist issues and riots. Why not for our causes, too?"

After the Woman Suffrage Procession, Alice Paul, the Washington, D.C., organizer, overheard rumors of a war soon to come and felt there might not be a country left to vote in after it, so the issue of women voting was left in the cold. But we needed to figure out more than just voting rights; we needed to save our community from racial inequality and, by increasing women entrepreneurship and focusing on sustaining our wealth, we could gain the power to overcome some of our issues. Our involvement in larger organizations would certainly give us a foundation for a conversation. When we pulled together, we always got the attention of the government.

"What do you want us to do? I'm too old for some of the things you want from us, Maggie," Mrs. Sarah said softly.

"I want the women in this room to come together and brainstorm what we could be doing for our community. I think that is something we all can do."

"I must say, these biscuits are simply delicious," Fannie interrupted.

Several of the women rolled their eyes. Fannie always had to be the center of attention.

"Can we think of some ways to get our families more involved, mainly women, in these organizations?" I asked.

"My husband is already part of the NAACP," Mary said.

"I know. Most of our husbands participate, but we need to go to the meetings ourselves to bring our own concerns to the forefront."

"Who's gonna take care of the children while we do that?" Edith asked.

"Good question," I said. "Let's bring them with us. If they are well-behaved, I don't think there will be a problem. And it would do them well to witness their mothers fighting for their rights."

"Mary, your children are growing up fast, but you might want to give them a talk before bringing them to any meetings. At times they seem a little untamed," Fannie said and threw her head back.

"My children are literally grown now," Mary said, then added, "I think it is time for us to push our agenda. We want more job opportunities, and should be allowed to own land, too. I want to feel as free as any white woman. We are always fighting for something. At times I get tired, but, Maggie, like you always say, God wants us to use our talents to partner with our husbands. How and when will women feel like they can do anything? Whites are constantly trying to keep us segregated from them. But then women are also segregated from their husbands, jobs, and even society!"

"Now you are going too far, Mary," Fannie said.

Following the Woman Suffrage Procession, I continued to come up with ideas to advance the colored agenda, working with the Independent Order of St. Luke and others like W. E. B. and his Niagara Movement and later the NAACP. Mary McLeod Bethune had begun to have meetings with groups of colored women across the nation. I had already worked to get all the women in Jackson Ward involved. I managed to convince the residents of Jackson Ward, but also more than 80 percent of the colored women in all of Richmond.

I pressed: "I am asking each of you to try to attend the monthly meetings. Bring your younger children along, if you must. We have issues of our own, and we will not settle for the way in which we are being treated any longer. Our only recourse is to work together and let our husbands, the community, and the white man know we are as serious as the white women about equality, and we are seeking the same opportunities in education, employment, and life."

"Maggie, I think we can come to the meetings and share our agenda with the members. The Order is doing its job, and I think we need to expand and be included in all the progressive committees and organizations fighting for equality," Fannie finally said with authority. I was glad to have her on board.

❖co❖

The next NAACP meeting was held on a Saturday evening. More than twenty women along with their children came in and sat in the back of the room.

When the leaders opened up the floor for questions, the women sitting in the back flooded them. Some politely stood up to ask a question and the others just blurted out their concerns in an unorderly fashion.

"We need rights, too!"

"Your agenda should also include women's issues."

A man yelled, "We take care of you! You don't have any issues."

"We *do* have issues, many you don't know or understand, and we expect to be heard!" Fannie yelled. Then she stood up so the people could see her dressed in the finest of clothes and a millinery felt hat.

Suddenly the crowd roared.

"Order, order!" The facilitator tried to calm the crowd. "We will hear you," the facilitator said, and the women let loose about voting rights and other concerns. Afterward, the men began to grow quiet and listen in earnest.

One man said, "Maggie, we talk about rights all the time. I didn't know our women were being neglected."

A chuckle was heard from the front of the room. But Mr. Smith, acting as facilitator on the dais, raised his voice and said, "Hold on, brothers," and lowered his hands to calm them down. "Now is the time to address their needs and come up with a plan."

I had already been attending the NAACP's meetings for a while. Most of the time, I was the only woman in the room. When their eyes would turn to me like a bolt of lightning, I would simply smile. But the magpies would whisper always anyway, "She thinks she a got-damn man."

That day, I was not alone!

CHAPTER 22

✦

1915

WE LOVED OUR HOME at 110 East Leigh Street, so near Second Street. It was distinctive, with a wrought-iron fence wrapped around the porch, large and stately. Jackson Ward had many beautiful homes. We were a well-managed community of professionals. All the homes were made of brick and had a carriage house, with an Italian flair.

Armstead had built many of the businesses and homes in Jackson Ward and was a wealthy man himself. Having access to a lending agency like our bank was what was needed in our community. People were able to borrow money for development and allowed to pay it back in installments as their businesses flourished.

Due to our bank loans, businesses were sprouting up everywhere along Second Street, thus adding more jobs for people in the community. Folks called the area where the businesses lined up and down the street "The Deuce." The Hippodrome Theater opened on Second Street as well. This area of Jackson Ward had grown to become an artistic, cultural, and economic mecca for coloreds. All the professional acts that would tour the country from New York to California would made a stop at the Hippodrome. Some called us "the Black Wall Street of the South" and others referred to Jackson Ward as "the Black Harlem of the South." All I knew was that Jim Crow laws were still alive and well, and we were going to do all we could to overcome their harsh influence on our community.

As Jackson Ward continued to thrive, I started receiving more and more threats. Some of them were so serious, they actually made me consider giving up. It was no longer the usual buffoons who occasionally approached me, but white men who would walk up to me and brazenly scrutinize me with a violent eye. "We are going to get rid of you, Maggie Walker," they'd say. At times my heart would shudder, and beads of sweat would form around my nose and forehead, but I would take a deep breath, reach into my satchel, and pull out one of my handkerchiefs—tucked beside my Colt pistol—to pat the sweat dripping from my face.

One day, as I was leaving the bank on the way to my car, two men came from nowhere. One of them grabbed me so fast I felt helpless. He put his hand over my mouth and locked his arms around me. "Just try and run your mouth now," he threatened, and dragged me behind a vacant building off Broad Street while keeping his hand over my mouth, preventing me from screaming while the other man assisted. They were strong as bulls, pushing me up against a brick wall with little effort. My chest heaved up and down as I tried to think of a way to escape them. I kicked out at them, but my feet didn't connect with their targets. Chills traveled throughout my body. For once, I truly feared for my life. But once they had me against the wall, the nerves in their voices became more evident.

"Maggie, you are a threat to the good white people of Richmond."

What on earth did he mean by "good"? I thought.

I was too nervous to answer, besides still having his hands over my mouth. Struggling, I tried to bite him, and he quickly removed his hand.

The other one, with eyes hidden behind bushy eyebrows and a pug nose, said, "We've been warning you for over twenty years to stop what you are doing, but you won't listen. You are one stubborn woman."

He tugged and pulled so hard on my jacket that it tore, and I felt the pain as he pushed me hard against the brick wall again. I began to squirm and push them away from me. They were strong, but so was I. I pushed until the other one finally released one of my hands.

I was huffing and puffing from the struggle. Once my hand was free, I put it in my buckled skirt pocket and pulled out my Colt. "Move back," I said, pointing my pistol directly at them.

"You have some nerve pulling a pistol on a white man."

I shook it at them. "You had better leave me alone before I take you down. I will drop you right where you stand."

One of them backed away and then took off running. The other looked me straight in the eye and didn't budge.

"Shouldn't you be following your friend?" I asked him.

"Mrs. Walker, I ain't mean no harm to you. But you see, us white folks don't like seeing you uppity Negroes strutting around here like peacocks."

"Are we bothering you?"

"Not personally. But you exist. That's crime enough."

"I am tired of people like you threatening me and mine," I said. "Put your hands down." He was holding his hands above his head, shaking nervously, yet his menacing eyes were still locked on me. He was scared, but he was also dangerous.

"Coloreds ought to stay in their place," he hurled.

"And I think you ought to stay in yours," I hurled back, and his eyes grew wide. He had never had this much resistance from a colored woman. He attempted to move closer, but I cocked my pistol. "I told you, sir, I am a God-fearing woman, but I will kill you. I'm sure the good Lord would understand. Now, don't make me do it."

Looking from left to right, I could see in his gray eyes that he was calculating whether to believe me and go, or trust that I wouldn't dare and lunge at me. I glared at him, unblinking, waiting for him to make a move.

After a beat, I said, "Go on about your business, and don't you ever threaten me again."

"Mrs. Walker, it's you who can't threaten a white man. Don't you understand we run this world?"

My heart was pumping fast. I was so scared I didn't know what to do. I glanced toward the sky for God, and suddenly I knew I had to survive. I moved and glared at him in the face, all the while my heart felt like it was going to jump out of my chest. I inhaled and conjured up an intentional scowl, showing him I meant business. "I will kill a white man, if I must," I said.

"You'll have no mo' problems out of me," he said, finally starting to slowly step backward.

I thought his partner would come back, but he didn't. My anxiety level was high, adrenaline pumping throughout my body. I could feel the tension in my neck and shoulders.

All I could think about in that moment was my daddy, Willie. I had followed the Good Book to the page. Reciting each word of the Bible I could hold in my memory, trying to live by it without wavering. How could I be troubled enough to consider shooting a man?

"I better not see you anywhere near Jackson Ward again," I said. "If I do, it will be your last time in the wrong part of the city."

He kept walking backward and sneered. "I'd heard that you act like a man. Now I see why." Finally, he turned fully and stalked away after his companion.

I released the lever on my pistol and slid it back into my buckle skirt pocket. I walked over to my blue Packard, got in, and drove around the corner and down the street to my home. I was so stunned about what had happened, I had to take a moment to gather myself before exiting my car. I gazed up at the moon and said a silent prayer.

I had convinced myself on the drive home to tell Armstead what happened to me, but not that night. All I aimed to do was to take a long, hot bath

and then crawl into a warm bed. I slid under the covers and snuggled as close
to Armstead as I could. He put his muscular arms around me, and I automati-
cally closed my weary eyes, trying hard not to think about the evening and
what had taken place. I cuddled up close to my husband, and a sense of forti-
fication immediately swept over me. The next morning at breakfast, I shared
my story with Armstead. Just like always, he took offense and fear rose in his
hazel eyes. This was the kind of threat we couldn't just overlook.

"Now they are angry enough to hurt me."

"I don't want you going anywhere alone," Armstead demanded.

For a minute, I had been afraid, thinking the men would take my life.
Now I knew that God would protect me, but even He needed a little help. "I
agree. I think it's time for more security. These white men feel like their status
is being threatened and they are angry with me for pushing our agenda."

"You've been working hard for years, darling," he said. "Look around you
at the progress we've made. We have storefronts of all kinds in Jackson Ward.
We are making strides. They are just angry because colored folk are improving their situation, and making things happen after being treated like animals,
and being enslaved for so many years. They are still at the top, and all we want
is a little of what they have. Remember, no man wants to lose to a woman,
either, and a colored woman at that."

The threats didn't stop. I always made sure to carry my Colt with me,
usually tucked in my jacket, satchel, or my buckled skirt pocket. White men
would stare me down as I walked down the street. Their wives would also
give me an unwanted look. But with time, it became as common as the burst
of sunlight in the mornings.

We had experienced burglars trying to enter our home, people trying to
scare us off. Momma was getting up in age, and I feared for her more than
myself, since she was always in the home. Polly was usually with her, but two
women on their own, one sixty-seven and the other twenty-five years old,
were easy targets for dangerous men. The market and church were Momma's
only outings these days. When we traveled across the state signing up new

members, the trips were too burdensome for an aging woman. At times our work took us to other places like Maryland, Pennsylvania, and New York, to continue to grow our membership, and we served colored customers everywhere. Momma would stay home with our grown children on those occasions now; all but Russell, who was determined to follow in our footsteps. Although Polly was our adopted daughter, she took care of Momma like she was her own grandmother.

"Maggie, if you must do things in the evenings, swallow your pride and allow me to go with you to these strange places. A woman shouldn't be out at night alone anyhow," Armstead said sternly. I nodded.

"Listen, we are going to be just fine," Armstead assured me. I believed him, as he cared more about his family than anything else, including the job he loved. Armstead's strong sense of responsibility for his family surpassed everything else around him and he expressed it to us daily without hesitation.

✦c❂✦

In the months of May and June, there were rumors of more break-ins throughout Jackson Ward. Members of the Independent Order of St. Luke were hysterical, and I called an emergency meeting. Just the suggestion of crime in Jackson Ward had everyone concerned about their welfare.

I knew my Russell would take things more seriously, since he sometimes filled in for his father, sharing his characteristics, looks, and ways. He was so focused, and now that he had gotten married himself in 1912, he also had his wife to consider and protect.

During a meeting of the Order to discuss the Ward's security, folks clamored to raise their concerns.

"What if it's the Klan? I heard of them coming closer to Jackson Ward," one of the attendees asked, anxious.

"I don't think so, but they are gaining territory. And rumor has it they are headed this way," Mr. Forrester said, as if he were still the leader of the Order.

"We've got to be ready," I agreed.

Anxiety was written all over the faces of the attendees. No one felt comfortable even mentioning the Klan. The flashback of two white men threatening me had beads of sweat forming on my nose. Just the thought . . . was grueling.

Rumors of the Klan being reestablished had been on the minds of progressive coloreds all across the States. In 1915, the Ku Klux Klan had been making themselves known in places like Atlanta, Georgia, and the rumors of their presence had spread like wildfire. The KKK was an organization that attacked Jewish people, Catholics, Japanese Americans, and African Americans. Colored folk had experienced their share of beatings and other violent behaviors from the Klansmen, who were increasing their membership across the United States. They reigned with terror, attacking innocent people whom they deemed a threat to political white supremacy. It was the same thing that had happened prior to the Civil War. They rampantly did all they could to commit genocide against anyone who wasn't Caucasian.

It didn't help that certain films were feeding the KKK's mentality on the silver screen. The nationwide release of *The Birth of a Nation* that February had brought with it a glorification of the Civil War and clear anti-colored sentiments while praising the KKK. It had been a hit. With such blatant support for their causes, the residents of Jackson Ward were right to worry that the KKK might be coming for us next, as they had other towns in the South.

"You've got to get the word out to the community as soon as possible," another man had urged us, breaking me out of my reverie.

We made sure to print concerns about the burglaries in the *Herald* and the *Planet*. We immediately went on the lookout for the Klan if any concerns of burglars or interruptions to the progress of Negroes came up. They were the last disruptors we needed in Jackson Ward.

❖❀❖

Several days later, Mr. Walter and his wife, Annabelle, our invited guests, arrived on time for dinner, as usual. For some reason undertakers were never late. Armstead and I would occasionally joke about their efficiency.

Over dinner, Mr. Walter confessed that he had been robbed, having never mentioned it during the Order meeting. I wasn't sure if he was ashamed or just plain ornery.

"Armstead, someone came into the funeral parlor and stole money I had in my desk drawer. It wasn't much, but who in their right mind would come into a parlor filled with dead people and not be scared?" Armstead peered over at me, and I subtly grinned.

Armstead smirked. "That is a conundrum, Mr. Walter. I would certainly think they'd be afraid of one of them corpses rising up and scaring *them* to death."

We all gawked and laughed at Armstead's response. We knew no one wanted to be in a funeral parlor for any reason, and it was seemingly the last place someone might think to burglarize.

"Most people hate being in there during the day, let alone at night," Armstead added.

A frown swept across Mr. Walter's face. "I had never given it a thought before," he said.

"Do you have any idea who might have wanted to steal from you?" Armstead asked.

"No, not at all."

"Maggie, do you think it is the Klan?"

"The Klan typically don't rob folk," I said. "They come to threaten and even kill coloreds, but not rob. Outside the city of Atlanta, two colored men on their way to the market were found hung on a tree, upside down and bleeding out like deer. Hate is the Klansmen's business and what they're intent on spreading. We suspect the attempts around our home are being done to scare us off."

"I sure hope not," Mr. Walter said. "The last thing we need in Jackson Ward is more hatred."

"I agree, Mr. Walter," I said. "There are more than enough crowds of hate-filled folks surrounding us already. Our progress has roused some ill feelings among some of the businesspeople downtown. They have felt for some time that we are taking money out of their pockets."

"It is strange how they can hate us so much yet love our money more than we do," he said. "We are still buying from them and spending our greenbacks outside the community."

"I know this doesn't help the burglary you've experienced, Mr. Walter, but if we could continue spending in our own community and depositing money in our own bank, we would be in a better place for negotiation."

"What are you saying, Maggie?"

"Your money should be deposited in our bank. We give returns on your savings, and you would be helping someone else seeking money to open a business. I have an application on my desk now to approve for a new cabinet and furniture shop."

"Are you talking about loaning my money out?"

"Oh, you know we have to do all we can for the community, and lending money is one of the things the bank does for Jackson Ward and others across the state. Stop putting your money in desk drawers and deposit it in a colored bank."

"He still uses a safe, Maggie," Annabelle answered, and Mr. Walter rolled his eyes at her to shut her up, but she never was one to keep her thoughts to herself. "Walter, you need to come up with the times. If they stole from you once, they would try again. Being around the dead does not bother an eager rogue. Besides, with enough manpower, they can take the safe as well."

It wasn't often that I agreed with Annabelle, but tonight she made sense.

"I guess I could move my money to the bank," Mr. Walter said pensively. Shortly he added, "Until we find out who is robbing around here, and they are locked up in jail, I will deposit my money in the bank." But it felt to me like it was just something to say since he was outnumbered by three adults who believed in safety deposit accounts.

He probably had money in his safe from thirty years ago. He had been a young man when he inherited the business from his father, and he had never once stepped into the bank. Annabelle spent her share of his greenbacks. She wore tailored dresses that flowed to the ground and those that came to the ankle showing her newly shined and purchased Italian shoes. She and Fannie were always adorned, and they wore wealth well. I didn't do too bad myself.

Armstead promised, "I will make some trips around Second Street to see if there are any others experiencing bouts of burglary. We will find whoever it is or scare them off. Either way, we are going to find a way to keep Jackson Ward safe."

"We are going to need more protection," Russell chimed in. "All we have is that little Colt that Momma carries with her."

We knew what he was saying was true. And we saw the concern in his eyes.

After Mr. Walter and Annabelle left, Armstead and I got dressed for bed and dropped to our knees and prayed as we did each night.

The very next night, an otherwise ordinary Wednesday after dinner, Russell heard a rumble of something in the attic. He pulled out a weapon his dad had just purchased earlier that day, for our protection, and climbed the back stairway to the attic. When he made it up, he could only see a silhouette in the dark. The shadow perplexed him. Nervously, he cocked the gun and fired a shot. The sound caused all the members of the house to scurry up the back stairs to see what had happened. When we lit the lantern, we found Armstead lying facedown in a puddle of his own blood. In an instant, I lost my bearings. I rushed to Armstead's side, desperately trying to resuscitate him. I did everything I possibly could to try to stanch the bleeding, but it was no use. Momma bent down with me and pushed hard on the wound, but the damage had been done.

In a corner of the room, Russell was crumpled against the wall, sobbing and staring at his father; at his own hand, the one that had pulled the trigger; and the gun, lying inert at his feet, that was meant to protect him and instead had ripped a hole through our family that nothing would ever be able to repair.

CHAPTER 23

1915–1916

TEARS BEAT MY HEAD to the pillow. I couldn't believe my Armstead was truly gone, and by the hand of our eldest son. I felt I was dying inside, my stomach churning, my head spinning. It was rare for anything to make me cry, but Armstead was my backbone and the only man I ever loved. My heart beat erratically at the thought of my son murdering his father. Only God knows the pain he felt at unintentionally committing such an act. Momma held me in her arms like she had when I was a child. Our roles reversed from when Daddy had died. She rubbed my back and rocked back and forth with me, but nothing seemed to help. Like a bird with an injured wing, we were all broken.

Russell had been handcuffed and arrested. He pleaded with me, "Momma, I didn't know it was Daddy. I didn't know." Then he wailed with the renewed realization of what he'd done, "Oh, oh! I have killed my father." He buried his head down on his chest. He couldn't look up for anything, tears streaming down his face. I didn't know how to comfort him.

"Son, we know it was an accident!" I yelled as the policeman put him into the Ford Model T paddy wagon. As they drove off with Russell, I slid down the baluster and sank to the ground. Momma helped me back up, though she was getting frail now. I could see shadows around her dark eyes. She loved Armstead and Russell. The night must've reminded her of when she lost Daddy, too. Both of us had lost a good man. One by whatever means unbeknownst to us, and the other by gunshot. She was experiencing that pain all over again, but remaining strong for me.

Later that same night, the two of us were left up in the kitchen, neither of us feeling like we could sleep, though we were weary down to our core.

Momma said compassionately, "I know your pain, chile. But, I promise, you will get through this, too." She put her hand on mine. "Day by day, new sunlight breaks the sky."

When she spoke, the tears streamed down my cheeks. I had lost my husband and my son.

Polly, silent tears rolling down her own face, set a mug of calming tea in front of each of us. She made a third to take to Hattie, who was inconsolable in the room she shared with Russell. She had lost her husband. None of us knew what Russell's fate might be after that night.

❖CƆ❖

Armstead was laid out for viewing at Fannie's mortuary, the only woman-run mortuary in Jackson Ward. Her family owned it, but it was Fannie who handled the business. She had a reputation for serving high-end clients, and she did a good job with Armstead's viewing.

Mr. Walter was angry because we'd chosen Fannie's funeral parlor instead of his, then remembered it was a dear friend we were observing, and he sobered. His outburst didn't matter at all. I had lost the one person who loved me regardless of my faults. Momma had often said I lucked out when I found him. I think God blessed me with the best, and for that I was extremely grateful.

The Walker family was upset when Armstead passed. They couldn't believe Russell had been so careless, but they still supported him. "Maggie, that boy is going to need us all," Andrew, Armstead's brother, had said, and immediately started going down to the jail to visit him.

"I know," I answered, knowing that losing Armstead was difficult for him as well. Andrew had worked beside Armstead every day, pouring mortar and placing bricks, and I know he missed his presence with all his heart. They were a cohesive family and their love for each other extended beyond blood kin and overflowed to me, their sister by law.

✦☙✦

I struggled to find the strength to carry on, but I had to. I dropped down on my knees and prayed to God for deliverance. My son was suffering. Russell was traumatized, and I couldn't help him. I couldn't hold him, and I couldn't say anything that would make him feel better. My poor husband lay dead in a funeral parlor, looking like he was asleep. I had to find a way to help free Russell.

I was anxious about going down to the police precinct and broke out in a cold sweat. I had to do the best negotiating of my life. I put on my brown skirt, bolero blouse, and a hat. I put my pistol in my satchel, though I knew the police would check me for weapons. Instead of taking it inside the precinct, I slid it under the driver's seat of my car.

I sat down with the police chief, a white man who offered me neither a welcome nor a smile. He stared at me from across a small desk.

"Your son will stay in here until we complete our investigation, Mrs. Walker."

"Sir," I said, "he made a mistake. He didn't know it was his father. There have been more and more reports of burglars in the vicinity, and he acted too quickly. He had no intention of killing his own father. You must see that he's innocent." I pleaded with all my might. Yet he didn't budge.

"We are going to investigate this like any other case. Just because you walk around Jackson Ward like you run this town doesn't mean you have any sway here. The law is the law."

"Can I at least see my son?" I asked kindly for fear of agitating him, though he seemed to already have a dislike for me.

The police chief considered me a moment. "Sure you can. I will get him."

Russell looked crumbled with grief, his eyes red with anguish. I could feel the pain in his soul. He peered at me with tears welling up in his eyes. "Momma, I am sorry," he said humbly.

"I know, son. It was an accident." I grabbed his hand through the bars that separated us. He squeezed my hand and didn't release it.

"Momma, I took Daddy's life," he said and broke down crying, tears flowing freely out of the corners of his eyes.

"Enough of that for now, son." I hushed him, tears springing to my own eyes again, but I refused to let them fall. "We will have you back home with us soon."

Chills traveled all over my body. My nerves were rattled, yet I had to be strong for Russell. I had to project strength to him. Any concerns about his jail stay had to be shoved aside. I knew there were people all over Richmond who would use this accident to bring me and my family down. They knew that my Armstead meant the world to me, and that Russell loved his wife as much as I did Armstead.

"Momma, take care of Hattie for me, please."

"Don't you worry, son. Polly hasn't left Hattie's side since . . ." I let my words trail away as I braced myself against the image of Armstead in our attic. Shaking my head, I gripped Russell's hands in both of mine and said, "Soon you will be coming home to take care of her yourself again."

He clung to my hands, and even though I was hurting way down in my soul, I held my head up high.

"I'll be back to see you soon, son," I said as the policeman told me my time was up.

As I was leaving the precinct, I noticed a subtle smirk on the police officer's face. I bit my lip and kept my mouth shut tight. I didn't want Russell to suffer any more than necessary because of whatever hatred the officers held toward me. Everyone knew coloreds were mistreated in jail.

❖c◗❖

It took me more than a week to let Armstead's body go. I just couldn't let them put him in the cold, dark ground. But Momma was adamant about his homegoing, as she called it. "Armstead knows Russell would never do anything to hurt him. He loved his father, just like you and me; we all are going to miss him."

We all cried a river of tears on the day Armstead was eulogized. The authorities decided Russell could not attend his father's burial. All of Jackson Ward was at St. Luke Hall afterward; so many people came to the service that many had to stand. A piece of me was lowered in the ground with Armstead's coffin that day at Evergreen Cemetery.

The days afterward were empty. I took time off work, and even took a break from my civil rights activism. I spent most nights on my knees, praying for my family and especially for Russell. My bed was cold, and although I embraced Armstead's pillow, it brought me no comfort.

After a week, Momma told me, "You've got to get back to work, chile. Your chi'ren may be grown, but they only have you now." I knew she was right.

"Momma," I told her, "I have got to get Russell home first. He is dealing with a guilt that is eating him up from the inside. Even after we do bring him home, I'm not sure how we'll be able to lift him back up."

"Them people will hold him for longer just to get back at you. They evil, I tell you," she said, sipping on hot coffee. "Ain't no one around who can help you there."

As I gazed at Momma, I could see her deteriorating, too. With Armstead and Russell missing from our home, the house appeared to be too big. Polly, Hattie, Melvin, and Johnnie were there. Usually it was Armstead and Russell challenging us at the kitchen table about one subject or another. Everyone was voiceless for a while. The silence seemed to encourage the melancholy.

Momma was as strong as a horse, and although she kept a stoic expression on her face most of the time, it was just a façade. None of the children could possibly know how much pain she was in. I had seen her deal with many things over the years, hiding her fears and never bowing her head. I drew my strength from her, and sorely needed it now.

The Richmond authorities kept Russell in jail for a long time. I knew that securing Russell's release would require great persistence, so I spent countless hours waiting to get an audience with Mayor George Ainslie. His secretary was a protective woman, and it took nearly six months to get to see him. He was an aristocrat with a social connection to Britain, and he wined and dined the elite, spending money meant for the improvement of the city. The mayor was a handsome man; he wore the best suits, and the finest bow ties. He appeared of royalty, and he was kind. But I had built an alliance with Mayor McCarthy, and hadn't needed to goad this new mayor yet in order to move our progress along.

"Mrs. Maggie Walker, to what do I owe the pleasure of your visit?" he greeted me as I strutted into his office. He was surrounded by the finest mahogany furniture, and the chandelier in the middle of the ceiling was more extravagant than the one in the governor's office. I had never met him before, but it seemed my reputation preceded me.

"Sir, may I sit down?" I asked, and he pointed to the chair in front of his desk.

"Mrs. Walker, I hear you're called the 'race woman.' Or, in other words, 'the mayor of Jackson Ward'!" He chuckled as if he'd made a joke. I gave him a simple smile.

"I am here to ask for the release of my son, Russell Walker, who is still in jail."

"Yes, I heard about that. My condolences for your loss, Mrs. Walker. I've been told your boy accidentally fatally wounded his own father. Is that right?" I could only manage a nod.

"That's just a double helping of grief there, now, isn't it? But you see, it is our right to hold Russell in jail until the investigation is concluded, and a verdict has been reached. I believe he was found innocent, is that so?"

"Yes, sir. And yet, he has not been released. Can you please speak with the police chief and have my son released from jail, so he can be cared for at home?"

"What's wrong with him? Has he been injured in jail?" the mayor asked.

"No," I said, taking a moment to collect myself before I continued. "We just miss him from our home."

"I will look into his release, but I cannot make any promises."

"But the courts found him not guilty."

"I will look into it. Is there anything else you need, Mrs. Walker? If not, I have a meeting with some city officials."

Graciously, I got up and thanked him for his time.

A month later, after being in jail for seven long months, Russell was finally released. But he was no longer the same man he was before. It was obvious that he had worried himself sick and was drained of confidence.

We brought him home, and Momma nursed him as if he were a child again. Telling him affirmations, making sure he was well fed, rubbing his back as he struggled to drift off to sleep. But he sank deeper into depression, re-playing over and over again in his mind that dreadful night when Armstead was killed. I wondered if he would have been so quick to shoot the gun had he not attended the Order meeting, which put a lot of fear in everyone, including me.

Once Russell was out of jail, his uncle Andrew would invite him out with him. Sometimes Russell would go, and other times he would stay home and drink whiskey until he was too numb to move.

I insisted that Russell try keeping himself busy, to keep his mind from lingering on what happened that night. But not even Hattie could fully comfort him. He spent most of his time self-medicating with the fine alcohol from our liquor cabinet. Even Hattie was at a loss as to how to help her husband.

"At least he is home," Momma said as she folded clothes. *But is he truly?* I thought. He had been severely punished in jail, in addition to the internal turmoil that plagued him daily. Though he was still alive, it was plain to see that he had become a ghost himself.

My son needed me, but so did our community. At a loss for how to help Russell, and to safeguard my own sanity, I went back to work. It was the only way I could cope.

CHAPTER 24

1917

TIME FLEW BY AFTER bringing Russell home. He went back to his job and continued to do all he could for the St. Luke Penny Savings Bank, at times working late hours to keep himself busy and his mind occupied. Hattie was elated to have him home, even though at times he solved his personal problems with a stiff drink of whiskey.

While Russell was pulling himself together, I ended up working day and night to sign up new members for the Order. By 1917, there were forty thousand adults and more than ten thousand youth members in the Independent Order of St. Luke.

Aside from my work at the bank, I had successfully aided the NAACP in chartering their Richmond Chapter. The organization had been growing in leaps, and I now served on the national chapter with W. E. B. Du Bois. My deliberate recruitment of Mary and Fannie had been helpful in inspiring women in Jackson Ward to join the organization, too.

"I'm so glad you came to me, Maggie. I can't take sitting in that cold funeral parlor all day for another minute," Fannie commented.

When she said it, all of us nearly choked to keep from laughing. Her funeral parlor was more popular than Mr. Walter's, and still she complained. We just glanced at one another and smirked.

Mary Bethune's work with the National Association of Colored Women's Clubs was also growing in Richmond. Mary had put together a group of women determined to address the issues associated with education and social equality.

Things were changing fast, and I was struggling to stay apace. I was starting to get headaches—bad ones. I knew something was wrong with me, but I couldn't stop. I felt compelled to continue to do the work for the good of the people. And burying myself in my work was the only way to deal with Armstead's absence in our home.

One night, Melvin said to me, "Momma, you need a change. All you do is work and now it is making you sick." My head was pounding.

I glanced at him and grinned. Lord knew he was right.

"Thank you, son, for the advice."

I worked endlessly, and there was always something needing my time. But the St. Luke Penny Savings Bank was steadily growing. With each move I made, I felt that Armstead was still beside me. The memory of him was my rock.

My children had found ways to cope, too. Polly had stepped up and was taking care of Momma and the home. The loss of Armstead was felt throughout the entire Jackson Ward community, too. Especially those who depended on his fine craftmanship in building. But his memory lived on in the buildings he'd helped to construct in life.

We'd settled into a bittersweet peace. And I desired to unwind.

❖�’❖

Pearl Brown, a local nightclub singer, had been booked at the Hippodrome Theater. Everyone in Jackson Ward couldn't wait to witness her stage magic. She could sing the blues, jazz, and scat, and W. E. B. Du Bois had a liking for the way she mesmerized men and women alike. If you were down and out, she could make you forget all about your troubles. I wrote to W. E. B. and Mary McLeod Bethune about the performance and invited them to join me.

Just the mention of Pearl Brown performing had the entire community ready for some relief. And I could use some good company, music, and food.

John Mitchell Jr., Mary McLeod Bethune, and W. E. B. Du Bois rode along in my Packard to the Hippodrome, which was only a few blocks away. As we stood in a line that wrapped around the block to get into the theater, one of the guards directing the traffic of attendees noticed me and my famous friends.

"Y'all come to the front of the line, please."

Mary peered back at me with a smile on her face. W. E. B. was accustomed to this type of treatment, so he didn't hesitate to come from the back of the line to the front. I don't feel the rest of us had his sense of entitlement, but W. E. B. called it "confidence."

As we walked past the other patrons, some recognized us and smiled; others frowned and made it known they didn't like us getting special treatment.

"They need to wait just like everybody else," some shouted. I simply smiled and went into the club. The owner seated us at the best table available. It was my first time out in a crowd since I'd lost Armstead. Suddenly the headache I'd had earlier disappeared.

The room was lit with table lanterns, which made for a subtle, sexy atmosphere. The waiter came straight to our table, swinging his arms as if we were in a hurry. He was cordial, introducing himself to us before taking our drink orders. Mary and I were social drinkers, so we each ordered a glass of red wine. The men opted for something stronger, scotch neat.

They sat us in the center of the room, and all night we kept being approached by people attempting to strike up a conversation. At times W. E. B. would stiffen at the interruptions because he wanted only to be mesmerized by the likes of Pearl Brown. Although it was a pleasure to be respected by so many, it was supposed to be a relaxing night and we only wanted to hear the silky and soothing voice of the community's favorite singer.

Pearl Brown was an inspiration to us all. A small-town singer with big dreams, she often came into the bank and sought my advice on investments and savings. I respected hard work and determination, and Pearl had an abundance of both. Just like the money she deposited weekly, she was growing as an entertainer.

She'd say to me, "Maggie, eventually I am out of here."

I believed her, since everything she wanted had become a reality so far. She had the kind of faith others dreamed about and she carried it with confidence.

The Great War was raging overseas. Rumors of the United States joining the fight had some of the folks concerned. How would joining the war affect their businesses? Would colored men be required to enlist? Would colored folks be the sacrifice for all that was in the making?

"Maggie, is everything all right?" Mary asked. "You are looking a little tired this evening." I had been losing sleep for months. Nothing had been the same since Armstead passed. Some nights, I didn't sleep at all.

"I'm a little worn out, I suppose," I answered without mentioning the headaches I was having from time to time.

"Well, you are going to have to sleep in tomorrow morning while I prepare breakfast for you and W. E. B."

W. E. B. smiled. Mary was an amazing cook, and she seasoned her food to perfection.

John overheard her and immediately spoke up. "I believe W. E. B. is staying at my home."

W. E. B., a man with so much class, simply smiled at John's comment and replied, "I think I'll stay at Maggie's tonight."

The crowd at the Hippodrome seemed so sophisticated that night. Women were dressed in hats and chemise dresses that draped their frames like Grecian goddesses. They had on rouge and lipstick, and reminded me of well-styled mannequins. The men were dressed in dark suits with bow ties, their mustaches trimmed and hair neatly cut. Noticing how debonaire the men looked reminded me of the beauty of my dear late husband and how just gazing into his light brown eyes sent chills down my spine. But those days were over. There would never be another Armstead. No one had his touch.

When Pearl Brown started to stroll from the back of the room, winding through the crowd with a sensuous smile on her face, we all stood up to applaud her entrance. She was tall and statuesque, and a magnet for hungry eyes. The applause was generous, and everyone graciously smiled. A few women whispered, "Pearl Brown is always trying to seduce somebody's husband." I turned toward them without smiling. It always bothered me when women put each other down.

Pearl was certainly the talk of the town. Her performances were better than Bessie Smith's or any of the other entertainers who had stopped through Richmond recently. Her voice lit up the room. All night, W. E. B. swung his head from side to side. He loved her voice and how she could send rhythms and beats all through your body.

Pearl knew how to stimulate the crowd and get folks swaying. At times, in the middle of her song, she'd look in W. E. B.'s direction and say, "This is for you." He would raise his glass to her before taking a sip of his drink and leaning back to enjoy the attention.

As the evening came to an end and the pianist and drummer left the stage, Pearl strutted over to our table. She spoke to all of us, but it was clear she had a certain affection for W. E. B. She wrapped her long, slim arms around him and embraced him as she said good night. Her red chemise dress was beautifully darned and sparkling. It appeared to be one of Mrs. Sarah's creations. A small smile adorned his face the entire trip home. Mary shook her head and so did I. How could a visit to a nightclub have that kind of effect on a grown man?

The next morning, I did wake up late, and found Mary, Momma, and Polly in the kitchen. They each had aprons draped around their waists. The succulent aroma of ham, fried potatoes, and apples filled the whole down-stairs area. One whiff and you started to salivate.

"I told you a little rest was all you needed. You look like you're feeling much better," Mary said. "Now sit down and let's eat."

W. E. B. was already seated at the table and so was John Mitchell Jr., who had invited himself over to our breakfast. Momma and Mary served hot bis-cuits, apple butter, and coffee along with the ham, potatoes, apples, and eggs. It was enough food to feed an army, but we never worried about wasting anything, since we had plenty of mouths to feed and could always have any leftovers the next day. Sometimes my children would eat in the kitchen in-stead of the dining room.

Once we were all served and the dining table was full, we began discuss-ing the awful rumors floating around about the Great War.

"I'm afraid to print about it in the *Planet*," John commented.

"We must let the people know what is coming if we can, and have the sources to back it up," I said.

"I'm not sure why we are joining the fight," Momma said. "It is time to make peace in this ol' ugly world. Lord, after all these years . . ."

The more Momma aged, the less likely she was to hold her tongue. I sup-pose being quiet all those years had been hard, and now she really didn't mind saying how she felt. The "ugly world" was something I had never heard from her lips before.

"I think coloreds need to consider how fighting in this war would benefit us," W. E. B. said. "The Negro will gain recognition as being patriotic, and it should certainly help our position in society."

For a minute, no one uttered a word.

"We should not be fighting any wars," I said. "There is a war going on right here in Richmond and across the South. We are fighting for our survival and sta-tus every day of our lives. Why must we prove our patriotism to anyone else?"

W. E. B. wasn't used to being challenged, but he was certainly wrong. I refused to allow him to inflict pain on top of pain on our people.

Mary swallowed. "I agree with Maggie. We've done all we can to fit into this America. Why must we fight?"

W. E. B. broke his statement down into a long soliloquy. We listened, but not one of the faces at the table seemed convinced of his reasoning for a war.

Mary changed the subject to the action of her organization and school in Florida.

"We are making progress. We have the attention of the politicians, like the assistant secretary of the Navy, Mr. Franklin Delano Roosevelt, and we are not going to stop until every woman in the state is educated and given opportunities."

She had worked tirelessly for the advancement of all people and especially young women. We were all very proud of Mary and the strides she had made in the last decade. No matter how much work there was to do, none of us were able to stop the fight for economic and social justice.

Our breakfast ended when Mary reminded W. E. B., "You know, Pearl Brown may stop by here today. I heard she's been asking about 'the man from the North.'"

He shook his head and grinned. "Stop teasing, Mary. She is just an illusion."

We all broke out in laughter.

CHAPTER 25

⁓⊙⁓

1917–1918

ON APRIL 6, 1917, with the support of the U.S. Senate and the House of Representatives, President Woodrow Wilson declared war on Germany after they had bombed U.S. merchant ships. We would officially join the Great War, which had been raging since July 28, 1914, when Archduke Franz Ferdinand and his wife, Sophie, were murdered and the Austro-Hungarian government declared war on Serbia. Immediately afterward, other European countries had declared war upon one another. America was nearly three years late.

W. E. B. Du Bois had been writing about the Great War from his point of view since it began. He didn't consult many on his compilation of the war, and very few colored leaders participated in his self-serving printings. We had always consulted him on grave matters, but for some reason, at times he would feel he had an upper hand on intelligence and would overlook the concerns of the people. He felt strongly that participation in this war would benefit the Negro.

My immediate concern was for our colored soldiers. Would they be able to fight? Or would they be treated like the enslaved colored battalions had

223

during the Civil War? Many colored men agreed with W. E. B. and wanted to fight. They felt that showing their patriotism would give them leverage in a country filled with hate.

The *Herald* printed all the ports at which colored soldiers could join the war. Most of them were up north and hundreds of eager colored men migrated in carriages, trains, and automobiles to get to a port where they could enlist.

At the influx of volunteers, I immediately called a meeting with the members of the NAACP. "We need to talk to our people," I said, standing before them at the pulpit of the First African Baptist Church.

"We have people traveling long distances to join a segregated army in a war in which no one is sure who is the enemy. Is it the Germans, the French, the Dutch, or the Europeans? I am not sure."

Mr. Walter, who was beginning to grow more feeble, stood up and shook his cane at me. "Now, Maggie, before you start, understand that these men need to know they can make a difference. And fighting is one way to prove their value in this country."

I smacked my lips. "We've been fighting right here in this country for more than two hundred years, and what good has come of it?" I shot back at him.

"Why is it so bad to fight?" Mr. Eugene Thomas, who ran a shoeshine stand, said.

"It is not bad to fight," I answered, "but our fight *here* isn't over, and we need every man, woman, and child to be a part of the colored war on economic inequality and injustice. We need them to continue supporting our banks and insurance companies, and the growth and advancement of our businesses. I strongly believe that going overseas to fight for this country is not the answer. It will not magically resolve all our troubles here. But I really am trying to understand your point of view."

"Your friend, W. E. B., is all for our involvement in this Great War. I hear one of the troops out of New York will actually do some fighting. They won't be just a cleanup crew."

In wars past, colored soldiers had been the laborers and cleanup battalions. Honor did not come with all the work they were given, yet they held their heads high.

One man yelled from the back of the room, "I will be getting on the train in the morning and going to Harlem, New York, to enlist in the 93rd Division in hopes of joining the 369th Infantry Regiment."

Eugene followed: "I think I'll join you in the morning."

"We'll be sad to see you go, for many reasons," I said, thinking of their degree of involvement in the NAACP.

"Maggie Walker, what on earth do you mean by that statement?" Mr. Walter asked.

"We are the National Association for the Advancement of Colored People. We work with the courts and the government to effect policy and law changes to protect you from abuse and provide justice. Fighting for our rights has been a hard battle. And knowing you will be joining segregated troops—segregation being one of the very things we've been fighting so hard against—saddens me. And not knowing how you will be treated worries me."

The man at the back of the church spoke up again, saying, "The 369th Infantry is a regiment that is supposed to be deployed to Paris, France. I've heard the French treat coloreds better than Americans do, and we's born here."

The French had always been more progressive and respectful of different races. I expected them to continue with the same disposition during times of war. Booker T. Washington's secretary, Emmett Jay Scott, had been given the task of ensuring that colored soldiers were treated fairly. It was the passing of the Selective Service Act that had allowed men from twenty-one to thirty years of age to enlist. It included coloreds. But no war was truly ours unless it was fought on American soil.

"All I can say to you is good luck and may God bless your journey into war."

After taking a few more questions, it was time to leave. Trying to save humans from their own demise took away all my energy. Although the sky was darkening, I couldn't go straight home. After the meeting, I went back to my office and wrote a letter to be printed in the *Herald*.

When I finally made it home, I had to take a seltzer for my headache. There was also a wound on my leg that stubbornly would not heal. I had tried a salve of tobacco and aloe vera, but nothing seemed to do the job. Momma said it was because I had eaten too much sugar. Although we loved it, it was not good for us.

When I got down on my knees, I prayed for the soldiers and the men, hoping that entry into a war would help them be accepted once they returned to American soil. When the soldiers would come home, the St. Luke Penny Savings Bank would be the one colored bank willing to take their war bonds, even if the white banks wouldn't.

❦

A few months later, I received a letter with an overseas stamp from Eugene. His letter was weathered from all the travel in cargo ships across the sea. It read, "Mrs. Maggie, I lucked up and got put into the 369th Infantry. We are in France fighting for our lives. We are in the trenches, just like them white boys. Some people call us Doughboys, the French call us Bronze Fighters, but I overheard someone say the Germans call us Hell fighters. Mrs. Maggie, it is strange, but the French people treat us better than the Americans."

My prayers had been answered. Eugene Thomas had found his way to New York and joined the 93rd Division and ended up in the 369th Infantry Regiment, just like he'd hoped. Booker T. Washington had made sure we were all informed about the activities in the Great War. He was determined to see to it that Negro soldiers were treated well. I could feel the joy of finding that overseas in Eugene's letter.

The right to vote was one of the expectations the soldiers felt would come out of serving in a war in which they were as misunderstood as the reasons for fighting. Coloreds were not allowed to vote, based on the Grandfather

Clause. The clause was unfair in that it maintained that a man could only vote if his grandfather had voted before him. Poll taxes, literacy tests, voting fraud, violence, and all sorts of intimidation tactics kept Negroes from voting. But the NAACP successfully fought against the Grandfather Clause in court. Before the war, the U.S. Supreme Court's *Guinn v. United States* ruling in 1915 had granted freed people in Maryland and Oklahoma the right to vote. Hopefully the war would inspire many of the other southern states to follow suit.

I wrote back to Eugene, yet I was afraid the war would be over before he received my response, or that it wouldn't reach him because he might have been left for dead in a trench in France or Germany.

Eugene's letter lay heavy on my heart. That night at dinner, I read the letter to the family. Everyone listened with eager ears. Just knowing a war was being fought across the waters had me and everyone in the house concerned.

"I just hope my letter reaches him," I said. "I have prayed for the troops and especially for the colored boys, who I hope are being treated fairly."

"Me, too, Momma," Polly said.

Russell just listened without commenting. Hattie occasionally shook her head in disgust as I read his letter. Then, just when we had ingested it all, Polly couldn't contain her thoughts.

"Do you think he will make it home?"

"I certainly hope so."

Finally, Russell leaned back and said, "I guess now is as good a time as any. I have planned on enlisting into the service, too."

When he said that my entire being stood still. I was numb. What was my son doing?

Hattie was so upset, tears welled up in her eyes and trickled down her cheeks.

Melvin just gazed at us in silence. I wasn't sure if he already knew or was thinking about what his brother had just said.

"You can't go, Russell," I said.

He peered over at me. "Why not?"

Before I could answer him, Hattie blurted it out: "Because I'm pregnant, that's why."

Hattie being pregnant was a symphony to my ears. She probably had said the one thing that would save my son from the tragedies of war.

We were all elated to learn of the new addition to the family, and Russell couldn't contain himself.

Hattie asked him, "Do you want to leave us, Russell?"

Russell did not hesitate to answer her. "No, I will be with you, Hattie. I will be with my family."

Russell got up from the table and went over to his wife. He wiped the tears from her face with his hand and kissed her on the cheek.

I finally could breathe. My joy came from being around my family. And seemingly everybody at the table was suddenly put at ease.

✦c✦

While our men fought on foreign soil, the fight continued in Richmond.

Annabelle, Mr. Walter's wife, had become a valued friend. She was devastated when Armstead passed and felt that the least she could do was try to comfort me during my time of bereavement. Over time she had been of great assistance to increase the membership of the NAACP and our women's organization.

One of Mary's sons had attempted to sign up for the Selective Service, but was turned away because he wasn't quite old enough. He missed being twenty-one by one month. A lot of men had changed their ages to fit the Selective Service requirement. I was glad to hear his unfortunate news. Mary was happy as well. Just like any mother, she wanted her child home and out of harm's way. Too many intelligent and able-bodied colored boys would never see American soil again.

"Maggie, I am not going to stay cramped up in this house any longer. The children are grown now," Mary told me.

Mary shared her concerns with me in a conversation in her kitchen while we sipped our evening tea. Otis was listening from the other room. He was always lurking whenever I visited. When he overheard what she said to me, he came into the kitchen and pulled up a chair, scraping it across the wood floorboards, the sound shrill against my eardrums.

He peered over at me. "Maggie," he said, "you's a single woman now. I don't want you introducing Mary to any of them mens you encounter. Armstead understood you, but I don't. You ain't never acting like a woman. You's hanging around talking business with men most of the time."

Mary's face was perplexed; her eyes were slits, and I could see the anger stirring up with each breath. Suddenly her smile had been replaced with a scowl. She gazed over at Otis in silence, anger and embarrassment seething beneath the surface.

I answered before Mary could utter a word. "We have people fighting overseas—colored men—and all you can think about is Mary meeting another man? We have things going on in this community right now that need our attention. The last thing we need to worry about is your insecurities."

He stuttered, "Now, Maggie Walker, you are not going to talk to me that way in my own home. You can leave right now." He pointed to the door.

I rolled my eyes and continued to speak. Otis was always making idle threats and then apologizing for them. I meant every word I had said to him. There was nothing to hide or be ashamed of. It was time he paid attention to the liberation of colored people and stopped watching Mary like a hawk.

"Otis, we have troops in Europe fighting a war just so the United States can claim authority over countries like Germany, Spain, Belgium, and France. But as the war continues, I am getting word that our colored soldiers are not being given the proper clothes to wear and very little training. This is a bad situation. The members of the fraternal orders, the NAACP, and the National Colored Women's Clubs must print this and write to our government officials demanding things be equal. All I'm asking is for someone to help me. And I know I can count on Mary."

With veins bulging from his neck and a stiff face, Otis could barely contain his anger. "Didn't you say a few months ago that Eugene said he was treated better in France than he was here in the States?"

"He may be treated better there, but that is not the case for all our troops. We want equality in training and treatment. Do you know more than twenty thousand colored boys left the country from Virginia alone?"

"What difference would it make for my wife to work with you on this?"

"Otis, look around you! Aren't things better than they were twenty-five years ago?"

He was silent, gathering his thoughts. His facial muscles contracted; his beady eyes twitched as he searched his mind for counterarguments.

"I need your help, too, Otis," I told him. "The NAACP needs *all* of us to work for equality for our soldiers. There is hard-core separatism and segregation here *and* in the U.S. Army, wherever they may find themselves. Yet our men are overseas fighting for a cause that is not theirs to fight."

Finally, Mary got tired of our arguing. Though she had a temper of her own at times, she was mostly soft-spoken. Even in the heat of the discussion, her tone remained calm.

"I want to help Maggie and whomever else is helping her on this. We are one people, and the least we can do is stay together and try to make things better for us coloreds. Now, in the past, from time to time, I have volunteered and even worked at the Order part-time, rushing home to fix dinner for you and the children immediately after. But our children are grown now. And Otis, it's about time you cook for me instead."

I took a deep breath, knowing Otis was going to blow a gasket at her last statement. And yet, for the first time, he surprised me. Instead of shouting in anger, he solemnly said, "I would do anything for you, Mary. Even cook. But Maggie, don't you go and introduce her to any of them old men that are part of them organizations you work with."

I cringed, wondering why Otis was so set on thinking that this was my goal. At times, I wished I hadn't introduced Mary to Otis! We had work to do, and appeasing Otis was not one of our tasks.

In the evenings, a group of us would gather and write letters to the governor, the mayor, and even to President Woodrow Wilson demanding that our troops be treated with the same attention and respect as the Caucasian soldiers. Besides, they were fighting for the same country.

As expected, John Mitchell Jr. printed these concerns in the *Richmond Planet*. We all had to stand up and present a united front. Oftentimes, he was the only man around our meeting table, and he didn't seem to mind it one bit.

We called our renewed efforts for equal treatment the New Negro Movement. Word of it spread throughout the South and the North. Colored musicians, artists, and poets began to include commentary on the colored plight in their works.

✦C✦

Joy came into our lives on February 16, 1918. Hattie gave birth to a beautiful little girl. With the war still going on, this was what our family needed.

Seeing the little baby brought tears to my eyes. She was the prettiest child I'd ever seen.

When Hattie handed her to me to hold, I had almost forgotten what it was like to care for someone so little. I held her close to my chest. Then Hattie said, "We named her after you, Momma."

I couldn't believe my ears. "What is her name?" I asked, staring down at the precious new addition to our family.

"Her name is Maggie Laura."

Russell didn't say much, but he puffed his chest out like a bird. He was a proud man.

Maggie Laura seemed to enjoy being in my arms. She balled up and cuddled as close as she could to me. *My namesake*, I thought.

Russell immediately began to change. He stopped drinking and took on being a father as his dad had done. He loved Maggie Laura and held her often. At night he would rock her to sleep and feed her an occasional bottle of cow's milk. At his job, he worked exceptionally hard. The staff raved about a modernized report on the insurance tables he created, and how the tables changed the insurance payments to a better cost-benefit analysis for our patrons. All his intelligent and smart efforts had directly increased the success of the Independent Order of St. Luke's insurance policies. Russell finally had something to live for.

We enjoyed exactly four months of sobriety and productivity before Russell announced once more that he had enlisted. When Maggie Laura was just four months old, Russell took his sweet child and wife with him to Fort Wayne, in Detroit, Michigan, to begin officer training in June 1918, leaving us somber all over again just as the world was beginning to contend with another threat.

CHAPTER 26

1918–1919

WHEN THE SOLDIERS returned home in 1918, with a few following in 1919, some of them had their chests puffed out and all of them had wide smiles spread across their faces. They were proud to have served in the Great War. The end was celebrated around the world with fireworks and guns fired in the air. It was the signal of the final closing of a war no one really understood. There were parties everywhere. Folks played music and paraded down the streets as if they had conquered the enemy, though the true enemy had not yet been vanquished.

Back home, colored soldiers couldn't find the jobs that the government had promised them for serving. And yet white men were granted government positions, and it tore them to pieces. They soon fell back into the same disheartening rut.

Still, during it all, the bank kept growing. The amount of money we lost during the war wasn't large enough to hurt our business or compromise the quality of our services. I made sure that we continued to focus our efforts on job equality and economic security. I asked the soldiers to deposit their war bonds and cash in our bank. Though they did, I noticed that the smiles they'd come home with were slowly starting to falter until they disappeared entirely.

The members of the Order were terribly upset by how the war had turned out. And how the government had not followed through on their promises to the colored men who had fought bravely for their country, just as the white men had.

After the war was over, some twenty-five race riots were reported throughout the country. Nothing had improved, other than the amount of liquor being sold. The soldiers were drinking away their troubles, and their anger was being taken out on their wives and children. Abuse was on the rise, and colored women needed support and liberation more than ever. I took it upon myself to speak to the owners of the liquor stores and lounges. I begged the barkeepers at the establishments to set a drink limit. I knew some of the libations came from bootleggers, and I couldn't do much about them.

"You are messing with my money now, Maggie," one barkeeper said.

"Your pockets won't suffer that much," I replied. "I promise. Just help me keep families together by sending husbands home less liquored and less inclined to take their grievances out on their wives. Women have been fleeing their homes because their husbands are sick with alcohol, the stench of it oozing out of every pore."

"Don't blame me for their thirst," he said. "Blame the white politicians who broke their promises to them. As a matter of fact, weren't you and the NAACP supposed to be protecting them from this very problem?"

"Ridding the nation of racial disparities takes time."

"More like the government never intends to make any changes. I'm telling you, it's all for nothing."

He struck a nerve. With my voice low but my words sharp, I said, "Look at our community. We are one of the richest colored neighborhoods in America. *We* are doing our part. *You* need to help me by keeping our men sober. We are nothing without family and support."

He shook his head. "Are you joking? You can't stop a man from doing what he wants to do."

"Just watch me," I said without the hint of a grin.

I knew that just asking men to practice moderation was not going to stop them from drowning their sorrows in whiskey, but I knew the bartender could tell the drinker why he couldn't continue serving him the booze, and that might change his mind. For most of them, their family was all they had.

Before my efforts could take effect, a deadlier sickness came knocking on our doors: the Spanish flu. The *Richmond Planet* ran a headline that read, "The American Influenza Epidemic Is Here."

A neighborhood friend, Mae Ellen Calloway, blacked out and fell on the cobblestone street, blood gushing from her head. They tried to slow down the bleeding, but she had been stricken by the influenza and the head injury had made it worse. She never recovered.

"She got that disease, the pandemic that's floating around here—the respiratory one," one of the bank tellers told me.

❦

August 1918 had been a scorcher in Virginia. The heat and humidity of Petersburg was at an all-time high, beads of sweat dripping from the brows of the soldiers twenty-five miles south of Richmond. The first case of influenza was reported in an army base—Fort Lee. A new inductee had been admitted to the infirmary on a Friday evening in September with symptoms of severe respiratory disease; he was struggling to breathe and prone to coughing. The Army doctors suspected it was the flu. Within a few hours, ten more cases of the new malady were reported in different parts of the base. By mid-September, that number had grown by five hundred people. Though Russell was nearly seven hundred miles away at the time, I prayed the Spanish flu wouldn't reach him in Fort Wayne, Michigan.

Just like in Petersburg, Richmond's epidemic spread like wildfire. Al-

though the first case was reported in February 1918, it hit Richmond hard
that summer. Within a few days, the city had more than six hundred con-
firmed cases. A plea went out for every man or woman, white or colored, with
any nursing experience to lend a hand.

Jackson Ward residents were afraid. They didn't know what to do. And
trusting the government left a sour taste in their mouths. They had already
been left out of jobs and now a flu was circulating without a cure or a real way
to keep people from getting sick.

Doctors were crying, "Ventilation is key! Use fans to keep the air circulating out of your home." But people were still getting sick. Word of Mae Ellen
Calloway dying had spread throughout Jackson Ward, and people were confused by the diagnosis of a respiratory infection. The disease was unpredict-
able. Folks sprang their windows wide open, but no matter what they did, the
number of fatalities kept increasing.

Mary stopped by my house with a handkerchief over her nose and mouth.
So anxious, she held her chest when she sat down at my kitchen table.

"Maggie, what can we do? Folks keep being claimed by this disease. I can
hardly breathe myself. I've been putting camphor oil on my chest and drinking
hot tea every hour. It is getting better, but Mr. Walter's funeral parlor is full of dead
colored folks. He can hardly keep up with the demand for funeral services!"

"Calm down, Mary," I said as she gasped for air. Her chest was heaving
up and down.

Her eyes were bloodshot. It was obvious she was sick. I put a handkerchief around my face like a mask to protect myself. With how fast the
disease was spreading, I was sure it was highly contagious. I reached for the
kettle and filled it with water to boil on the stove. Mary sipped at the mixture
of apple cider vinegar, honey, and hot water that I served her, and I waited
until her breathing slowed down and her anxiety subsided. The warmth of
the drink had soothed her cough for now.

When she could talk without hacking, she said, "We've got to do something, Maggie."

"I know, but right now you need to go home and get some rest," I said, patting her vigorously on the back as her cough returned. "You won't be any good to anyone sick." She nodded and I walked her to the door, watching her go in her Ford Motor Company Model T.

On October 5, with outbreaks in nearly every community across Virginia and more than two thousand cases in Richmond alone, the Virginia Department of Health issued a recommendation advising local health departments to ban all public gatherings and close churches, theaters, movie houses, and other such places. School closures were not recommended; instead, teachers were asked to monitor students and to send home sick children. It wasn't long before they realized the schools needed to be closed also.

I promptly went into the *Herald* office and printed stories about the disease and how it was affecting the Negro community. John Mitchell Jr. did the same, but he warned me, "Maggie, this is something we need to get to all the people."

"I already have a plan in mind," I told him. "I am going to drive to the homes and businesses in Jackson Ward and other colored neighborhoods to spread the word in the morning. Winter is around the corner, and we need to work as quickly as possible." John agreed to do the same.

The next morning, after a breakfast of oats and tea, Momma laced up my corset and I headed to the businesses and homes in Jackson Ward. It was misty outside, a northern wind gust blowing the cold that would soon take hold of the South, as the frost lined the ground. But with the flu in the air, I was a bit fearful. I knocked on doors and sat in unwanted chairs and scolded the people about what was happening, pleading with them to stay out of crowds and places where the flu could be transmitted easily.

"Maggie, we have businesses to run and things to take care of," Amos Hart said. Instead of trying to convince him to stay home, I asked him this question: "Amos, do you want to live?"

Afterward he tucked his head and said, "I suppose you make sense."

It wasn't long before influenza cases approached their peak in Richmond. The ill-funded city health department launched a fifty-thousand-dollar fund-raiser for influenza care. These funds were used to convert the city's John Marshall High School into an emergency hospital. In keeping with southern patterns of racial segregation, white patients were treated in the main area, while colored patients were treated in the basement. People from all sectors of Richmond society stepped forward to volunteer at the hospital.

One day, Governor Westmoreland Davis telephoned me, and then his wife paid a visit to my office at St. Luke Hall. "Maggie, we need your help with the colored people," she said, standing in my office after refusing to take a seat, her small way of "maintaining" that she had more power than me, even though she was coming to me for help. Governor Davis had been accused of liking me too much, and Mrs. Davis wanted to make it clear that she would not take such rumors lightly and they did not earn me any favor.

I cleared my throat and said, "What help are you looking for, Mrs. Davis?"

"We need someone to inform and help the Negroes who are sick. We need y'all coloreds to do your part about stopping the spread of this disease that's going around. They must take the precautions necessary to survive. And if you can get a few of your nurses to volunteer, I think we can get a hold on this terrible disease."

I immediately volunteered.

Mrs. Davis had never been one to converse with me on my previous visits to the governor, yet she had always been cordial. Her tone was that of a true southern belle, polite with a syrupy southern drawl.

When she left my office at the Order, I began the task of making sure my people were given the necessary care to survive the pandemic.

I drove over to the emergency hospital based at John Marshall High School. I knew about the importance of care, as I was a member of the American Red Cross and had established a colored branch in Richmond. Anything the whites had, we had also. At times I was tired, but there was no way I could allow Jim Crow–minded white folks to impede and prevent colored folks from the care we all deserved.

The hospital was in complete disarray. No one knew how to treat this disease and the nurses at the hospital did all they could to make sure the patients were fed, hydrated, and drenched in alcohol to lower their fevers. More than two hundred patients occupied the building, all being attended by just a few nurses.

I persuaded Mary and Edith to come along with me to volunteer at the hospital. Mary had thankfully recovered. Edith was reluctant at first but gathered her things and came along anyway.

"Finally, the white people admit they need us. Can you imagine serving beside the white nurses?" Mary commented on our way to the hospital.

"When there is a great enough need, I suppose color can be put aside," I replied, and Mary grunted.

But that thought was short-lived. Inside the hospital, there were people everywhere. Some were coughing, others barely breathing. We put on masks and began to assist in the care.

"Where are the colored patients?" I asked.

The nurses ignored me. Again I asked, "Where are the colored patients?"

I looked one of them dead in the eyes and forced them to make eye contact with me. Before I could ask again, she said, "They are being cared for in the basement."

Immediately, Mary, Edith, and I took off down the stairs to the basement. The chill from below blasted us as we made our way down, as all the windows were wide open. The wind was blowing the thin sheets covering the patients, making them shiver besides exhibiting the same symptoms as the white patients upstairs. It was clear they wouldn't survive long under these dire conditions, and I had to hold back tears. *How could they ask us to help save the white community and overlook our own?*

I began to ask more questions of the nurses while attending to the coloreds who were dying in the basement.

At one point I had to raise my voice. "Why are they separated from the rest of the patients? Why are they freezing to death? That's not ventilation, it's torture!" The nurses listened, but not one of them had an answer.

Without hesitation, I left the hospital and went straight to Governor Davis's office. Because of our business relationship, his staff was used to me and didn't give me any problems entering his spacious office, adorned with fine Italian furniture similar to what was in my own.

His eyes gleamed at the sight of me. "Well, what can I do for you, Maggie?"

He wasn't wearing a mask, but I kept my own on for safety reasons.

"There has been a huge oversight down at the John Marshall emergency hospital."

"I am aware of the need for more nurses and health care assistants." He ran his hand through his hair and straightened up his bow tie.

"Governor Davis, the colored patients are not receiving any care. They are being thrown in the basement, basically left to die," I said matter-of-factly, cutting right to my reason for barging in unannounced.

He peered at me with seductive eyes, as he usually did, not seeming to really pay attention to what I was saying. Ignoring his gaze, I forged ahead.

"I need supplies and a place to house the colored patients where they can actually heal rather than freeze to death. I cannot allow them to be mistreated like this."

"So, what do you need from me?"

I provided him with a list of things I needed, including money to fund the purchase of medical supplies and medicine.

On October 15, I converted the Baker School in North Jackson Ward into an emergency hospital for colored folk. We were still segregated, but that was a battle for another day. At least here, coloreds could be treated without discrimination. Then I requested staff members. Only the best would do for us.

A group of twenty-two Black physicians met to organize the staff for Baker, and elected Dr. William H. Hughes as their chief, with others volunteering their services. Colored emergency hospitals were being set up across the nation. In Philadelphia, they solicited the best physicians as well. We were not going to let our people succumb to the racial disparities in health care. I put all my supporters to work. Some tended to the bank, and others worked with the NAACP, National Association of Colored Women's Clubs, and all the organizations for our betterment.

With social distancing measures in place, officials turned their attention to the city's health care system and its overworked nurses and physicians. Dr. Roy Flannagan, Richmond's chief health officer, divided Richmond into four sectors and assigned a doctor, nurses, and volunteers to each to eliminate duplicate efforts. The Richmond Academy of Medicine and Surgery issued an appeal for all specialists to lend their aid, as did the Red Cross and the Visiting Nurses' Association. The latter worked with Richmond's churches to establish soup kitchens to feed families too sick to feed themselves or where the primary breadwinner had fallen ill and the family had lost those wages. At the request of the United States Public Health Service, the Red Cross had fifteen thousand pamphlets printed with recommendations on how to keep healthy.

Richmond's resources were being taxed to the limit. Milk was in short supply, partly owing to the number of sick dairy and distribution employees and partly due to physicians recommending it as nourishment for the ill. The shortage had grown so severe that city inspectors visited the Richmond jail to select inmates for work in the dairy farms. Some even expected the city to take over the dairies. The city was frantic, everyone concerned about their lives and survival. As I worked, I prayed for my family and their health.

A lot of good men and women were lost in the pandemic. Brilliant minds who'd helped keep the bank going through everything that had been thrown at them, but had ultimately been claimed by the virus. There was not enough time to mourn them properly; hospitals were full and so were the funeral parlors. I was doing everything I could to stanch the flow of bodies to the parlor. But I wanted to honor them, as I was grateful. I would honor them as soon as the pandemic was gone and time allowed.

As promised by Governor Davis, masks and alcohol were sent to the Baker School and we went to work. It took education and effort, and lives were being saved.

As we gained control over the sickness, the undertakers were elated. They had so many dead bodies stored in their parlors. It took days to embalm them, and a pungent stench had begun to encircle the air around them. Many people were afraid of this flu, which the Americans blamed on the Spanish. It was a sad time in Richmond.

CHAPTER 27

1919–1921

THE WAR OFFICIALLY ENDED on November 11, 1918, but a few of the colored soldiers stayed in France to help clean up the mess. Not all of them returned. Some were left across the sea in unmarked graves, and others were shipped back to the States in body bags.

The war affected our soldiers in so many ways, harming not just their bodies by claiming limbs or worse, but their minds as well. And yet, they all felt like they had not suffered in vain.

Those who returned were dubbed the "Harlem Hell Fighters," and they marched down the streets in Manhattan like heroes. We were all there to cheer them on. I drove to New York with my family for the occasion, although I was skeptical about taking my son Russell.

However, God had answered our prayers.

The war had ended before Russell could be deployed and he never saw a day of combat.

All of us were silently happy. Then, during the trip to New York City, Russell boldly announced that he was not going back to Richmond with us. He had made plans to stay in the city for a while.

"I just need a break," he said, shaking either from nervousness or alcohol withdrawal.

I was not happy with his decision. However, I realized he needed to be away from the ghost of his father and the constant reminder of what he did if he ever had a hope of truly getting sober. We all understood, with the exception of Hattie. She longed to have her loving husband, the businessman and caregiver, back for good.

Russell was on all our minds. How on earth could we ever help him?

Before leaving the state, I visited my friend W. E. B. Du Bois and asked him to keep an eye on him. As usual, he was glad to do it.

When we came back to Richmond, we had a celebration of our own. Pearl Brown headlined at a nightclub called the Colored Virginian, and everyone showed up, including her husband, Willie Brown, outfitted in his Army dress uniform and boots to his knees. It was a jolly good time.

❖○❖

I fell on my knees and prayed so fervently, my knees grew so stiff I could barely stand. I had been experiencing leg pain, and at times it was getting worse. But I had so much to be thankful for, and I was grateful to God. My job as bank president at times was grueling. My health was failing, but I had said many times, "I would rather die trying than give up." So, I lived by my mantra and prayed my children would have the same tenacity.

The Spanish flu was finally being contained. No one knew its true origin, but most believed it had traveled to the States with the returning soldiers of the Great War. By wearing masks and using alcohol as an antiseptic, we had managed to control the death toll, which exceeded 675,000 people across the nation by the end. It took two years for the virus to extinguish itself. And the rebels who refused to comply with safety precautions fell to their death regretting that they had not listened to the physicians and health officials from the start. I knew it was the grace of God that had kept me and my family from catching it ourselves.

Back home, Momma was getting on in her years. She had begun to slow down, and her mind wasn't as sharp as it had been. Melvin and Polly did their best to take care of her whenever I was away. Russell was in an almost constant daze, his eyes bloodshot from the cheap liquor and wine he was always drinking. It was difficult to have a conversation with him at all anymore.

Russell was drinking liquor like water to drown his guilt and feed his depression. After spending more than a year in New York City and then another six months in Alabama at the Tuskegee Institute, auditing their books, he had found his way back home.

"Russell," I begged, "please have some water, son. It's not healthy for anyone to cling to the liquor bottle the way you do."

He glared at me with Armstead's hazel-brown eyes and said, "You know why I just can't do that, Momma." Tears welled up in his eyes.

It tore me apart, watching him dwindle down to nearly nothing, physically thin and bent—his body transforming to match the way he felt inside. It was shameful to be able to care for everyone in Jackson Ward, yet my own home was out of sorts. Russell might be the only one I'd failed. We all tried to help him, and at times we could see him improving, going for weeks without a drink, yet he was never the same. And soon the ghost of Armstead Walker would call him back to the bottle, and he was never strong enough to tell the devil to go. Not even his precious baby girl, two-year-old Maggie Laura, could keep him from self-medicating with liquor.

Over a meal I'd prepared of corn pudding, turnip greens, and sliced ham, I gathered my children and apologized for not being home enough. "I hope you can forgive me."

Melvin said, "Momma, you make it home for dinner every night and we travel with you whenever you are called away. We don't feel your absence, so there's nothing to be sorry about." He was so much like Armstead, always supporting and uplifting me.

"There's still so much work to do," I said. It was my constant refrain. "We have done a lot in Jackson Ward, but there is always plenty more that can be done."

"Is something in particular weighing heavily on you, Momma?" Polly asked me.

"I have been doing this my entire life. I started attending church and familiarizing myself with the Order around twelve years of age. We've done a lot of good over the years. Our community is almost completely self-sufficient now. But something horrible has happened to a neighborhood just like ours in Tulsa, Oklahoma, and I hear that other communities like ours are also falling under harsher scrutiny . . ." I trailed off and rubbed my forehead before continuing. "When will this racial divide end?"

"Momma, because of people like you, it *will* end. It might just take a bit more time," Polly said, knowing it would take a village to get anything done.

Russell listened, and then asked, "Are we going to have any wine with this meal?"

I quickly responded, "No, son. This meal does not call for wine. It is one of sober minds and love." Russell shook his head.

My son was gone. He was not the same man anymore, and even his family had fallen apart. His wife's smile had been replaced with a frown and Russell had not noticed any of it, but he smiled at the sight of Maggie Laura. Even though he literally drowned in guilt. Armstead would have spoken to him and said he'd been forgiven if he could, but the ghost of guilt showed up instead.

Momma bowed her head and silently prayed to herself. Her lips moved, but nothing came out.

"Are you all right, Momma?" I asked her.

"Yes, I am fine. I just wanted to have a brief talk with God." And whatever she prayed about, Russell seemed to notice, and his disposition changed. It was a miracle, for sure, because he even appeared to enjoy his family for the first time in months. No one knows what Momma said, but Russell loved her so much, he would do anything to try to please her.

Polly giggled as she said, "We all need a talk with God!" I just shook my head.

My children were all grown, yet they still lived in my home. I loved it that way and had insisted on them adding their spouses. We all took care of each other. And because of my bold business moves, I had been approached with many threats. None of them were substantial enough for me to quit. Besides, the Bible said, God had given us the power to conquer over snakes and scorpions and no harm would come to me. I believed and had faith.

Mary McLeod Bethune and I had been writing detailed letters back and forth concerning the facts and rumors about the Greenwood community. The massacre had us all upset and in a frenzy about what was happening in Tulsa, Oklahoma.

"Children," I said, "if hateful folks can attack the 'Black Wall Street' in Tulsa, I fear they may do the same to our 'Black Wall Street' here in Richmond. Like them, we own our businesses and purchase from our own merchants. We're much the same."

"Momma, you wrote about this in the *Herald*. We read your newspaper, too. What is the concern about Jackson Ward?" Russell commented, as he was always reading everything.

"This type of behavior from jealous racists is spreading across the nation. Mary McLeod Bethune is concerned about Rosewood, Florida. There are rumors they want to dismantle everything we have put together. I can't let them take us backward, children."

Melvin and Polly looked concerned. Russell appeared to be tuned in to the conversation also, glancing up at me from time to time. He had been quieter since his daddy's death, yet I knew he had lots of grand thoughts floating through his mind. He was intelligent and sensitive. Momma focused on her plate.

"Do you know what really happened in Greenwood?" Polly asked.

"When it comes to these things," I said, "no one really knows the truth. However, it was reported that a young colored boy raped a white lady and took advantage of her without her permission. At least, she made it seem that way. But in this world people make up stories all the time."

"Whatever happened to the man?"

"He was eventually incarcerated, but the evidence was not very clear. Although the colored men, including veterans, guarded him while in jail for fear of a lynching, a cruel group of white men sought to destroy the town to which the man retreated after being attacked by more than fifteen hundred white men. They burned down the place just last month. We can't let that happen here. More than twelve hundred homes and businesses were destroyed. And hundreds of people were killed."

Melvin stood up and walked around the kitchen table to put his hands on my shoulders. "Momma, we know you will think of something to do. Everyone around Richmond and the country knows how strong you are. You make me want to do better, too. The only thing missing is how you and Daddy would put your heads together during these times"—he glanced up at the light fixture—"but I'm sure he is watching over us."

I put my hand on Melvin's. "I think you are right, son."

"What about Ms. Mary? Will she be all right down in Florida?"

"Yes, child. Right now, things are stable, but only God knows what might happen. They are angry everywhere we are gaining in economic independence. They are watching Harlem, Atlanta, and North Carolina, too. You see, jealousy is a strange bedfellow. Whenever we try to relieve them of any care for coloreds, there is a struggle for control. Only God knows why, my child!"

Russell and Momma were silent most of the meal, but everyone enjoyed the food, especially the corn pudding, which was loaded with sugarcane syrup. It was mighty tasty, if I did say so myself.

After the meal was over, we all cleaned the kitchen together. Polly washed the dishes, and Momma and I put the leftover food in containers and placed them in the icebox for the next day. Russell handled the trash and Melvin mopped the floor. Before retiring to bed that evening, I sat in the parlor alone and sipped on a glass of red wine, something I rarely did, but it was for a me-dicinal purpose, to relax the jitters inside.

The next morning, even before the birds started chirping, I put on my navy-blue dropped-waist dress, adorned with my butterfly broach and hat, ready for a visit with Governor Davis.

"You look very nice this morning, Maggie. To what do I owe this visit?" Governor Davis's eyes twinkled at the sight of me.

"Governor, may I have a seat?"

"Yes, of course," he said, gesturing to the chair in front of his large ma-hogany desk.

"It's a pleasure seeing you, as always," he said. "The way you handled the pandemic in your community, well, I don't think we could've done as well without you."

"Thank you, sir," I said, smiling, and added, "It took a lot of effort from everyone to get some control on it. We appreciate your contribution. The supplies you sent us saved many lives."

He smiled. "Now, Maggie, you are one of the few colored people that have my full respect. You know that."

"Why is that?"

"I admire your tenacity and persistence," he said with a small smile.

"Thank you, sir." As his gaze lingered on me a minute too long, I cleared my throat. "Governor, I know you must be aware of the atrocities being committed around the country. For example, the massacre that took place in Tulsa, Oklahoma, just recently, destroying the Greenwood community there."

"Yes, I am aware of the unfortunate situation in Tulsa."

"And, what are you planning to do?"

"Frankly, I have not given it much thought. My time and energy are best spent keeping this state running. I don't have a mind to interfere in another governor's jurisdiction. Why do you ask?" he said nonchalantly.

"I have worked tirelessly to make sure the members of our Jackson Ward community feel they are safe, are treated well, and have the opportunity to be productive in prosperous ways."

"I'm quite aware of this, Maggie. There is no need to convince me of your self-worth. I know you are one of the most progressive people I know. Nothing can stop you when you put your mind to it. Not even me," he said, chuckling.

"I want your assurance that nothing even close to resembling the situation in Tulsa will happen in Jackson Ward. It is a good place with good people. We do not interfere with the other merchants and homeowners. We tend to keep to ourselves and take care of our own."

"Maggie, have I told you that you are one of the most beautiful colored women I have ever seen?" He took a moment to gaze at me for a little too long again, then continued: "It is so difficult to say no to you. I will do my best to keep anything even close to what happened in Oklahoma away from Jackson Ward. Besides, I don't need any of that kind of trouble here in Richmond."

I always had to brace myself before meeting with Governor Davis. The way he gazed at me sent uneasy chills down my spine. I didn't like it, yet I knew I had to tolerate it if I was to keep him on my side for the sake of our community.

Governor Davis was a man of his word. Each time I had asked for his help, it was rendered. When he was elected in 1917, he was a welcome change from the other Virginia governors I had done business with, yet all of them eventually worked with me. It was rumored that Governor Davis had been poor prior to finishing law school and earning his wealth in progressive New York City. I always thought maybe his experiences there had allowed him to be more sympathetic to colored folks' economic growth. Most of the time, he complimented me on how well the bank had prospered, which I always thanked him for. But he was still a politician.

"Thank you, sir. I do appreciate your time and consideration," I responded graciously, and stood to leave his office. But before I made it to the door, he shuffled past and opened the door for me.

That evening, I wrote a letter to Mary, Booker, and W. E. B., letting them know I had started to build my fortress against the destruction of Negro wealth in Jackson Ward. I informed the community in the next issue of the *Herald*, and John Mitchell Jr. followed suit in the *Planet*. We were going to retain the progress we had made, and with God's strength help inform other progressive colored communities.

CHAPTER 28

1921

ON SEPTEMBER 5, 1921, the Black Republicans meeting was attended by more than six hundred colored delegates from across the United States. We had decided it was time to run for office. On an all-colored ticket, the nominees listed were John Mitchell Jr. for governor; Theodore Nash of Portsmouth for lieutenant governor; myself, Maggie Lena Walker of Richmond, for superintendent of public instruction; Joseph Newsome of Newport News for attorney general; Thomas E. Jackson of Staunton for treasurer; F. V. Bacchus of Lynchburg for secretary of the commonwealth; J. L. Reed of Roanoke for state corporation commissioner; and A. P. Brickhouse of Northampton County for commissioner of agriculture.

Just the thought of one colored person on the ballot would certainly draw attention our way, but an entire ticket? Besides, Governor Davis had said he would endorse my one nomination, but I was not sure if he would support a colored slate.

We decided to run on a "Lily Black" slate, as opposed to "Lily White," which made people chuckle. Besides, the white Republicans did not want any Blacks on their slate, so we decided to create our own.

"I'd never thought any one of us would call ourselves Lily Black Republicans," F. V. Bacchus said, tickled by the name we'd given ourselves.

The white government officials were infuriated by our audacity. Governor Davis told me, "Now, Maggie, this has gone too far."

I smiled at his comment, knowing this was a monumental event across the entirety of the Jim Crow South.

"Don't worry, sir, you will not regret it if I am elected."

There was plenty of work to do before the election. As usual, I hit the road to garner support, this time for myself. Melvin agreed to drive me around town and across the state to campaign.

"Maggie, you are getting too old for these trips," Momma grumbled as she packed up biscuits and mason jars of drinking water.

"Momma, I'll be fine," I assured her, even though she had to be exhausted by these excursions of mine. Momma was always trying to get me to stay closer to home.

"Melvin, just make sure you put the shotgun under the front seat," Momma demanded.

Melvin grinned and got the shotgun for the ride. He dusted it off, since it had been put away for years; Russell had grown fearful of guns since the accident. The sound of a gun going off during their annual hunting trips with their uncle Andrew made Russell shake like a leaf on a tree. The boy was traumatized.

At the newspaper office, I printed out flyers to ask our neighbors to vote for me, and on the bottom of the flyer I included all the others running for office, too.

A team of mobilizers had gathered at my home. We'd pulled out a map and together marked out a campaign trail for each of the nominees to caravan in a city of their choosing. We had members from the National Association of Colored Women's Clubs, the Independent Order of St. Luke, and the NAACP there. Everyone was excited about what we were attempting to accomplish.

With the ratification of the Nineteenth Amendment giving women the right to vote, I had brought my sister friends into the fold of all the political and financial actions going on in the city. It was finally time for them to exercise their rights, and I was always thrilled that women's intelligence and wisdom would finally be brought into voting booths across the nation.

The recent Tulsa Race Massacre in Greenwood also still had people on edge, and they were more than ready to defend our rights by any means. Having people who identified and resembled us on the ticket was a good place to start.

Several cars hit the road along with me. My caravan had decided to visit places in central Virginia. We traveled to Lynchburg, stopping at all the small towns along the way.

Strangely, many of the people in the countryside were oblivious to colored struggles. They were so used to sharecropping and taking care of white people, it was the norm for them.

I spent hours explaining to some of them the value of their vote and how putting their money in a reliable bank would increase their savings over time.

"We don't vote around chere," said an old lady with braids wrapped around her head and a wad of tobacco in her mouth.

The paint was peeling off her house and her surroundings appeared unkept and disordered. After an hour of talking, she went into the chicken coop and came back with a can the size of a watermelon. When I opened the can, there were many one-dollar bills in it. It was astonishing! Most of the people who banked with me didn't have this amount of money saved in their St. Luke Penny Savings Bank account.

"How long have you been saving this money, ma'am?" I asked her.

"I've been saving ever since I was a little girl. When my daddy give me a penny, I save it. When someone else give me money, I save it. I don't use it. I just make do with what I have. You see, we've got plenty of food around here.

I can grow everything I eat, and my husband, he kill a pig once a year and we smoke the meat. We in good shape."

Her name was Ruth Parrish, and I made sure to take note of it. She handed me the can and told me to open an account for her at my bank. I couldn't help wondering how many other country folks had hidden money somewhere that needed the security of a bank.

"Mrs. Parrish, will you be voting in the coming elections?"

"I don't vote, but my husband do. I'll tell him about you stopping by and get him to vote for y'all."

"Does your husband know about your savings?"

"Hell no. This is the money my daddy told me to keep for me. You can't tell a man e'rything. He ain't gonna tell you e'rything. An' he might see fit to keep what's yours for hisself." I smiled. I liked Mrs. Parrish's spirit.

We refilled our jars at the well by Mrs. Parrish's house. She gave us a cake she had made earlier in the morning using flour from the mill up the road and butter she'd churned herself. It had to be the best cake I'd ever tasted. My children ate greedily of it, too, leaving nothing but crumbs. Momma was a little upset by how much we loved Mrs. Parrish's cake. She had baked a pound cake for our journey as well.

"We will eat your cake on the way home," I assured Momma, trying to soothe her hurt feelings.

"Your children act as if this is the first time they've had a pound cake in their lives."

I could see her frustration, but Mrs. Parrish's cake was simply delicious. The farm-fresh eggs, churned butter, and recently collected cow's milk added a freshness to the flavor of the cake we hadn't tasted before. She even told me she had ground a bit of fresh vanilla and nutmeg for it.

We thanked her for her hospitality and went on our way to make it to the home of Anne Spencer, a civil rights leader and poet, in time to rest there. She gave us beds to sleep in and a dinner of beef and potatoes. I loved stopping by her home during my travels, getting to admire her beautiful garden and, most importantly, listen to her recite her poetry.

Once we made it to Roanoke the next morning, we turned around and started back down the road to Richmond.

I was so proud of our efforts. We had killed two birds with one stone—expanding our banking clientele and rallying people to vote in the upcoming election.

On the way back to Richmond, we took some time to inform country folks of their newly granted rights. Most of them knew only work and were oblivious to the voting processes. However, a few of their eyes gleamed at the thought of a slate of people who looked like them running for government positions. They offered to volunteer to spread the word and bring people out to vote.

Two days before the November 8 elections in 1921, the excitement of voting had newspapers singing. The fervor had taken the capital by storm, with people talking and whispering about nothing else everywhere. Colored folks' eyes danced with excitement while our white compatriots' eyes were solemn with concern.

A mass meeting was called at Richmond's Moore Street Baptist Church to rally voters to support all the colored candidates. Everyone was there, including my good friend Mary McLeod Bethune, who had come in from Florida just for the occasion.

"There wasn't a chance of me missing this historical moment!" she said as soon as she exited the colored section of the train. The porters recognized her and handled her luggage as they would if she were a white person. She smiled and greeted them with a tip.

"I am so glad you are here," I said, and we embraced as sisters do.

That night, people cheered and some even cried as they called out our names. It was the same kind of celebration we had provided for our troops when they came home from war, except this time we were going into political battle.

On Election Day, of course there were people deliberately placed by our opponents to intimidate colored voters as they stepped forward to cast their votes for the Lily Black ballot. We had our poll watchers, too, but the power of skin color at times superseded us, and many of the voters turned around out of fear.

Mary stood at one of the main voters' stations and dared anyone to intimidate colored voters. Her stare unnerved many; she could look right through you without blinking.

One white man said, "Ma'am, you, a colored woman, are daring to glare at me?"

She didn't say a word, just continued to stare. He decided she was a demon. "You's a nigga devil," he muttered, but Mary didn't open her mouth or break eye contact for a second. He ran off with two other men following him.

After he left, we glanced at each other and continued the task of the day: getting every eligible member of our community in to vote. Neither one of us was afraid, nor did we carry ourselves in that manner.

At the end of the day, when the votes were tallied, none of the Lily Black nominees won. But we surprised them with our determination to get a seat at the table and to exercise our right to vote. They knew for certain we would be back again.

CHAPTER 29

1922–1923

MOMMA DIED PEACEFULLY in her sleep on a cold February day in 1922. She had been tired and worn for the final years of her life. She had worked tirelessly for me, making sure my children had a home-cooked meal every evening and someone to greet them at the end of the day while I was working at one office or another.

I knew this day would come. God had shown me in a dream. He'd whispered in my ear softly, "Your mother is getting tired. She is ready to come to her heavenly home with Me."

Momma had been so worried about Russell and his constant drinking in her final days. Seemingly nothing could prevent him from finding a bottle to drink, and nothing else would relax his unsettled nerves.

My parlor and kitchen were cozy safe havens, where we found solace in my home. At times I'd catch Russell sitting in the parlor glowering at his daddy's photograph, unblinking. I knew it was a reminder of that awful evening for him, but for the rest of the family it represented great memories of love and support.

"Russell, can I sit with you?" I asked him, wondering if he would allow me to.

"Sure, Momma," he replied without looking at me.

The parlor had the most comfortable furniture in the house. I had chosen the best pieces from a merchant in Jackson Ward, though some of it was actually custom made. We had a piano in the hallway, which I sometimes played to amuse the family. But not tonight.

I sat down beside Russell. He was a grown man now, at least six feet tall, and had a mustache just like his father. He favored Armstead more than Melvin did, with his hazel-brown eyes.

"I've notice you are spending a lot of time alone," I began. "Maggie Laura and Hattie are wanting your attention, son. Is there anything I can help you with? Maggie Laura beams at the sight of you."

He turned to peer at me. "Momma, I killed my own father. There is no helping me. I just need to think, sometimes."

"Son, we all make mistakes. Had I been the one to sense there might be a burglar, I probably would have aimed and fired as quickly as you did. I would be feeling like you do now. Please, don't be so hard on yourself. Robbers were taking over the neighborhood, and you were defending our family."

He shook his head. "Why can't you understand? There is no healing from this grief or guilt."

"Russell, you have got to put these thoughts out of your head. It was an *accident*. None of us can predict how we will act in those situations. We were all afraid of what could happen to us, including your father. Why do you think he purchased that gun in the first place? It was for our protection."

He put his hand on my arm. "Mom, I love you."

"I love you too, son." I let our love wrap around us for a moment before continuing. "Now, it is beyond time for you to straighten up and enjoy your life. Try to forget what happened and start *living* again." For the first time in years, he smiled.

"I will try, Mom. I promise."

I hugged him so hard, he yelled, "Ow, Mom!" We both giggled.

Afterward, we went upstairs to bed.

After brushing my teeth and bathing, I knelt beside my bed. My prayer that night was for Russell. "He needs You, Lord. Oh, he needs You," I sang out, hoping God could hear my plea and give Russell the strength to fight the demons that were in his head and had taken over his body for years.

It was a terrible feeling to be able to assist everyone around you while you were helpless when it came to your own child. God knows I tried, and so did Momma. She gave him all she had, but Russell could not forgive himself.

The next day, Russell seemed to be showing progress. He joined his brother Melvin to work with their uncle Andrew, who had been their father's partner and an important part of the family business. The Walkers had always taken business seriously, and Armstead had surely passed the torch to his sons. Both were fine construction craftsmen, as was their father. Russell had found more satisfaction in following in my footsteps and worked at the St. Luke Penny Savings Bank. However, the time with his uncle was important to his healing.

That evening, Russell participated in our dinner table conversation. By the look of the faces around the table, we were all surprised but thrilled that he seemed relaxed enough to talk.

"Melvin, Uncle Andrew made sure we earned our wages today," he said.

"He works like a bull himself, and he will not give you a break. But neither did Dad."

"I thought my legs were going to give out from under me. Carrying those bricks is more than a chore."

As I listened to them talk about their day, I quietly thanked the dear Lord for giving Russell the strength he needed to push through his depression.

Russell worked with his brother for a full month, and each night I thanked the Lord for his mercy.

Momma was so thankful for the change in Russell that she made a confession at the breakfast table just days before she died.

"You know I don't have long here on this ol' earth."

"Momma, what are you talking about?"

"Maggie, I am ready to go home to live with the Lord. I done did all I can around here."

"What do you mean, Momma?"

"Well, I asked the Lord to keep me around long enough to see Russell get on his feet."

"Russell is not the only one who needs you."

"Maggie, you are a strong woman. In truth, the woman I always wanted to be. You don't need me. God has always favored you from when you was a tiny little chile. Your curiosity and audacity have steered you well. Though it certainly gave me heart palpitations at times! Lord, I can remember you asking Mrs. Thalhimer about her house. I didn't know what to do! You know we didn't talk that way to white people."

"I got my courage from you. You know, Momma, you are one of the best women in this ol' world. You were my first role model. You taught me how to run a laundry business, and what it truly means to support your family. We never missed a meal thanks to you. You are everything I have ever aspired to be." When I looked up at her, teardrops were sliding down the side of her face.

I knew this was it. Momma had never been so talkative. We spent the rest of dinnertime talking about her days with Ms. Elizabeth Van Lew, and all the people at the mansion.

Afterward, she and Russell played checkers in the parlor and chatted as if there were no one else in the room. She loved him with her whole heart. He was her first grandbaby and had made her a great-grandma. She always went the extra mile for him. He was her heartbeat, and she was his. I left them there and went to bed. Finally, Russell was living again and Momma loved it. His renewal made her perk up in a way she didn't for anyone else.

The next morning, when Momma didn't come downstairs for breakfast, I went upstairs to check on her in her room. I found her lying in bed asleep.

When I shook her foot to wake her, she didn't stir. As I shuffled closer to the side of the bed, I realized she was not breathing. I felt her wrist for a pulse but couldn't find one. She had one hand at her side and the other one on the family Bible. Before going back down the stairs, I closed her eyes and slid in bed beside her, and hugged her body as tears streamed out the corners of my eyes.

We buried Momma near Armstead.

Russell tried to stay focused on work, but losing Momma broke something in him again. Immediately, he started missing days of work. When I approached him, he would say, "Momma, I just didn't want to go today."

"Russell, your grandmother died thinking you had changed and were on the right track." He continued to stare at the photos above the fireplace of Armstead, Momma, and the rest of the family.

"She's not here anymore, either," he said.

Russell loved his grandmother, I believed, more than he did me. I felt their love and I was never bothered by the beautiful bond they shared.

Now he was slipping away again, back into that state of nowhere land. He was drinking again, and there was nothing his wife could do.

Melvin tried to have a conversation with him, while I listened.

"You are going to kill yourself if you don't get it together, Russ."

"I'm not going to kill myself, Melvin," he quickly replied.

"Well, come back to work then. It will help to keep your mind off things."

Russell nodded and joined Melvin the very next day. He got up and dressed for work. He left with Melvin as he had the month before Momma died. But it didn't last more than three days. Missing work had become a habit, and his uncle was getting a little tired of his erratic behavior.

Although it was a family business, his uncle was not one to play when it came to work. Just like Armstead, he was a stickler for quality, and he had a strong dislike for slackers or workers who didn't think earning your wages with a hard day's good work was important.

"Russell, do you even want to be here?" Andrew asked Russell when finally he reappeared at work in the middle of the week.

"Yes, sir," Russell responded.

"Well, just because you are my nephew does not exempt you from doing your job well. The Walkers are hardworking people. We value our family and our trade. Now I know you are dealing with a lot, but we have work to do all over Jackson Ward."

Andrew was loving like Armstead, and had a deep passion for the community and Jackson Ward. He wasn't going to let his own nephew compromise that relationship or the integrity of his work.

Russell went to work every day for about a week, but eventually took a few days off from work again, during which he drank whiskey and did absolutely nothing else.

Again, he spent hours sitting in my high-back paisley chair gazing at the photos of our family. I'd stand in the doorway and watch him look at his daddy and his grandmother in turn. It was the worst feeling. The doctors gave him a pill to make him drowsy, in hopes he would forget about his pain. Nothing worked.

After months of instability, his uncle Andrew fired him.

"You can't fire me," Russell argued with his uncle. But Andrew was tired and realized he would never be the same eager young man who wanted to follow in his daddy's footsteps.

Russell didn't handle it very well.

At home, he stayed in bed until noon. Once up, he'd eat some of the leftover grits and eggs and sit at the kitchen table to eat alone. His wife was so fed up, each day she packed more and more clothes. She was going to leave him, and I didn't blame her for the thought.

Russell began to spend his evenings in the local bars and nightclubs. When he would make it home, he was at times drenched in urine, and so drunk he could not walk up the stairs.

Polly and I would bathe him and put him to sleep like a child. Momma had done it many times before. It was hard on me, seeing my son take his own life for granted. But I did about all I could do.

Polly would whisper to him, "Come on, you can do it."

He would just shake his head.

Soon Russell was in New York working in their branch of the Independent Order of St. Luke while Hattie got a degree at Columbia University. Russell would oscillate between New York and Philadelphia.

On November 23, 1923, I received a phone call from Hattie, who was in Philadelphia.

"Momma, Russell is gone."

I fell apart again. We hadn't been able to save him.

During the 1925 conference of the Independent Order of St. Luke, Russell was honored with a eulogy for all the good work he'd done for the St. Luke Penny Savings Bank. The members signed a memorial card. Russell was now with his dad.

CHAPTER 30

1924

SUGAR SWEETENS UP EVERYTHING, but it was my mortal enemy. Russell's death took a toll on me. At times, I experienced such a loss of energy. I thought it was from grief. But when I finally went to see Dr. Hughes, he informed me I had developed diabetes.

There was still plenty of work to do in Jackson Ward and the surrounding communities of colored people. As the pain increased and the medicine he gave me didn't seem to work, I was left sedentary in many ways.

My main focus had always been on improving the situation of the Negro woman. I had deliberately added them to the workforce at the bank, the insurance company, our newspaper staff, and the emporium. Over the years, they had proved they knew what to do and would work as hard as any man to get things done. Women were not created just for domestic work. Most of the women thanked me when they married, as they added a degree of completion to the marriage. Of course, old-fashioned men still existed, but deep inside they also longed for a woman who was able to think on her own.

Mary had a difficult time getting out the house and working away from the home. Otis was set in his ways and clung to her coattails as a young child would. Still, she managed to go to the Juvenile Branch meetings at the Independent Order of St. Luke when her children were old enough to attend. At times, she would work at the *Herald* with me. But Otis was a selfish and insecure man. Not like my Armstead at all. He needed control and Mary succumbed to his nonsense without flinching.

Armstead, Momma, and Russell were now gone from our home. I missed them with every part of my being. Settling down and retiring was something I would never consider, no matter how dire my health had become.

Memories of meeting Mrs. Parrish in my travels stayed with me. There was something about a woman living on the bare minimum but loaded with cash that could make her life so much easier that kept working at my thoughts. The St. Luke Penny Savings Bank had not even scratched the surface of the amount of people still out there that we could help.

I pulled together a team of women at my home. It was much easier to gain the support of my sisters than to try to convince men of the expansion of the bank. I had overheard Mr. Walter whispering behind my back at an Order meeting, "She's not a real woman." I had ignored him. I could do as much as any man, especially him. I had created businesses from nothing and grown two more businesses from it. Mr. Walter had inherited his funeral parlor from his father. I knew my ways were different than most women's, but I was as much of a lady as anyone. Aside from Fannie, I was the best-dressed woman in Jackson Ward. My hats came from Fifth Avenue in New York City and my clothes were tailored by the best seamstresses in town.

Polly had taken on Momma's role since she passed. Seeing her in the kitchen every morning was my joy. Now Polly would call me down to eat. I shuffled down the stairs into the kitchen just like I had when Momma was with us. Although Momma was missing, Polly had taken on all her characteristics. I would not allow anyone to take her place at the table for a while, then I moved into her seat. We all felt Momma's presence in the kitchen as we sat down to eat.

With her hands in her apron pocket, Polly said, "At times, I believe she is directing me on what to cook for dinner. Because I am doctoring up the taste with a pinch of salt, just like she did."

"I feel her, too," Melvin commented after sopping his eggs over easy.

She was my strength.

One Saturday in 1924, nine women came to my home. I invited Mary, Edith, Fannie, and six other women who worked in the businesses I'd established. I should have written to Mary McLeod Bethune, but I knew she was busy. She had written me from Harlem, where she'd spent time with the leaders in New York and had been invited to Washington, D.C., thereafter.

Polly had learned how to cook as well as Momma, and she had spent the night in the kitchen with me baking tiny biscuits while I shaved ham to put into the bread. Although mayonnaise was sold at the corner store, Polly preferred to make hers from scratch.

Polly warned me, "Now, Momma, you can't have any of this chocolate cake I am baking. You'll just have to let the ladies enjoy it themselves."

I smirked at her. "Now you know I want to taste it."

"Just a taste, and no more!" Polly said, like Momma would, moving around the kitchen like a professional cook.

Before my guests arrived, we made rooibos tea from the bags W. E. B. brought me from Africa. And of course, water was the best chaser for sweets and biscuits.

Everyone showed up around two in the afternoon. With everyone assembled, it felt like a salon of great minds coming together to ponder our community's troubles and find solutions to them. The parlor was scented with lavender, rumored as it was to relax anyone who inhaled it. I wanted my guests to feel comfortable enough to give their honest opinions. We all gathered around the room sipping on hot tea and munching biscuits.

After we had spent time chatting, updating each other on children and general life, I shook my crystal bell. When it chimed, everyone gazed up at me, and one of the ladies just burst into laughter.

"Well, Maggie, what a way to call the meeting to begin."

Suddenly little Maggie Laura showed up at the meeting, and I had to pause for a few minutes.

"Hi, Grandma. I just dropped in to tell you I love you," she said, smiling. I grabbed her and pulled her to my bosom and squeezed her.

"How long will you be here?" I asked her, hoping she would say "For a long time."

She walked over to the table and got a piece of her aunt Polly's chocolate cake. She smiled as she took a bite. "Grandma, it is time for us to take a ladies trip, just you and me. I need to pick your brain."

"Stay for the meeting and afterward we will make a date for a trip."

What a joy! I thought.

I took a deep breath and smiled. "Yes, it is time to discuss a few things, ladies."

They all turned to me.

"While I was campaigning for superintendent, I was exposed to all kinds of people. One of them was a lady who appeared to have absolutely nothing but gave me a tin can full of money to deposit in the bank that surpassed the funds of a lot of our middle-class patrons who have saved regularly for years. Also, I found out many of the people in the country are not aware of the organizations we belong to, or even how to go about voting. There are so many people who are misinformed or have been kept in the dark—either purposefully or due to lack of access to city resources while in the country. They need us."

"What can we do?"

"Jackson Ward is progressing. New buildings are always under construction and more shops are opening all along Second Street."

Fannie grunted and snobbishly said, "You've surely seen to that personally, Maggie. I don't think there is one business, shop, or new dwelling that you and the Walker Company have not touched."

Ignoring Fannie, I continued: "I feel we have made significant improvements over the last forty years. And the reason I've invited you here today is to make sure we continue to build on the progress we've made so far and expand to more remote areas of the country."

Edith put a hand to the side of her face. "What do you mean by that?"

"We have clients from across the United States who deposit their funds in our banks, and borrowers as well. It's time for us to reach people in rural areas and teach them about banking, investments, and their voting rights. We've come a long way, but every day proves how much more work there is yet to be done, and I can't do it without you."

"Are you asking us to travel to these rural cities and do some informing?"

"Exactly."

"I know my husband is not going to allow that," Edith said.

"Mine, either," one of the other ladies echoed.

"We need to get word out to them about the organizations we have that can help them," I said. "The NAACP should be everywhere. So, with that information, we must include the advantages of bank deposits. They need to know that the St. Luke Penny Savings Bank is here for them, should they desire to start a business, need to borrow money for their farms, or want to protect their life's savings."

The ladies continued to chatter among themselves about whose husband would or wouldn't allow such a thing or what they would say if they even heard they were considering this.

"How many of you have taken a vacation lately?" I asked, interrupting the scattered conversations and bringing our focus back to the task at hand.

We were on the verge of another year passing in which no one had gone anywhere to relax, think, do extraordinary things like swim in an ocean, or even visit a sick relative. It was as if staying home and doing the things their husbands deemed necessary had become the irrefutable norm.

"I haven't traveled outside of Richmond in years," Edith said thoughtfully. "I believe the last time we took the car out onto the open road was before the epidemic hit the area. Oh my, that's been years!"

Many colored folks tended to head north for a long trip to the Bluffs, which required a trip by boat as well as the drive. It was a beautiful place where colored folks got to take in the warm sea breeze while enjoying the success of their businesses.

"Lord, we haven't been anywhere in years either," Fannie exclaimed. "Not even to Harlem, which is my favorite place to visit. The people, the lights, and the nightlife are something to see. Am I getting old?" Fannie asked out loud, and not one of the women dared to respond. We all were getting old, now in our late forties and fifties. It was as if life was just passing us by.

Mary cleared her throat to speak. "Otis and I have not been anywhere at all. We've only ever raised our children. I would like to at least go to Washington, D.C., once."

"Certainly convincing him of a vacation shouldn't be too difficult?" I murmured. "Your children are long grown. Besides, wherever you will be traveling, you are likely to encounter many small rural towns in between home and your destination, somewhat of an adventure," I said, smiling.

Their eyes began to light up at the mere thought of planning a trip. And I knew all their husbands needed a break as well. Most of their children were grown and trained in how to run the family business. They would not lose any income over a few days' rest and travel. It would be business as usual at home.

One of the ladies stood up. "Put my name on the list, Maggie," she said. "I can help make people aware of our organizations and the importance of colored representation. And we'll encourage folks to deposit their money at the St. Luke Penny Savings Bank, too. It won't hurt that along the way I will get to dip my beautiful self in the Atlantic Ocean." That stirred all the women to laughter and exclamations of joy.

All of them agreed we needed a planning meeting, and everyone needed a vacation.

I had decided I would drive south and take my family to visit Mary McLeod Bethune in Florida. After stopping in Norfolk, Hampton, Portsmouth, and Suffolk, we would spend a couple of days relaxing on the beach with my dear Mary. Maggie Laura would be with us.

CHAPTER 31

1928–1929

WITH THE EXPANSION of the bank to rural areas, word was quickly spreading like wildfire across towns and into the surrounding states. We were a bank with plenty of cash for lending and our self-sufficiency policy allowed patrons to be able to pay money back.

With the help of the ladies and their husbands, our bank flourished. We had deposits in excess of $2 million, and more than forty thousand adult and twenty thousand junior members. Our insurance division had paid more than $1 million in benefits, and the *Herald* had more than six thousand subscribers. We were expanding despite the rumors of an economic crash on the horizon.

Members of the community borrowed money and built stately homes all along Marshall and Clay Streets. My impressive home with its wrought-iron and brick took up a substantial amount of space on Second Street.

Some of the other banks, controlled by men, were not doing as well, but try telling a man how to do business and you will get your feelings hurt. I could approach John Mitchell Jr., a good friend most times, but an adversary when it came to business. He had voiced his disapproval of me managing a bank several times, but whenever we needed him for matters of social justice, he was the first to volunteer.

One steamy hot day in August, I stopped by the Mechanics Savings Bank on the corner of Clay Street to see John, who served as the bank's president. John and I had similar business accomplishments. Most of our interactions had revolved around news headlines and cries for civil action. When it came to social justice, lynching, or any defamation of the Negro people, we flooded our papers with news to keep our people informed. But when it came to banking, John was always suspicious of me and my motives, when all I wanted to do was help and offer friendly advice.

"Maggie, why don't you have a seat," he told me and I sat down in front of his desk. It was an extremely neat office, with few ledgers and white paper on his shiny desk. His bookshelves were almost empty.

"To what do I owe the honor?" he asked.

"Now, John, you've visited me many times, yet this is the first time in years I've come to your establishment." I looked around me, appraising his office. "And I like what I see," I said, though it didn't have much personality. It lacked photos or extra file cabinets, or the personal touch of a davenport like I had in my office for those who preferred sitting on a comfortable couch while we did business. As always, I would offer them a cup of tea. But his office was neat and organized, something I found challenging with all the work I did.

"What is it you need?" he asked me in a tone much more authoritative than usual.

"We are on the verge of an economic depression," I said. "All the New York papers are saying so. Although we still have money in our banks, I believe we need to put our heads together, since the price of everything is creeping up."

He crossed his arms over his chest and leaned back in his seat. "Now, I know you haven't come here to tell me how to run my bank."

"Oh no, you are a capable businessman. I just want us to think ahead about what is coming. And you know being colored in a white man's world, we've got much more to lose."

"Maggie, we have fought hard for the freedom of our people. I have been threatened, as you have. We've seen things done in which we have not had any control. And yet, we've done it all. But, when it comes to the business of the Mechanics Savings Bank, I believe I have a good grasp of things."

I forced a smile across my face, knowing his business would be the first to go down if the depression was as devastating as analysts were predicting. It was already rumored that the Mechanics Savings Bank's assets were dwindling. But I had to honor his request.

Less than a year later, John's bank filed for bankruptcy, just as the Great Depression was beginning.

❖c꞊❖

At Order meetings, my name rang out whenever something was reported. It wasn't because I needed the attention; it was because I couldn't stop working. Although my body was breaking down from the diabetes, and the doctors lacked the knowledge to treat it, I remained vigilant. When the pain became unbearable, I sought the assistance of my brother-in-law, Andrew.

"Maggie, I will find something to help you get around. I know it is a burden for you to leave anything undone. I will work with the man who makes wheelbarrows and together we will get you a proper wheelchair. Now, when we get this chair made, you must promise me you will let me know whenever you decide you'd like to go out of town. Melvin or I will go with you and Polly. You are too independent for your own good, but this illness has made that harder," he muttered as he walked away.

"Andrew, I need my seat adjusted in my car as well!" I yelled after him.

"We will handle that, too. Just be careful until we can get it done," he hurled back at me and took off to do the work. I was grateful for my family, especially the Walkers.

Traveling up and down the road had been arduous, yet profitable for our bank. At times, I'd been turned away because I was a woman and had to beg the colored folks in rural areas to trust me, and it had been grueling at times. So many people had been brainwashed and taught to turn away from other colored folks. Slavery had made them vulnerable, and afraid of trusting their own. Eventually most folks allowed me to teach them. And some who showed talent in the skills I was sharing agreed to come back and train properly in the work we were doing, which sparked the idea to set aside an education fund.

Education had always been a priority of mine. So I worked with women in the community in addition to my service as a trustee of Nannie Helen Burroughs's National Training School for Women and Girls in Washington, D.C. I was also a trustee of Hartshorn Memorial College, a Richmond school for African American women that later became part of Virginia Union University. I created the Educational Loan Fund, an endowment to provide financial aid to colored students at 6 percent interest. To help build the $10,000 fund, the Independent Order of St. Luke distributed more than two thousand customized dime banks to its local councils. But I couldn't stop there. I also worked with Janie Porter Barrett at the Industrial Home School for Wayward Colored Girls.

"Maggie, you've been more than a friend," Janie told me after I had volunteered my time and efforts. "What you are doing is affecting us all. We need you around. We need a place for our girls to grow into women. The Wayward home is a godsend and anything I can do to help I will."

Janie and I prepared the meals for the girls. We always made sure nutrition was included. Square meals that included fresh vegetables and meat were served daily. I insisted on milk for their bones and teeth, even though milk was becoming scarce. Farmers couldn't keep up financially with the demand.

Being on the verge of a nationwide financial crisis was causing people to be concerned about their investments. I assured them they had nothing to worry about. The St. Luke Penny Savings Bank was stable.

The 1920s had been a prosperous time for Jackson Ward and the country. From afar, Jackson Ward was being hailed as the "Harlem of the South," a name given to many successful Negro communities. We had made a difference, but worry haunted me. A financial crisis could destroy our banks and all the progress our community had made. When I talked to God, He could sense my wavering confidence in my people. All I knew was that I could not allow us to fall backward. Letting my community down was the last thing on my mind.

One day, the owner of the welding company informed me, "If people don't start spending money again, I am going to have to close my business. You see these wrought-iron fences around here? I built them with my own hands. Now I don't want to have to use the money I have in your bank to survive."

Day by day, someone was reporting about the financial struggles they were experiencing in their business, and our deposits were taking a hit as well. As less money was earned, less was being deposited. Folks needed every penny they had left to weather the storm ahead.

It seemed like the only people with a foolproof business were the undertakers, and they were complaining about not receiving payments from their clients.

The stock market crashed as stock prices fell overnight in September 1929. The nation was shaken. It was amazing how quickly a thriving community's stability could crumble based on the repercussions of the New York Stock Exchange. People everywhere panicked.

As word traveled, businesses in Jackson Ward and those managed by Negroes worldwide began to feel the pressure of doing business with less.

I called a meeting with several bank presidents who were also feeling the decline due to the stock market crash on what was being called "Black Tuesday."

"We must merge in order to survive!" I cried out to them. "We can no longer do this alone." Every banker in the room nodded.

"We have lowered our interest rates to a bare minimum and patrons are demanding money from their accounts. I purposely will not allow my bank and its patrons to be wiped out by one storm."

The men nodded in agreement.

One murmured to himself, just loud enough that I overheard him, "Are we really going to take orders from a woman?"

I smiled to myself.

Amid the Great Depression, the St. Luke Penny Savings Bank and two others merged to become the Consolidated Bank and Trust Company and maintained stability in our community. Though the bank was no longer part of the Order, I stayed on as chairperson of the board of directors of the newly consolidated company. If we had attempted to survive on our own, we all would have lost the miles we had traveled on the road to self-sufficiency and prosperity.

I had begun volunteering at the Independent Order of St. Luke when I was fourteen years old. Being a girl, I was faced with many challenges, but I couldn't let that stop me. I had a goal. With faith in God and tenacity, anything is possible. After fifty-six years of belief in self-sufficiency through economics, I learned something new from the story of the fig tree in the New Testament, where Christ saw a fig tree with full leaves and tried to pick its fruit. Though fully blossomed, the tree had no figs. Christ cursed the tree because the tree was a living lie. It stood there . . . claiming by its appearance that it was fruitful. But when the test was made—there was nothing (the tree was a deception). A brazen hypocrisy. Do more than just talk about improving your personal situation and that of the community. Talk without action is a modern fig tree. "Appearance but no deeds; shadows but no substance."

As I thought of my journey, I often thought about Maggie Laura, who often stared at me with curious eyes. When I look at her, I see myself. So I took her by the hand that spring evening and led her to the front porch. "Sit with me for a spell."

Maggie Laura glanced up at me. "What is it, Grandmother?" She was a proper little girl of eleven years, almost the age I was when I started attending the Independent Order of St. Luke meetings.

"Do you realize you can be whatever you want to be?" I asked her.

"Yes, ma'am," she cautiously said.

The reflection in her eyes was of a curious little girl, who had dreams. She was so much like me. She was fatherless now, and most of her strength had to come from within.

"Tell me how you feel, child."

"Grandmother, there is nothing I can't do. I am just like you," she answered, smiling.

"You are, huh," I said, seeing her father, Russell, in all her mannerisms. She had been her daddy's joy.

"I just have a question," she hesitantly said.

"Okay."

"Do you think we will get through the Great Depression, Grandmother?"

I supposed all the talk around the dinner table had her thinking.

"Certainly, child. Us colored folk are fighters. And colored girls will fight to the end for our family, our economic standing, and social freedom. We will never give up."

She gazed up at me and smiled. "Me neither, Grandmother."

Then she took my hand in hers.

AUTHOR'S NOTE

MAGGIE LENA WALKER strongly believed in the voice of God. She transformed her life from that of an enslaved woman's child to a laundress, then teacher, and finally an entrepreneur, leader, and bank president. She was what one conceived of as a natural-born leader.

She loved being a woman and was determined to show Black women what was needed to survive in a "post"-Confederacy Jim Crow world. She was quoted as saying, without stumbling, "Whatever I have done in this life has been because I love women. I love to be surrounded by them. Love to hear them talk all at once. Love to listen to their trials and troubles. Love to help them. And the great love I bear for our Negro women, hemmed in and circumscribed with every imaginable obstacle in our way, blocked and held down by fears and prejudices of whites—ridiculed and sneered at by the intelligent Blacks."

I came upon Maggie Lena Walker as I was researching my first novel, *Blackberry Days of Summer.* I was enthralled with her tenacity and her belief in economic self-sufficiency. With further investigation, I realized this was someone we all needed to know about, and I've included her in all my novels. Thankfully, my literary agent and Simon & Schuster asked me to introduce her fully to the world. She is more than I could ever write about, but as I channeled her spirit, I hope to have captured the woman people referred to as "the race woman."

She argued that marriage should be a partnership in which both husband and wife participate in decision-making and the contribution to the family's financial stability. Women should be able to use their God-given talent and choose a vocation in which they can bring something to the partnership. If not money, a trade, or business, and certainly more than her clothes and a warm body.

There were men who felt she was too assertive, and that the things she did were "unladylike." In the 1800s, women were supposed to stay home and care for their children. She didn't have a problem with that, but she felt everyone had a brain and a talent that God wanted them to use. When speaking about prejudice and the Jim Crow laws, she believed that by building and supporting their own businesses, African Americans could "kill the lion of prejudice by ceasing to feed him."

She called for men to stop hiding their talents, and she would quote Matthew 25:14–30 often, saying, "For whoever has will be given more, and they will have an abundance."

She spent her life fighting for rights for all, especially women. She begged men to fight for their freedom. Control where their money is spent, and then you can control the prejudices.

After being credited for the sustainability of a major community in America, she also was a maverick in starting many organizations in Richmond, Virginia, that expanded and evolved throughout the state.

The St. Luke Penny Savings Bank, which she founded and led, helped fund more than six hundred businesses and financed the construction of many stately homes in the Jackson Ward community. At one time, her bank was the only functional one on the East Coast, and the only one in the world run and managed by a woman.

After spending time with a school, and bringing quality education into the community on the edge of a depression, Maggie Lena Walker was inducted as an honorary member of Zeta Phi Beta Sorority in 1926. They charted a course of action for the 1920s and beyond, raising the consciousness of their people, encouraging the highest standards of scholastic achievement, and fostering a greater sense of unity among their members.

Three years before Maggie's induction, her best friend, Mary McLeod Bethune, a prominent educator, became an honorary member of Delta Sigma Theta Sorority—the same group of twenty-two ladies who flooded Pennsylvania Avenue as members of the Woman Suffrage Procession marched on Washington, D.C.—at their fifth national convention. Both of them paved the way for women everywhere.

We must know about Maggie Lena Walker, because she was the only woman to run a bank until she died in 1934. She was a maverick and spawned from the influence of her strong mother, Elizabeth Draper Mitchell. She held dear to her heart her stories about an unselfish and daring white lady, Elizabeth Van Lew, who felt enslaved folks should be treated like human beings and be paid for their services. Ms. Van Lew died in 1901, and some of the Jim Crow followers spit on her grave, but her legacy continued through smart and strong Black women like Maggie Lena Walker. Maggie was a soldier in a time of war. Like all men who fought in war, death was the only way to take her down.

I'm sure you had moments of great thought as you were reading *A Right Worthy Woman*. Not everything written is truth; some of it is completely from my imagination. However, she was a pioneer, a scholar, an entrepreneur, and one of the most prominent bankers to ever live.

According to history, the first brown mannequins were made in 1964. Well, that is up for debate, since in 1905 Maggie Lena Walker's St. Luke Emporium was known for showcasing her clothes on brown-hued mannequins that resembled the community. So, it leads us to believe they were custom-made for her personally. She was a visionary, and it seems to fit with the character she displayed her entire life.

Maggie Lena Walker became a well-established and respected leader in the Richmond community and worked tirelessly for equal rights. Walker founded the Richmond Council of Colored Women to raise money for education and health programs. She was a member of the International Council of Women of the Darker Races, the National Association of Wage Earners, and the National Urban League, and she cofounded the Richmond branch of the NAACP. She also joined in the fight for women's suffrage and the ratification of the Nineteenth Amendment.

With a reputation as a powerful speaker and entrepreneur, she engaged in major civic issues and became an activist against discrimination and segregation. She was cofounder of the Council of Colored Women and was a major contributor to the Virginia Industrial Home School for Wayward Colored Girls as well as the Virginia Union University, where Mrs. Walker was awarded an honorary master of science degree in 1925. In 1934, the city of Richmond declared October to be "Maggie L. Walker Month" in honor of all her accomplishments.

By 1924 the St. Luke Penny Savings Bank had expanded to other parts of Virginia and included more than fifty thousand members. While other banks collapsed during the Great Depression, Maggie's bank survived by eventually merging with two other large banks to form the Consolidated Bank and Trust Company and moved to downtown Richmond. It is still in operation today.

After an illness in 1928, Walker was forced to use a wheelchair. Although limited in movement, Walker remained a leader in Richmond's African American community. She fought arduously for women's rights as well. For much of her life, Walker served as a board member of the Virginia Industrial Home School for Wayward Colored Girls.

Throughout her life, Walker devoted her energies to changing and improving working conditions for women and girls in domestic service, increasing home ownership and employment opportunities, supporting a safe haven with instruction for at-risk young women, and creating opportunities for upward mobility for women in professional careers. She led by example and became the best-known African American woman in Virginia and was nationally recognized as an advocate for women, children, and education, as well as a successful business executive. George Washington Carver, W. E. B. Du Bois, and Booker T. Washington, and even Virginia's governors, acknowledged her through their publications as the smartest Black business professional they'd ever met.

Maggie Lena Walker has influenced entrepreneurs all over the world to achieve their goals. Her great-granddaughter, Liza Mickens, is continuing her mission today. Liza was quoted by AfroTech as saying, "I think that making sure that we are really in the political arena and making sure that we realize the true power of our vote . . . African American women have always faced the double-edged sword of oppression and to really continue to make sure that we highlight those stories and uplift this group is something that's really important to me." Now, Mickens and her family have joined forces with Pay-Pal, who is on a mission to uplift Black women and share the stories of hidden figures like Walker.

(Below, left and right) The Virginia Department of Historic Resources (DHR); African American Registry

Maggie Walker with her colleagues in front of the St. Luke Penny Savings Bank (left) and a sample cheque from the St. Luke Penny Savings Bank (right).

Established in 1978, the Maggie L. Walker National Historic Site in Richmond, Virginia is the country's first national park devoted to the story of an African American woman.

(Above) Photograph by Calder Loth, courtesy of the Virginia Department of Historic Resources

The Maggie L. Walker Governor's School for Government and International Studies in Richmond is a living monument to her passion for education. This public school ranks in the top five in the nation for academic excellence, according to *Newsweek*.

In her businesses, Maggie highly favored employing Black women, and made sure she employed more women in well-respected positions than any other business, as she knew they had few other work opportunities. She didn't leave out the men, loaning money to fund the businesses that provided for their families. For all these reasons and more, she should be remembered by all.

RESOURCES

I have included some of the sources I found valuable in understanding the laborious and successful life of a true maverick, Maggie Lena Walker. These sources will allow for further research into a person who deserves to be known across the map.

Arts and Culture. "A Woman of Fine Presence, Maggie L. Walker's Style." https://artsandculture.google.com/partner/maggie-l-walker-national-historic-site.

BlackPast. "Maggie Lena Walker (1864–1934)." https://www.blackpast.org.

Cate Lineberry. "Elizabeth Van Lew: An Unlikely Union Spy." Smithsonian Mag.com, May 4, 2011. www.smithsonianmag.com.

Encyclopedia Virginia. "Maggie Lena Walker (1864–1934)." https://encyclopediavirginia.org/entries/walker-maggie-lena-1864-1934/.

Jim Hare. "Maggie L. Walker: The St. Luke Penny Savings Bank." Maggie L. Walker National Historic Site, National Park Service. https://www.nps.gov/mawa/the-st-luke-penny-savings-bank.htm.

National Park Service. "Jackson Ward and Its Black Wall Street." https://www.nps.gov/articles/000/jackson-ward-and-its-black-wall-street.htm.

Arlisha R. Norwood. "Maggie Lena Walker." 2017. National Women's History

Museum. www.womenshistory.org/education-resources/biographies /maggie-lena-walker.

PBS. "Maggie Lena Walker: Civil Rights Activist and Entrepreneur." March 3, 2020. https://www.pbs.org/wnet/americanmasters/civil-right-activist -maggie-lena-walker-75lx9t/13814/.

Virginia Changemakers. "Maggie Lena Walker." Accessed May 17, 2022. https://edu.lva.virginia.gov/changemakers/items/show/104.

Wikipedia. "Maggie L. Walker." https://en.wikipedia.org/wiki/Maggie_L._ Walker.

Shanique Yates. "PayPal and Liza Mickens Continue the Legacy of Maggie L. Walker, the First Black Woman to Charter a Bank in America." AfroTech, March 26, 2021. https://afrotech.com/paypal-and-liza-mickens-con tinue-the-legacy-of-maggie-l-walker-the-first-black-woman-to-charter -a-bank-in-america.

ACKNOWLEDGMENTS

"TO GOD BE THE GLORY for the things He has done." Is not utopia a moment of gratitude? I would love to acknowledge all the brave women and men who fought for social justice and economic equality. Let us not forget the women who were determined to take the helm and make something happen in uncharted territory.

Maggie Lena Walker was way ahead of her time. She was a maverick and a renegade in a period when it was not popular for a woman to even speak. I give honor to the hardworking colored folk, Jewish people, and immigrants who stood face-to-face with the devil and would not allow him to win. Maggie Lena Walker deserves to be known across the world.

I am blessed to have the best agents in the world, Marly Rusoff and her partner, Mihai (Michael) Radulescu, who took me on after my querying her for many years. It was worth the wait. She worked tirelessly to rebuild my writing career and provide the opportunity for me to write about one of my sheroes, Mrs. Maggie Lena Walker.

I'm thankful for the intelligent eyes of my wonderful editor, Melanie Iglesias Pérez, who inspired me to get this story right.

My gratitude extends to my family and friends, who were my greatest cheerleaders. I do not have the time to thank them all because I'm positive someone will be left off. Yet I can't help mentioning the people who would not let me keep this story inside: Edna Moffitt, Jennifer Walton, Charis Johnson, Vera Lewis, Marva Greene, Marcia Purvis, Dawn Cobb, Maria "Rhea" Bumbry, Johnnie "Brooks" Booker, Eric Wherry, and my son, Wayne J. You don't know how much those little chats meant to me.

Last, I'd like to thank Beverly Smith, the twenty-sixth national president of Delta Sigma Theta Sorority, and Valerie Hollingsworth Baker, the twenty-fifth international president of Zeta Phi Beta Sorority, for supporting this project from its inception.